Love, Secrets & Pearls

ब∽ਟ

JC Conrad-Ellis

For information about Provision Press please visit our website at
www.blackdiamondseries.com.

Library of Congress Cataloging-in-Publication Data

Conrad-Ellis, JC,

LOVE SECRETS & PEARLS/ JC Conrad-Ellis
ISBN 13: 978-1-957593-05-0
Teen Fiction

Copyright Registered: 2022
Published by Provision Press in the USA

Printed in the USA

January 2022

10 9 8 7 6 5 4 3 2

DEDICATION

This book is dedicated to
My black diamonds:
BJE, BJE & BWE-the sequel

& to

JTC, KBC, RAC
(my pickle juice grits & gravy buddies)

Love,
jtc-e

ACKNOWLEDGEMENTS

To my faithful readers who pushed me to continue spinning the "Tanisha Carlson - Black Diamond Series" chronicles. Thank you for keeping me company on this journey. When blog comments appeared to be written in invisible ink and book sales were sick and shut in, I wrote anyway knowing that you were anxiously waiting to finish the journey spinning in my "head is so big that I have to have hats custom made" head. Thank you for waiting. I hope this book meets or exceeds your expectations.

Namaste! jc

CONTENTS

"The Lord will fight for you; you need only to be still."

Exodus 14:14
The NIV Study Bible
New International Version

Love, Secrets & Pearls

Chapter 1

Driving under the Influence

Tanisha's stomach tightened into a knot. She glanced into the backseat, Maria was digging through her purse, and not listening. "Why didn't you bring Mr. Belvedere?" Teenie asked quickly.

"I was going to bring him, but when you told me that Maria was coming, I remembered that she was allergic to him, so I thought I better leave him at home."

Teenie smiled that David remembered her friend's allergies.

David stared into Teenie's face. "Wow! Your teeth are gorgeous," he observed. "I didn't even notice that you needed braces before, but now that you have them off, your teeth really stand out. They make your face pop," he grinned.

"Thanks." Tanisha settled into her seat and buckled her seatbelt. Pretending to stare at Maria, she watched as David walked to the driver's side of the car, a wide grin on his face.

"I'm starving," Maria whined from the backseat. "My flight was so early that I missed breakfast, and I would rather die than eat airplane food."

"What are you looking for, Maria?"

"A mint or some gum or something to take the edge off my hunger."

Teenie reached in her purse and handed her friend a granola bar.

"You are such an old soul," David smiled as he settled into his seat and buckled up. "You're like a little mother who anticipates her child's every need. What else do you have in that purse?"

"Are you calling me a child?" Maria asked snatching the granola bar from Teenie's grasp. "It's so good to see you, Teenie!" Maria grinned. "I can't wait to see Rashanda and Justine too. I hope my little Jeni Kaye didn't forget who I am."

"She won't. She's your baby sister. She'll remember you."

"Justine called me and told me that Grace..."

"Eat your granola bar," Teenie smiled.

"Do you want to drive, Teenie? You could probably use the practice. You haven't driven in three months or so, huh?"

"Something like that," Teenie smiled. "Thanks, but I'll pass." She'd driven Brian Kraft's car when he'd driven to Yale from Princeton. He also drove a BMW, but she thought better of sharing this news with David.

Teenie settled into the leather seats and watched as David deftly maneuvered through the airport traffic. The granola bar silencing Maria's hunger pangs, she laid across the backseat and closed her eyes as David weaved in and out of the Chicago traffic on the Kennedy Expressway.

"David, you really don't have to detour through downtown. Maria's asleep and the traffic is going to be crazy today."

"It'll be fine. You want Garretts, so Garretts you shall have. Lean back and take a nap, Teenie," David encouraged. "You have a long weekend ahead of you."

"I've got to stay awake and watch you drive," Teenie yawned. "I'll probably go to bed early tonight though."

"I'm looking forward to finally meeting your parents," David said.

The Chicago skyline was visible as they hit stop and go traffic near the Oak Park exits. "Why?" Teenie asked. She stared at David's profile.

"Because I've known you for almost five years and I've never met your parents."

"Oh." Teenie turned and stared at Maria, who snored softly on the backseat.

"I think it's pretty cool that your parents are back together," David smiled.

"Yeah, I guess it is. My dad couldn't believe that I didn't need him to pick me up at the airport. He'll probably give you the third degree, like you're my boyfriend," she smiled.

"Good. I like that."

"You're looking forward to the third degree?"

"I like that he thinks I'm already your boyfriend."

"David, let's not go there, okay?" Teenie whispered.

"I'm not going there. You brought it up. We have thirty seven more days before our deal kicks in, but who's counting?" he smiled. "Before I forget, my mother wants you to come over for dinner on Friday night. She and my sister always go shopping downtown on black Friday, and after that we have pizza since no one wants to eat Thanksgiving leftovers the next day. We eat those on Saturday. You'll finally get to meet my sister, too. She's pregnant by the way. We just found out a few weeks ago."

"That's cool," Teenie smiled. "You're going to be Uncle David!"

"She and my brother-in-law are really excited, and my parents are psyched about having their first grandchild."

"Maria and I are training into the city to shop with Justine. Justine is going to train back to Newberry East with us so we can all go to this party Friday night at the Illinois Institute of Technology. Grace is going to drive us."

"Okay, Yale nerd. It's IIT. Only geeks and foreigners call it the Illinois Institute of Technology." David spat the words slowly, enunciating every syllable. "You'll get beat up if you call it that." He leaned into the window to avoid her swat. "But you're right," David remembered. "I forgot that the annual black Greek party at IIT is Friday night. That's always really packed. All of the college students who pledged always wear their Greek paraphernalia."

"Aren't you going?"

"I might. I went to that my freshman and sophomore year. The party doesn't start until about ten o'clock, so you could come over for pizza to meet my sister and then go to the party after that. My grandmother was asking about you."

Teenie smiled at the mention of his elderly grandmother. "How's she doing?"

"She's fine. She'll probably outlive us all. We converted my parents' first floor office into a bedroom for her, and we have a nurse who comes and sits with her during the day while my parents are at work. They play cards and knit together."

"When's your sister's baby due?"

"Sometime in the spring. Speaking of babies, when's Rashanda due?"

"She's due in the spring too. Grace told me that she's really huge. But she's all baby."

"I can't imagine being a parent at nineteen," David whistled.

"Me neither, but Ian is almost twenty-one now," Teenie added.

"He starts medical school next year."

"That's going to be an interesting ride."

Teenie lurched forward as David slammed on the brakes, his right forearm thrust across her chest, pinning her to her seat. David laid on his horn. "Are you okay?" he asked. "Did you see that? That idiot just pulled right in front of me! No signal or anything. He just pulled right in front of me!"

"I'm fine," Teenie replied. She glanced at the backseat at the still sleeping Maria.

David laid on his horn again at the offending vehicle in front of him. The car pulled up and weaved into traffic again.

"No harm no foul," Teenie smiled. "Maria didn't even wake up. Breathe, David."

David smiled at Teenie. "I get road rage when people drive like idiots. That guy is lucky you were in the car or I'd be chasing him down the Kennedy."

In the distance, Teenie could see the Chicago skyline. The John Hancock Building and Sears Tower served as bookends to a concrete display of different size buildings in between. The sight made her homesick. She seldom admired the skyline from this vantage point. Her normal view of the skyline approached heading from the south side going north on Lake Shore Drive, past Soldier Field.

"Earth calling, Teenie," David said. "Did you hear me?"

"I didn't. I was just admiring the skyline."

"I asked if we should wake Maria so she can see the skyline."

"Oh. Good point. But I think we should let sleeping beauty get her beauty sleep. She can see it after we get the popcorn."

"What had you all consumed with thought?" he asked.

For the first time, Teenie realized that the radio wasn't playing.

She smiled at David's profile, glad that he'd picked her up from the airport.

"I was just thinking that I really never get to see the skyline from this view. I normally see it approaching downtown from the Southside. It looks different from this angle."

"It's a beautiful concrete jungle," David smiled. The car slowed to a crawl as they joined the other inbound commuters heading into the city. The inbound express lane resembled a parking lot. Teenie hoped there wasn't an accident up ahead. She had to go to the bathroom.

"Are you going to come over on Friday evening? You didn't give me an answer."

"Of course I will. I think it's sweet that your mother invited me and that your grandmother asked about me. I can always have Grace pick me up from your house for the party if that's okay."

"Of course that's okay. You can change into your party clothes in my bedroom."

"I didn't think about that," Teenie paused. "I probably will need to freshen up after shopping all day."

"You can shower at our house, the whole nine yards. Just don't change into a hootchie dress or my mother's opinion of you will change. She thinks you're a good girl," he teased.

Teenie pinched his bicep. "It's November, chucklehead. I'm going to wear jeans and probably a Yale sweatshirt. And I'll take a shower at my house, thank you very much. By the way, is your sister going to give me the third degree?"

"Under normal circumstances she would, but now that she's preggo, she's mellowed out considerably. She's a piece of work that one. She's edgy like my father. But Claire will like you, especially when she learns that you plan to pledge Delta."

"Her name is Claire? That's pretty."

"Dr. Claire Elliot Barton-Bishop. It's a mouthful. Her husband is a surgeon so she uses Dr. Barton professionally. It's almost like a generational curse," he smiled.

"Do you have a problem with her hyphenating her name?"

"No. I didn't mean it that way. I think it's funny that she also married a doctor. I think it's cool that she hyphenates her last name. I wouldn't care if my wife kept her maiden name to tell you the truth."

Teenie tilted her head at David. "That wouldn't bother you?"

"Not in the least. She'd still be my wife even without my last name. That's her personal choice. It's her name."

"What about the children? How will that work?"

"The children would definitely have my last name. I am very traditional about that. And Claire too. The baby will be a Bishop. In fact, if the baby is a boy, they're going to name him Barton. Barton Bishop," David repeated. "I think that's a cool name to have. Sounds like a movie star name or a quarterback. And Claire said that she can't wait for her child's friends to call her Mrs. Bishop instead of Dr. Barton. She's excited about her new identity."

Smiling, she found herself surprised by this disclosure. David was a very chivalrous guy, he always opened doors for her and opened her car door and closed it once she settled into her seat.

The traffic had now halted to a complete stop.

Teenie peered into the backseat. Maria was still knocked out. "Wow! I'm surprised to hear you say that. You seem like an old fashioned guy with your 'I'm a man, I have needs machismo,'" she mocked in her deepest male voice, her fists beating playfully against her chest. "You can be quite caveman like when you want to be and now you sound so current. So progressive. So not like yourself," she laughed.

"My old man is cool with my mom hyphenating her name, so that's good enough for me," he paused. His brow furrowed, his face took on a serious tone. "Teenie, there's something that I want to tell you, but I'm not sure if now is the right time." David glanced in the rearview mirror at the sleeping Maria who purred softly. "It might not matter anyway." His teeth were clenched, his brow tight.

"What might not matter?" she asked. Following his eyes, she also glanced over her shoulder at her sleeping friend. The urge to pee now consumed her. She felt like her bladder was swelling to the size of her backpack. She wished she'd taken David's advice and gone to the bathroom at the airport. She stared out the window and squeezed her knees tighter as they sat in traffic.

When she turned to face him, she noticed his serious expression again. "What's up, David? Maria's knocked out. She sleeps like a log."

"Never mind. It's not important." David shook his head from side to side.

"Are you sure? You look pretty serious." The look in his eyes reminded her of their trip to Buckingham Fountain before he left for Georgetown. His eyes were misty and soft. That day, she thought that he was going to kiss her, but instead he took her picture. "Why are you looking at me so seriously, is something wrong?"

"Because you're pretty," David stammered softly.

Teenie bit her upper lip, unsure how to respond. David had never called her pretty before. She'd seen that look before and thought back to the day when they met. When he introduced himself to her, he'd stared at her with a similar soft look on his face. Then, she'd feared that he'd seen her decayed tooth. He'd told her that she reminded him of Grace Kelly or Doris Day. She'd been grateful that he hadn't seen her cavity and accused him of being blind to think that she looked like either of the actresses. Teenie had also seen him looking at her like that when she found herself on his driveway the night of his seventeenth birthday party and again before he left for Georgetown. But he'd never said that she was pretty. She blushed.

"Usually when someone pays you a compliment, you say thank you," he coached.

"Thank you," she blushed. "And of course I know that. You just caught me by surprise."

"Of course you know that you're pretty? My, my, Yale has turned you into an arrogant monster!" he grinned. Teenie noticed how pronounced his jaw line was.

"I know to thank someone after a compliment, Dodo brain. But I wasn't expecting you to say that," she whispered.

"You say that like it's a surprise. You know you're pretty, right?"

Teenie wished she had a witty comeback to toss out. His flattery made her uncomfortable. Thirty seven more days. He knew the exact number of days before she had to make a decision about their friendship. She didn't know if she should be flattered or frightened by his compliment.

"Pretty is a relative term, so thank you. And I think I'm going to take your advice and try to grab ten minutes of shut eye," she fake yawned without answering his question.

"Good idea. This traffic is a monster. At this rate, it'll be another fifteen or twenty minutes before we reach Garretts. I'm going to see if I can find a traffic report." David switched on the radio and turned the volume down.

She leaned her head against the head rest and closed her eyes while David searched for a traffic report. Teenie recognized the call letters for Lite FM 93.3. David pushed more buttons. A jazz station and classical station were next in rotation, finally the R&B station was last on the dial. "It's too early for traffic reports," he said aloud. Teenie pretended to be asleep. He switched to the AM channel. The familiar sound of static appeared as he pressed the pre-programmed station buttons in his mother's car. "I can't believe that Elle doesn't have the traffic station pre programmed in this car," he muttered to himself. He stopped at 720 WGN and listened to a sports update.

Elle Dudley Barton, my mother's psychiatrist is David's mother? How did I not connect these dots before? Why would I have known this? I've only met his mother a couple of times. But didn't I ask her what her specialty was? Did she not say psychiatry? Or maybe she did and because I didn't know she used Dr. Dudley it didn't ring a bell. As if mocking her, her bladder seemed to swell. She found herself squeezing her eyes and her bladder simultaneously. Her thoughts volleyed in her head like an imaginary tennis match against herself. He thinks you're pretty, Teenie. You knew that. You just didn't think that he thought you were pretty because of your tooth. But he didn't know about my tooth. Would he have thought I was pretty even with my bad tooth? Glen thought I was pretty even with my bad tooth. And what about Brian? Brian kissed you with the bad tooth. But Brian didn't know about the bad tooth either, and then when you saw him again you had braces. What does it matter, stupid? He thinks you're pretty! She felt the car moving faster and opened her eyes slightly to peer through the window at the traffic. She could see the Rock & Roll McDonald's sign and knew they were close to Garretts.

"That was fast. My eyes were barely closed and now we're almost downtown."

"There was a disabled vehicle in the express lanes, so it went down to one lane and then it opened up and the traffic was wide open. I should have known it was an accident or stalled car, it's too early for that type of gridlock."

Teenie squeezed her knees together. "David, I really need to tell you something. I don't know how to say this, so I'm just going to say it," she paused.

"It sounds serious." David's Adam's apple moved slightly as he swallowed. His serious look returned. She'd never noticed how pronounced his Adam's apple was before.

"I have to pee like a racehorse!" she squealed. "Can you please pull into the Rock & Roll McDonald's parking lot, or I'm going to pee my pants," she panted.

His palm slapped the steering wheel, his voice boomed in laughter. "I knew it! I knew you had to go when we were at the airport," he laughed loudly steering the car into the parking lot. "See how well I know you?"

"Whatever, dude!" she screamed as she hit the middle console door lock button and jumped out of the car before he'd placed the car in park.

"Good memory," David yelled through the partially cracked driver's side window. "Most people forget that the BMW door locks are in the center console."

"I'm not most people!" she screamed over her shoulder as she ran toward the door.

"No you're not," David smiled.

"Where are we?" Maria squinted. Her voice startled him. "Ooh, Mickey D's," she squealed. "I'm gonna run in and get a snack. That granola bar did nothing for me. I'm starving. Teenie had to pee didn't she? I'll be right back. You want something, David?" Her statements ran together in rapid fire succession.

"No, I'm good, but thanks for asking."

Alone in the car, David watched as Teenie walked toward the registers, guessing that Maria had seen her and waved her over.

"Should I tell her? In thirty seven days it might not matter. Besides, the jury is still out on that one. If you tell her now, it will definitely influence her decision. But if I don't tell her, she'll be mad. I wish I knew which way she was leaning. She's so hard to read. A deal is a deal, David. Enjoy the weekend. She's finally taking you to meet her parents. She's coming to hang out with your family Friday night. Keep your mouth shut."

Chapter 2

The Game of Life

The taxi was lost. The construction detour and one way streets proved more than he could manage. As the cabbie slammed his fists in frustration, mumbling in a language unfamiliar to Justine, her eyes stared at the bright red numbers on the dashboard meter that seemed to tick away nonstop. Her "ten dollar including tip" cab ride was already costing her almost eleven dollars, and she had no idea where they were. She felt like a tourist, and she was afraid.

Years had passed since the Lakeshore Drive mugging and bike theft, but she still thought about it, especially at night. I got thrown off my bike on a Sunday afternoon in broad daylight! There's no telling what a motivated mugger could do to me on a dark, one way street at night! What if the taxi driver is pretending to be lost so he can harm me? She felt herself holding her breath. The taxi swerved to avoid a car that slammed on its brakes.

"I no charge you more than eleven dollars, okay lady?" he stammered in broken English. He slammed the meter, freezing the red numbers in place. "I'm lost is not your fault. Streets closed off. Two way is now one way. Is a mess! I call my dispatcher." Justine breathed. She interpreted his comments as a positive sign that he was not driving her to a doomed fate.

Exhaling, she wished that she knew her way around Chicago better. She knew that Kendal's condo was less than ten miles from hers, but she didn't know exactly how to get there. All she knew is that Kendal lived in the Wrigleyville area. She knew that Wrigley Field where the Cubs played was somewhere in the area, but she couldn't remember the streets. She was embarrassed by her lack of direction. Kendal scolded her often, reminding her that she'd lived in Rogers Park long enough to know her way around the city by now. "Fish, you are not a tourist, and you do not live in Newberry East anymore! Learn your way around Chicago. It's pathetic that you don't know how to get around."

On her daily commute to work, riding the Howard Street L, she forced herself to pay attention to the streets as Kendal had instructed. "You're never going to learn the city if you ride the train with your head buried in a book, fish. You have to buy a map and study it at home. Don't pull out a map on the L or you will look like a lost tourist. Just pay attention to the conductor and read the signs. Chicago is on a grid system. All of the major streets are eight blocks apart. Learn the major intersections first. It'll start making sense soon enough if you put some effort into it. And carry your map with you in your backpack just in case," he encouraged. "Just don't read it on the bus or the train or you're signaling that you're a tourist or an idiot," Kendal laughed. Justine was reminded of the kind lady who'd helped coach her on safety rules while riding the L for the first time after she'd gotten her bike stolen along the lakefront. Out of habit, Justine only kept five or ten dollars in her backpack or purse. If she had more cash than that on her, she tucked it in her bra as instructed.

Her life coach, Kendal, had been right, and Justine was slowly learning her way around the streets of Chicago. On the train, she always tried to sit nearest the main door so that she could discreetly study the train grid posted above the doors. She found herself repeating the street names before the conductor announced them. She'd tried this technique on the bus, but she hadn't mastered the bus street routes yet, there were just too many streets to remember, and the CTA bus drivers didn't always call out the street names, the way the train conductor did. Tonight of all nights, she'd left her map at home, assuming that a taxi driver would know how to navigate the city. When Kendal heard about this, he would scold her. She decided to blame the abandoned map oversight on the tiny party purse that she carried. Kendal would forgive her for the sake of fashion.

Since she'd never been to Kendal's house, nothing looked familiar. All she knew is that Kendal lived on Halsted Street and that Halsted Street ran north and south. "I live in the heart of Boys' Town, fish!" Kendal boasted. She also remembered him mentioning something about taking the Irving Park or Addison Exit from Lake Shore Drive. But she couldn't remember which one and didn't want to confuse the already confused taxi driver any further. Justine decided not to share this sliver of information with the driver. She knew that the Belmont Exit was too far south, that much she knew. Belmont was too close to Fullerton, and Fullerton was in the Streeterville neighborhood which was next to the Gold Coast. She knew that the Wrigleyville neighborhood was further north near Addison. Or was it Irving Park Road? Her courage fortified, she wondered if she should mention Irving Park or Addison to the taxi driver who muttered into his radio in his native tongue.

"I know now how I go," he grinned. "We're almost there. You nice lady. You not yell at me for being lost," he smiled in the rearview mirror.

Justine smiled back. "Are you new?" she asked, wondering if it was wise to engage a lost taxi driver in conversation, distracting him from his focus.

"I drive taxi for six months, but some streets are hard for me to know about construction. New rules. My guy says we near. Just two minutes near."

Justine read his taxi name badge: Arik Wojochowski. She wondered where he was from. Poland? Czechoslovakia? Russia? She wanted to ask, but feared distracting him. I wonder why he came to the United States? How is he learning English? Is he studying to become a citizen? Is he a student driving a taxi to put himself through college?

She shifted to the right as the taxi turned left on to a street that was lit up with bar and restaurant signs and people milling about. Justine hadn't bothered to fasten her seatbelt. Seatbelts were another stress trigger. She forced herself to take several deep breaths. Not tonight, Justine. No panic attacks tonight. You're going to a party. You will NOT think about the shooting, the car accident, the mugging or AM! Ignoring her self motivational thoughts, her index finger floated into the air, resting on her forehead. She pulled it away. Her therapist had told her that her urge to rub her hairline was similar to other nervous habits that were difficult to break: smoking, thumb sucking, teeth grinding, nail biting. She'd never held a soft spot in her heart for smokers before, calling them weak willed and stupid for deliberately inhaling toxins into their lungs that they knew had the potential to kill them. She thought nail biting was disgusting, and thumb sucking childish. And now she was thrown into the same category of weak willed people. "You suffer from Post Traumatic Stress Disorder or PTSD, Justine. After all of the things that you've been through, it's very common. Shooting, divorce, death of a friend, your own injuries from the accident, a move, new school, mugging, and a break-up with your boyfriend," she listed. "Jeesh! I'd think something was wrong if you weren't showing signs of stress! Justine didn't like the therapist. She thought she smelled funny. Her name was Dr. Fitzgerald but she encouraged her patients to call her Tori. Seeing the therapist had been her mother's idea.

The bangs had covered up the bald spot for awhile, but one day while Justine snuggled with her mother on the sofa, her head in her mom's lap, Andrea had noticed it. The stress spot was the size of a quarter, smack at the top of her forehead, concealed by bangs. Surprisingly, Andrea hadn't freaked out. "Justine, I know you're still sad about AM. I want you to talk to someone. She's on staff at Evanston Memorial, and she has an office a few blocks from here. You could walk to her office on your way home from school. I've already called her and told her that you'll be calling her to set something up. Her number is on the refrigerator. Do it for me," her mother encouraged. She stopped rubbing Justine's head. "I never told you and the boys, but I talked to her after your dad and I got divorced. I was having nightmares about the police gunning down your dad's girlfriend in the doorway."

Justine lifted her head from her mother's lap and stared into her mom's face. They'd never discussed the shooting. Ever. When Justine tried to talk about it, her mother silenced her. "The past is in the past. No one was hurt, so let's look forward."

"I know now that it was wrong not to talk about it before, especially with you since you were there. I'm sorry, baby." Andrea reached for Justine's hands and placed them in hers. "She fell back into me. When the police shot her, she slumped back and fell on my foot. I never told you that. I still sometimes have nightmares about what happened, but not as frequently. Moving to a new place helped a lot," Andrea smiled. "But talking to Dr. Tori really helped me too. I wanted your dad to go to jail. I wanted him dead actually, but I blamed him. I still do, but through Dr. Tori, I found a way to forgive him in my heart. And now I'm dating Bob and I'm as happy as a clam," she grinned. "So, things work out for a reason. You've been through a lot, and I know that the break-up with AM is hurting you. Talk to her, okay?"

She'd shared her mother's suggestion with Maria and Grace. "Do it, Justine. Dr. Dudley was awesome. It's nothing to be ashamed of. I'm glad I talked to someone," they both encouraged.

Tori smelled like stale cigarettes and dirty clothes. The musty smell in her clothes gave the impression that she hadn't washed her clothes in a long time or ever. Her office was in the basement of a brownstone walk-up on Jarvis Street. It was at the end of the block near Sheridan Road. From the street, Justine could see her apartment.

Her mother had paid for five sessions. Justine made it to three. She couldn't take the smell. The furniture in Tori's office also smelled of cigarette smoke and wet dog hair. Justine never saw a dog, but there was dog fur on the furniture. The only thing redeeming about Tori was her voice. It was soft and soothing. It reminded Justine of a sleep aid. She wanted to suggest to Tori that she record her voice and sell it as a sleep aid. Justine dozed during all three visits. Tori took this as a good sign, that Justine felt relaxed. When you feel the urge to rub your hairline, just redirect that energy. Use a stress ball, bend a paper clip or twirl a pen. Will yourself not to rub your hairline. You have to want to stop doing it. Justine didn't remember if there were any instructions after that. She'd nodded off. She thought it ironic that Tori, the smoking doctor, doled out stress reducing tips.

The green stress ball had been a gift from Kendal. That too

wouldn't fit in her small party purse. She balled her left hand into a tight fist and looked out the window, clenching her teeth to resist the urge to rub her hairline. She remembered that Kendal had described Halsted Street as a north side version of North Michigan Avenue, alive with people at all hours of the day and night. She noticed open boutiques up and down the street, many with tables displaying their wares on the street. This must be Halsted Street. Her suspicions were confirmed by a street sign. She breathed deeply, happy that she was nearer her destination. She pulled out her wallet and counted a ten, a five and several singles.

"Fish, keep singles in your wallet so you don't have to feel pressured to give a taxi driver a five dollar bill, 'cause the driver will make you feel like you should give him the extra singles as a tip. Or they'll act like they don't have change. Don't fall for that trick, just always keep at least five singles on you at all times," Kendal coached. He was always coaching her on life skills. She was Eliza Doolittle, and he was Professor Henry Higgins. And he was usually right.

"It's the building right there. I only charge you ten dollars. You nice lady. I'm sorry I lost you," Arik stammered facing her.

Justine smiled at him. "No problem. Be safe out there and good luck to you," she offered, not sure why she was wishing him good luck. She handed him twelve dollars and exited the taxi street side as instructed.

She watched as the yellow cab pulled away from the curb. From the street, she could see into a party. In the taxi, she'd been too anxious to check her hair or make-up. She remembered the tiara that she'd crammed into her small party purse. She pulled it out and placed it on before crossing in the middle of the street. She confirmed the building's street address as Kendal's.

"If I had a fly condo like his, I wouldn't let people smoke in my place either, chile," the tall blonde man said. "You have to replace your carpet padding once you get cigarette smoke in your place. Or cat pee too," he added.

"When I get my first place, I'm not doing any carpet. Just hardwood floors and ceramic tile or marble if I can hit the lotto," the short, round guy said. "Don't move your foot from the door cause it's so loud up there it'll take them a minute to hear the phone to buzz us back in."

"Excuse me, is this the 'denim and diamonds' party?" Justine smiled timidly.

The tall blonde smoker returned her smile. "Well, that depends. What's the password?"

"The password?"

"The password. What's the password?" he repeated.

"I don't remember him telling me a password. I work with," she stopped herself mid sentence, another Kendal "thou shall not" ringing in her ears. "Fish, do not give out more information than necessary. You do not have to answer every foolish question asked of you."

"On second thought," she replied boldly. "The password is get out of my damn way so I can get my party on!"

The men laughed. "Good answer! You are a feisty little fish, aren't you? I like you. I was just messing with you," the smoker grinned, blowing smoke away from Justine's face. "I almost wore the same tiara tonight, but I decided to wear my blue one instead. I don't want there to be any confusion who the royal blue queen is up in here tonight!" he finished.

"Okay?" his short, stocky friend replied. "Come on up with us. You'll be down here for twenty minutes waiting to get buzzed up. You're dressed in tonight's theme, so I know you're on the guest list."

Tall smoker snubbed his cigarette butt into the stoop and pushed the door open for Justine to enter. She instinctively walked toward the elevator sign. "Walk this way, we're going to take the stairs," tall blonde smoker announced. "Teapot needs the exercise."

"Your mama needs the exercise!" Teapot replied.

"Teapot? Is your name teapot?" Justine asked.

"No. He just calls me that because, as you can see, I'm short and stout," Teapot explained. "I'm just big boned. My body mass index is less than fifteen percent, so I'm all muscle, I'm just short."

"I'm Teapot and this is Killer."

"Killer? Why does he call you killer?" Justine asked.

"Because he's killing himself smoking those cancer sticks," Teapot explained. He opened the stairwell door. Loud dance music wafted through the stairwell. Two girls wearing the exact same tiara as Justine walked down the stairs. "You ladies aren't leaving are you?" Teapot purred. "We didn't get our dance with you yet!"

"We'll be right back. We just have to meet a friend who's lost. We're going to stand on the stoop so she can find the building."

"Hold the door open with your foot or you'll be locked out. The music is too loud to hear the phone buzzer," Teapot reminded.

Justine wondered if the two girls were chapter members. People are people, Justine. Not everyone at the party will be gay. You're not gay, and you're going to the party.

"Do your families call you Killer and Teapot?" she asked walking up the stairs.

"Our families don't call us anything," Killer replied. "I haven't talked to my family in three years. How long has it been for you, Teapot?"

"Almost five."

"Why?"

"After I came out, they didn't want to have anything to do with me. You're not a chapter member are you?" Killer asked.

"No, I'm not."

"I didn't think so. Not everyone is as welcoming and embracing to chapter members," Killer explained. "Our party host complains about his old man all the time, but at least his mom and dad accept him for who he is."

"Amen to that. I know his parents probably don't like it, but at least they didn't disown him. So no, honey. My family does not call me Teapot. They don't call me anything at all. My grandmother still talks to me, but my parents act like I'm dead."

Justine stopped on the stairwell causing Killer to bump into her back.

"Keep it moving girlfriend. Killer needs some more joy juice in his veins."

"So when you told them that you were gay, they disowned you?"

"Pretty much. You seem shocked. Don't you have any friends that are gay?"

Justine bit her lip.

"How old are you? Twenty or twenty-one?"

"I'm twenty, I'll be twenty one this year."

"And you don't have any gay friends who've been disowned by their peeps?"

"Where'd you go to college?" Teapot asked standing on the landing.

"I was attending DePaul, and then I dropped out to work, and now I'm thinking about moving to Dallas or Houston," she said softly, her words barely audible with the loud bass booming through the stairwell.

"That makes sense then. You never lived on campus so you missed the coming out rush. Most kids come out in college. Tell your story, Killer," Teapot encouraged.

"You tell it. You've heard it enough times. And tell the quick version."

"Killer's parents had no idea he was gay. They knew he had a roommate, but they didn't know that he had a "roommate" if you know what I mean," Teapot winked.

"So when they came down for his graduation from college, they went to his apartment and saw that the apartment was a one bedroom unit with one bed!"

"I don't get it," Justine said.

"Get it? A one bedroom apartment with one bed, and his roommate was a guy named Greg!"

"I didn't know how to tell them so I thought I'd show them. I was done with college, and I'd landed my first job and was moving to Cincinnati so I figured what the hell?" Killer continued.

"Did your parents flip out?"

"Yeah. My grandparents were there, and some of my aunts and uncles, so I think my old man was more embarrassed than anything. My uncles kept asking if the sofa was a sofa sleeper. But they could tell by the art in the apartment that Greg and I were a couple. The gig was up."

Justine was mesmerized. "So they had no idea before that night that you were gay?"

"I think they had an idea, but they just tried to pretend like I wasn't. I dated a few girls in high school, but it was all for show."

"Well, how do you know that your parents knew you were gay? How would they have known?" Justine pleaded.

"My mannerisms and things that I liked to do. From the time I was a little boy, I liked talking about fashion and jewelry and make-up. I used to have fashion shows with my sister's dolls. My friends were ripping their sister's dolls heads off, and I was coordinating fashion shows. By the time I was ten, I was picking out all of my mother's clothes."

"Well, some men are just into fashion," Justine challenged, unsure why she was challenging his comments. "Not all men that are into fashion are gay."

"True, but I never liked playing with boys. If given the chance to play with girls or boys, I would choose the girls. And I played girlie games with the girls, not boy games with the girls. Trust me, the signs that their little boy was gay were definitely there."

"Well, what about the Bible?"

"What about it?" Teapot asked.

"Doesn't the Bible say that homosexuality is a sin?" she offered.

"The Bible also says that a man can have more than one wife or that he can stone his wife."

"It also says that we can take an eye for an eye," Killer offered. "Or that a man who divorces his wife is an adulterer and should never marry. And if a man's wife dies, his brother should marry her. It says all of those things. And we don't apply those things into today's culture. And don't forget, the Bible talks about slavery and accepts it as just the practice of the times, and now no one in their right mind would condone slavery."

"Amen. My parents threw the Bible at me when I came out, but I was ready for them and told them what Killer just told you. They didn't know what to say," Teapot added.

"And don't forget, until very recently, a lot of states banned interracial marriage," Killer said.

"That's right," Teapot agreed. "I forgot about that one. Look, I'm a Christian, and I'm a good person. I just happen to be gay. It's who I am, I didn't choose this for myself. God made me who I am, and God has me here for a purpose," he paused smiling at Justine. "I can't believe we're standing here having this deep philosophical debate with you, and we don't even know your name, fish."

"Justine. Justine Wellington," she grinned.

"Why are you so concerned about gays, Miss Wellington?" Killer asked.

"I just found out that my best friend is gay. I've known her since we were ten years old."

"I knew this was personal for you," Killer admitted. "Does that bother you, sugar, learning that your friend is gay?"

"It did at first," she admitted hesitantly. "It's just hard to believe. I don't have anything against gays. I work with Kendal, and he's become one of my closest friends, it's just that I was surprised to find out someone I've known all my life is gay, and I didn't know it."

"Who's Kendal?" Killer asked.

"Kleo," Teapot replied. "Kleo's real name is Kendal, remember?" His gaze directed at Justine. "None of the chapter members call him, Kendal. We call him Kleo."

"Kleo? Why, Kleo?" Justine asked.

"Kleo Elizabeth to be exact," Killer added.

"At the theme parties, all of the chapter members use nicknames or their stripper names."

"You guys are strippers?" Justine replied shockingly, staring at Teapot's short, squat stature.

Don't be looking at me like that. I know I'm short and stout, but I could work it if I needed to, chile," Teapot laughed. "It's for fun. Killer and I have nicknames, but if we have trouble coming up with a good nickname, we do what the strippers do and just use the name of your first pet and pair it with the street that you lived on as a child. Kendal's first pet was named Kleo and he lived on Elizabeth Street, so his chapter member name is Kleo Elizabeth."

"You try it," Killer encouraged. "What was the name of your first pet?"

"I had a fish when I was little, but we didn't name it."

"The first pet you named, fish," Killer said, his irritated inflection resembling the tone that Kendal used with her.

"We got a cat when my parents divorced. We still have the cat. His name is Fudge."

"Okay, that's a nice start. And what's the name of the street that you lived on as a child?"

"Sycamore Lane."

"I love it!" Teapot squealed. "I officially knight you Fudge Sycamore. At every chapter member party from now until forevermore, you will be Fudge Sycamore."

Justine laughed. "But I'm not a chapter member. Will people think I'm a chapter member since you gave me a nickname?"

"Who cares what people think? You know what you are. Not everybody at the party is a chapter member, Fudge. People are people. If we like you we give you a nickname. It'll be our private joke. I'll introduce you as Fudge Sycamore, member-at-large."

"Member-at-large status means that you're straight, but we like you well enough to nickname you," Teapot said. "It's a very special status."

"You guys are fun," Justine smiled.

"One more thing, Fudge Sycamore," Teapot said seriously. "Another reason we use nicknames is to protect the privacy of some of our chapter members. Some members are still in the closet. You know what being in the closet means, right?" Teapot asked.

"It means that the person isn't openly gay."

"Exactly. So we don't use their real names in case someone overhears us talking. Chapter members do not expose or "out" other chapter members."

"It sounds like a secret society," Justine said.

"It is, honey chile. Teapot and I both lost our families when we came out," Killer reminded. "People have to come out when they're good and ready. Girl, the stories I could tell you about how folks acted when they found out their star quarterback son was gay. Chile, it would blow your mind. Now let's get upstairs, I need more punch."

"And I have to pee!" Teapot squealed leading the trio up the stairwell. They were greeted with loud voices that wafted down the stairwell screaming over the loud music like an echo chamber.

"I'm really concerned. She told me she would be here thirty minutes ago. I've called her apartment and there's no answer. I told her to spend the ten dollars and take a taxi. I hope that girl didn't cheap out and get on the bus at this time of night. We can take my car," Kendal screamed.

"Are you sure she doesn't know that I'm here?" the voice asked loudly.

The voice was vaguely familiar, but Justine thought it was her imagination mixed with the loud dance music.

She lifted her head and locked eyes with the voice.

"Justine?"

"AM? What are you doing here?"

Chapter 3

Shades of Blue

It happened on Tiffany's shift. Mrs. Hall, Ian's mom, was running late again. Barbara Ann Hall was always fashionably late, but she could usually be counted on for things that really mattered. Rashanda suspected that she was stuck in traffic on the Edens' Expressway. Ian had told her to take Lake Shore Drive to campus, but Barbara Ann needed to bop into Saks Fifth Avenue to return something.

Rashanda stared at her watch and tapped her foot. "I'm going to be late for my final. And if I'm late, I'm going to fail my class. And if I fail my class, there goes my GPA!"

"Why don't I take you, Shanda?" Tiffany suggested. "I can drop you off and come right back."

"But you need to be heading back, Tiff. I'll just walk."

"Don't be silly, you can't walk in your condition. Just leave the key under the mat, and leave a note in the lobby for her to let herself in. I can drop you off on campus, park the car back in the spot, and lock the key in the glove compartment. Ian can use his key to get in the car."

"That could work. But I feel bad just leaving without her."

"She should have been on time. Ian told her that you had a class."

"True."

"Let's go." Tiffany grabbed her weekend duffel bag and Rashanda's backpack. She watched as her pregnant sister waddled to the door.

"I have to go the bathroom again," Rashanda groaned. "And we have to write her a note."

"You just went to the bathroom!"

"I know that, but I have to go again. I'll be quick."

"That baby must be using your bladder as a pillow! I'll write the note," Tiffany suggested. She reached for a notebook on the table and ripped out a clean sheet of paper and wrote: "Mrs. Hall, I had to scoot to class. Key is under mat."

"Rashanda, can we leave her clues to figure out your apartment number in case she doesn't remember it?"

"Clues?" Rashanda yelled from the hall bathroom, the door wide open. Tiffany could hear her sister peeing. "She knows our apartment number."

"But what if she forgot it? Let's leave her a clue, just in case."

"I get it. That's a cute idea. She's been here twice, but she might not remember the number. Let me think of a clue that works for our apartment," she paused. "Write this down, Tiff, the three digit apartment number is the month of your birthday, the number of daughters you have and the number of boys you have."

"Daughters? I thought you said that Ian didn't have any sisters."

"He doesn't have any sisters, get it?"

"Oh, I get it, so the apartment number is 302. I didn't know that his mother's birthday was in March," Tiffany noticed.

"Yup, her birthday is ten days after yours. So add the clue to the note before I have to use the bathroom again."

Tiffany scrawled the clue on the paper.

"Did you write it legibly so she can read it? Not everyone can read your chicken scratch, Tiffany."

"I printed it, Shanda." Tiffany moved the stacks of papers around on the dining room table that served as a study desk. "Where's your tape, Shanda?"

"I thought I saw it on the table. But Ian may have put it back in the kitchen utility drawer. Keep looking on the table, and I'll check the kitchen."

"You are clearly not concerned with what your mother-in-law thinks about your housekeeping skills! You guys have papers scattered everywhere."

"What? It's a small apartment, and Ian is in the middle of grading papers, so things are a little out of order on the table since we use it as a desk," Rashanda dismissed walking into the small living/dining room with a roll of tape.

"Where do you guys eat with papers scattered everywhere?"

"We have these tv trays that we set-up," Rashanda pointed.

"Daddy would have a fit if he saw you eating on a tv tray, Shanda. 'Meals should be eaten at a table,'" Tiffany said in her deepest voice.

Tiffany's bad impersonation made Rashanda laugh. "Every time we use them I think of Daddy too. We don't watch television while we're eating. We just eat on the trays so we don't have to clear off the table. We connect two trays together to make a mini table, so we're facing each other," she explained. "And don't make me laugh, Tiffany, or I'm going to have to use the bathroom again." Rashanda let her eyes roam the small apartment living room, before reaching to straighten some of the haphazard stacks of paper on the table. Just as quickly she backed away, her hands in the surrender pose. "Ian has the papers he's grading in some kind of system, so if I move them, it might mess up his organized chaos. I'm sure Mrs. Hall will probably say something about the mess, but she'll get over it. And if she says it while Ian is here, he'll straighten her out. The only thing that's really out of order is this table. Our bedroom and the kitchen are neat, and I even cleaned the bathroom sink and toilet. I couldn't bend over to clean the tub, so I just pulled the shower curtain back. It wasn't that dirty, but it could use a good cleaning, I'll have Ian take care of that tonight," she said, her voice panicky.

"It looks fine, Rashanda. It smells clean and fresh too," Tiffany reassured. "I was just teasing you about the papers. You and Ian are full time students, you're pregnant and Ian is working, so Mrs. Hall will get over herself. Is she spending the night? Why would she look in the shower?"

"No, she's not spending the night, but she's nosy."

"Why is she coming up for a visit again?"

"She wanted to bring us some stuff for the baby. I don't want to have a baby shower until after the baby is born, because Ian's old roommate AM says it's bad luck to have it before the baby comes."

"That's what Jewish people do, Shanda. You're not Jewish."

"I'm not Jewish, but I think it's a good idea. Can you imagine how sad I would be if I didn't come home from the hospital with a baby, but I had a stack of stuff here waiting for a baby?" Rashanda shook her head and waved her hand across her face. "Anyway, it's my baby and my decision, so the shower is scheduled for two weeks after my delivery date. But Mrs. Hall insisted on bringing us some stuff now."

"Well, that's awfully thoughtful. And why do you still call her Mrs. Hall?"

"Because that's what I've always called her."

"But you're married to her son now. She didn't tell you to call her Mom or at least Barbara Ann?"

"Nope. Ian's dad told me to call him Ken, and his mother was standing right there, and she didn't say 'you can call me Barbara Ann or Barbara,' so I just call her Mrs. Hall." Rashanda glanced at her wristwatch. "Maybe she doesn't like me."

"I'm sure she likes you, Shanda, she's probably just not ready to accept that her brilliant son is about to become a father. She probably thinks that you trapped him. You know how mothers are with their sons. Or there might be some Oedipal connection going on too," Tiffany winked.

"Not funny. I see you're reading European Literature in Humanities again. Let's go. If we hurry, I can still make it on time. I feel like the white students look at me funny when I waddle into class with my pregnant belly, especially now that my fingers are too swollen to wear my wedding ring, It feels like they're looking their noses down at me like I'm some dumb, unwed, black single mother about to get on welfare."

"Nobody thinks that, and who cares if they do, Shanda! You know that you're married. I swear, carrying that baby is making you paranoid! Did the baby steal your self confidence? I don't remember you ever exerting this much energy over what people thought about you before."

Tiffany grabbed Rashanda's backpack and walked through the door. Rashanda locked the door and handed the key to Tiffany who placed it under the small welcome doormat. "I'll take the stairs and pull the car around. You take the elevator, and I'll meet you out front."

"The car is parked in the back, near the alley." The girls

walked down the hallway toward the elevator and stairwell.

"I know that, Rashanda. I was with Ian when he parked the car after picking me up from the train."

"That's right, I forgot," Rashanda smiled. "Don't forget to tape the note to the glass door in the lobby before you go to the car. Mrs. Hall knows the code to enter through the main lobby door."

"If you gave her the lobby code, why didn't you just give her a key to the apartment too?"

"She asked for a key, but Ian didn't want her just barging in on us. At least she has to knock to get into the apartment. And besides, we didn't give her the lobby code, but we mentioned that the code was Ian's birthday, so she tried it one day, and the next time that she came for a visit, she just let herself up," Rashanda pushed the elevator button. "It would be too rude and obvious to change the code now."

"Hmmmph! I would. She needs some boundaries," Tiffany grunted. "And she needs a watch so she can be on time when people ask her to do something. I'll meet you in the front."

"I gave you the car key, right?"

Tiffany jiggled the car key in her sister's face before pushing the stairwell door.

৵৹৻

She couldn't tell if it was a police siren or fire department siren. The sirens made her heart race, her mind doing mental gymnastics to trace her steps. She feared that she'd left the coffee pot on again. She always forgot to turn off the new coffee pot. The last time that she'd forgotten to turn it off, she'd received a lecture about how it could cause a fire. She didn't quite understand how a coffee pot could cause a fire. He'd explained that if the coffee pot was almost empty, the contents could evaporate and the pot would then be heating an empty glass container which could crack, spark and ignite a fire. She found that highly unlikely. Possible, sure, but highly unlikely. But she'd promised to be more careful. She wasn't supposed to be drinking coffee in her condition anyway, but she hadn't slept well the night before, and she needed a pick me up to prepare for her exam. Rashanda trudged closer to the deafening sirens, praying that it wasn't a fire truck. She exhaled when she saw two squad cars parked in front of her dorm.

Drug bust? Was one of the students smoking pot and got caught? Occasionally, she and Ian could smell marijuana in the building. The first time it happened, she didn't know what the smell was. Like most of the residents in the dorm, they were accustomed to keeping their apartment door open when they were home, they liked to wave at the students loitering in the hallway. The apartment reserved for the resident hall coordinator was really three large dorm rooms that had been reconfigured into a one bedroom apartment.

Sometimes on the weekends, a strange smell mixed with incense wafted into their apartment and made Rashanda sleepy. The first time it happened, she curled up on the sofa and took a nap. Ian had called it a contact high. Now that Rashanda was pregnant, Ian was concerned about his wife inhaling any toxins or pollutants, so whenever he smelled anything foreign in the hallway, he closed their door. At their monthly meeting with the residents, he'd told them that any illegal activity that interfered with anyone else's enjoyment of their room would result in sanctions. Rashanda knew that a few of the students continued to partake in their occasional ritual and placed rolled up wet towels under their doors in an attempt to block the smell from getting into the hallway. "Do you smell that?" Ian would ask concerned. "Smell what?" Rashanda would feign. "I don't smell anything," she would fib in an effort to protect the residents whom she adored. Moments later, Rashanda would always say that she wanted to take a walk to stretch her swollen legs. Ian always obliged. Once in the hallway, he would ask her if she smelled anything again. And again her reply would be no. After their walk, their nostrils filled with the Lake Michigan scents and fresh baked goods from the corner bakery, the smell that had been the impetus for the walk was usually long gone and forgotten.

Now that Rashanda was in her ninth month of pregnancy, she'd cut a deal with her husband. She could walk one way to or from their off campus dormitory but not both ways. If she walked to class, she had to take the shuttle, the train or get a ride back to the dormitory. At first, she thought she could live with this restriction. But in reality, she didn't like the limits that it placed on her mobility. The shuttle ran ten minutes after every hour, so if she missed the shuttle, she had to wait fifty five minutes for the next one. In her third trimester, Rashanda could barely sit through a one hour lecture without having to relieve her bladder. So by the time she waddled to the restroom with her backpack and made her way to the bus stop, she found herself missing the shuttle on a regular basis.

The first few times she missed the shuttle, she walked to the library to study, not wanting to study alone in the empty lecture hall. But now that her gait was much slower, after walking to the library, and settling into a cubicle, it was time to visit the bathroom again. Sometimes she was able to read a few pages before it was time to pack up her backpack and prepare for her pregnant shuffle back to the shuttle bus depot. The walk from her last class' lecture hall to their dorm took less than twenty minutes in her pregnant state, so waiting an hour for a shuttle bus was silly to her. And taking the train didn't make much sense to her either. She had to climb thirty six steps, wait twenty minutes for the train and then walk from the train. Trying to bum a ride to her off campus dorm had proved futile. Only the commuter students drove to campus every day, and she hadn't befriended any with whom she felt comfortable bumming a ride home. Some days she broke the rule and walked both ways, fibbing to her husband so that he didn't worry. But today, Tiffany had dropped her off, so she was technically allowed to walk back.

Rashanda had made it to class on time and her exam had gone very well. She hadn't noticed any glaring stares from the students who were still not accustomed to her swollen belly. She'd also completed her exam without having to excuse herself to go to the bathroom. While taking the exam, the baby moved and squirmed as though trying to find a more comfortable sleeping position or poke Rashanda to walk around, but miraculously during the exam, the baby had managed not to compress her bladder. When Rashanda was active, the baby slept. The movement of her body and the sloshing of the amniotic fluid created a hammock effect for the baby, like being rocked in a rocking chair. When she sat still, the rocking stopped and the baby awakened. The baby's movements had gotten really animated at night when she tried to sleep. Normally a belly sleeper, she'd been forced to find a new sleeping position by the time she was four months pregnant. Ian also told her that she'd begun to snore now that she was pregnant. The only time that she didn't snore was when she slept on her left side. She hoped that the snoring phase subsided after delivery.

As she approached her building, she watched as a uniformed officer turned off the siren, but the blue disco lights atop his squad car continued to spin. Now she could see students mulling in the lobby, clearly sharing the play by play of events with each other.

"The police think that it was a townie who'd been casing the building for awhile. He had a backpack with him, so she probably thought he was a student."

"He didn't look like a criminal."

"Not at all! He was actually cute," one of the girls giggled.

"He had golden blonde hair and blue eyes. He was adorable."

Rashanda recognized the students as residents, but could only remember one of the girls' names. "Hey Alyssa, what's going on?" she asked.

"Hey, Rashanda. Where'd you come from? I didn't even see you walk in. Is she going to be okay?" Alyssa asked without thinking.

"Is who going to be okay?"

"You don't know?" Alyssa asked.

"I just came back from taking my final."

"Someone tried to break into your apartment," one of the girls shared.

Rashanda heard the words, but didn't comprehend the meaning.

"Did you hear what Denise said, Rashanda? Someone tried to break into your apartment. But they caught the guy. Ian is upstairs now."

Her feet were frozen to the carpet. Oh, my God! Tiffany! Her left hand cupped her large belly.

"You should probably sit down. You're pregnant."

"I need to get upstairs."

"I think the police turned off the elevator. Can you walk up three flights of stairs?" Alyssa asked.

Without answering, Rashanda walked toward the stairwell and climbed the stairs effortlessly without pausing on the landing. Alyssa and Denise walked behind her.

There were more police officers in the hallway. As she walked down the corridor toward her apartment, her heart raced again.

"Rashanda! There you are!" Ian blurted gripping his young wife in his arms.

"Where's Tiffany?" Rashanda gasped. "Is she alright?"

"Tiffany?" Ian repeated. "She's not here. And Mom's going to be all right."

"Your mom?"

"She sprayed the guy with mace and kicked him in the nuts!" Ian laughed. "Can you imagine? Barbara Ann Hall kicked someone in the nuts! She wanted a cocktail, so she's having a beer to settle her nerves."

Rashanda felt the baby kick again. She reminded herself to breathe.

"A beer? Your mom drinks beer?" Rashanda asked incredulously, almost more shocked to imagine Barbara Ann drinking a beer than she was to hear that she'd kicked someone in the nuts. "What happened?" Rashanda asked.

"Mom said that a student was in the vestibule waiting for his roommate so she let him follow her into the building. She got a kick out of your clue and was explaining the clue to the guy. She said she got suspicious when he also got off on the third floor, so she got her mace spray ready, just in case. And when she got off the elevator and started heading toward the apartment, she pretended to leave something in the car, so she turned back toward the elevator, and that's when he grabbed her arm so she sprayed him with mace," Ian explained. "And then she kicked him in the nuts and sprayed him with mace again. She said he crumpled over and didn't know whether to rub his eyes or grab his nuts. She ran down the hall, pulled the key from under the mat, locked herself in the apartment and called the police. The police said that he had only made it about a half block before they caught him. He could barely walk from the pain and he could barely see after being sprayed twice with mace."

"Is she okay?"

"I'm fine, Rashanda. I'm a tough old broad! Don't let the St. John suits fool you! I was raised in West Philly, so I know how to take care of myself," she boasted standing in the doorway and flexing a bicep. The students in the hallway applauded and whistled. Barbara Ann Hall looked like a well dressed police officer, her St. John pant suit the same rich navy blue color as the police officers' polyester uniforms.

"You're lucky that you weren't hurt, Mrs. Hall," the officer stated. "It's often best to give the perpetrator whatever he asks for so you don't get hurt."

"Had he not doubled over groaning like a girl, I would have kicked him in the teeth! Now if he had just ordered me to drop my Gucci, I probably would have," she paused as she described her purse by its designer name. "But I wasn't going to just hand him the Gucci. He would have still gotten sprayed. But the little creep put his hands on me. And once someone puts his hands on Barbara Ann, all bets are off! I had to take him down! West Philly in the house!" she hooted.

The students loitering in the hall applauded loudly. Mrs Hall took a bow, careful not to spill her beer on her expensive knit suit.

Rashanda stared at her mother-in-law as though she'd never met her. She watched as Ian's mother took another swig from her beer. "I haven't had a beer in ages. I used to love beer, but it was ruining my girlish figure and giving me a beer gut, so I had to cut it out of my diet. St. John was not designed to accommodate a beer gut. But there's nothing like an ice cold beer after you've kicked a guy in the nuts," she giggled.

This time, Rashanda noticed that even the two police officers giggled at Mrs. Hall's performance as the students squealed and hollered.

Barbara Ann Hall was enjoying her audience. "Maybe I should teach a self defense class for your residents, Ian. Kicking a guy in the nuts is really an art form," she explained, careful to direct her comments to Alyssa and Denise who stood against the wall. "If you don't kick them just so, they won't feel it," she continued, pressing her index finger and thumb together. "And believe me when I tell you, if you're going to bother to kick a guy in the nuts, you want him to feel it. You girls need to learn the proper way to disarm an assailant with an accurate kick to the nuts," she laughed. "It's a life skill, like swimming, because sometimes you can't always get to your mace."

Alyssa and Denise giggled and blushed. Rashanda was in shock. Barbara Ann Hall had repeated the word nuts three times.

"Have you sprayed your mace before, Mrs. Hall?" Rashanda asked.

Barbara Ann tilted her head and looked at Rashanda with a sideways glance, almost a frown. "Of course I have, little missy. I'm from West Philadelphia born and raised. I've sprayed plenty of mace on the mean streets of Philly. That's how I knew to keep my hand on the trigger finger when I was in the elevator with that young man. He was cute as all get out too. Blonde hair and the bluest eyes I've seen up close in a long time. But it was something about him that didn't smell right. The criminal "Pretty Boy Floyd" was a cutie pie too, and he was one of the worst criminals around. Not all criminals are boot ugly," she explained toward Alyssa and Denise. "Attractive criminals know that people get caught up in cuteness, and they use that as their secret weapon. But not me, I was suspicious about that young man from the word go."

"What do you mean, Mom?"

"This is finals week, and he was loitering in the lobby in the middle of the afternoon. If he were really a locked out student, he would have been sitting on the floor reviewing notes or something while waiting for someone to let him in. And when I asked him what finals he'd already taken, he stammered and said that his first final was tomorrow. That did it for me. I knew something was up right then and there. Today is Thursday of finals week, no one takes their first final on the Friday of finals week. He was a cute, stupid criminal, looking for an easy mark," Barbara Ann finished. "I'm just glad I came along when I did or one of these cute little co-eds could have really been hurt. They would have been entranced by his looks and next thing you know, it could have been a different ending altogether. Who knows what his real intentions were?" she said seriously. "Because if you'll lie you'll steal, and if you'll steal, you'll kill."

"My mother used to say that all the time," one of the students said.

"So, it's a good thing that I was late meeting you, Rashanda, or I wouldn't have been here to take down that guy. By the way, your coffee pot was on too. You could have burned down the building. You need to get a coffee pot with an automatic shutoff switch. And you shouldn't be drinking coffee in your condition," she added before taking a long swig of her beer.

This was the first Barbara Ann bee sting. Rashanda dropped her head, hoping her husband hadn't heard the last part of his mother's comment. A part of her wanted to lie and say that she'd made the coffee for her sister, but her mother's voice rang through her head. *You're a grown woman, Rashanda. You're as grown as she is. You don't have to defend your actions to her or lie about whatever you're doing. Just ignore her when she makes those comments. And don't let her intimidate you. You can't stop her from saying whatever she wants,, but you don't have to heed her suggestions or let it ruin your day either. Just learn to ignore her little comments.*

"Ian, I need another beer, please," Barbara Ann ordered. She patted her flat midsection. "I am going to have to increase my cardio tomorrow after chugging two beers. I'm surprised you don't have any red wine in the refrigerator, Rashanda. You know you can have an occasional glass of red wine now that the baby's fully developed. If you're drinking coffee, you can drink wine." Bee sting number two. "Heck, when I was pregnant with my sons, I drank and smoked during both of my pregnancies, and my boys were both over nine pounds and twenty-one inches long. But of course, that was well before the surgeon general put out those warnings about smoking and drinking while pregnant." She smiled at Rashanda. "My grandchild is just in there gaining weight now so a glass of red wine would help you both sleep better," she smiled, patting Rashanda's large belly. Ian handed his mother another can of beer. Surprise belly pat soothed the sting of Bee sting number two.

"Telling by the bags under your eyes, you're not getting much sleep."

Bee sting number three.

"I don't drink. And I'm not twenty-one yet, Mrs. Hall,"
Rashanda reminded. "So technically I'm not even old enough to
drink yet."

"Oh. I forgot that. You're old enough to have a baby, but
not old enough to have a glass of wine. Hmmph. You need a
license to drive a car, but anyone can just have a baby." Barbara
Ann mumbled under her breath, but loud enough for Rashanda
to hear.

Bee sting number four. The crowd pleasing, beer chugging
Barbara Ann Hall was an imposter, the opening act. This was the
Mrs. Hall that Rashanda knew, the Barbara Ann Hall who always
had a comment about everything, and the comment was usually
a negative one. Rashanda had slowly grown more accustomed to
her mother-in-law's sidebar comments, always mumbled within
earshot of her new daughter-in-law. Rashanda had nicknamed
them "bee stings" or "zingers." Behind her back, Rashanda called
Ian's mother "The Quon" which stood for "the queen of negativity."
Her criticisms knew no boundaries. Rashanda had decided that
her mother-in-law was incapable of holding her tongue or listening
to a story for the entertainment value. She always felt the need to
comment on every event, situation or experience that came within
earshot. Barbara Ann made a comment about everything. From
the way Rashanda washed dishes in the sink, folded the laundry,
dusted the furniture, prepared dinner, brushed her teeth, organized
her backpack or washed her hair. Barbara Ann had a different,
albeit better, way of performing every task, and she made sure
that you knew it and heard it from her. Once, Rashanda shared
a funny story about how her umbrella got caught in the wind

and how she chased it for almost a block. Instead of laughing at the story, Barbara Ann explained that Rashanda should purchase a "better" umbrella, one that was wind resistant and had a wrist strap. Rashanda nicknamed Barbara's comments "Barbara Ann band-aids." Every comment or experience received an annoying "Barbara Ann band-aid."

If Rashanda said that it was a beautiful sunny day, instead of agreeing with her, Barbara Ann would complain about the sun giving her wrinkles and share the level of SPF that was necessary to avoid wrinkles and skin cancer. At first, Rashanda took Barbara Ann's comments personally, her penance for marrying Ian. She thought it was the dreaded mother-in-law daughter-in-law tension that she'd heard so much about, but as she spent more time in Mrs. Hall's presence she learned that it was just her way. Barbara Ann Hall felt she knew best and was incapable of just listening to a story or observing an experience without adding an unsolicited "Barbara Ann band-aid" or highlighting the negative in a situation. Rashanda didn't dislike Mrs. Hall, but being fixed all of the time proved annoying and exhausting, especially now that she was pregnant and her hormones were out of whack. She found herself anxious in her presence, exerting way too much energy trying to anticipate what Barbara Ann would think about a situation in an effort to avoid the Barbara Ann criticism that was always cleverly disguised as a "helpful tip." Maybe Tiffany was right. Maybe carrying a baby had robbed Rashanda of some of her self confidence.

But today, Rashanda was seeing a different side of Mrs. Hall. She'd almost been mugged, yet instead of sitting on the sofa trembling in fear, or criticizing Rashanda for not being home when she arrived, she was raw and gritty, chugging beers from the can in a police officer blue St. John knit suit.

Rashanda understood that Barbara Ann's band-aids' were not reserved just for Rashanda. "You need door monitors downstairs at all times, son. I know you have them at night, but you need to hire someone to sit there during the day between nine and two. You could hire a retired person and pay them minimum wage to sit there and read their newspaper, watch a portable television and watch the lobby. With your dorm being off campus and not having the foot traffic of the on campus dorms, the housing office should give you extra resources for this security feature," she burped. "Pardon me! I haven't had beer in so long I'm forgetting my manners," she giggled.

One of the police officers chuckled. "I think we have everything we need in our report, Mrs. Hall. Thank you again for coming downstairs to identify the assailant. It always helps our case when we have a witness who can positively identify a suspect. And I think your suggestion for daytime security in the lobby is a good one. Criminals look for easy targets. With someone sitting in the lobby, watching the door, a criminal is more likely to choose another target."

"I think that's a really great idea, Mrs. Jordan," Rashanda suggested. "I'm sure there's probably someone at the senior center who would be interested in a job like that."

Mrs. Jordan smiled at Rashanda and took another swig from her beer can. Rashanda braced herself for the Barbara Ann band-aid or negative comment. "Rashanda, you can call me Barbara Ann, we're family now, and you're carrying my first grandchild."

Rashanda shifted her weight and stared at her mother-in-law like she'd seen a ghost. And then, her water broke.

Chapter 4

Ace

The giggle was mischievous, like that of a small child holding on to a secret, afraid that her private gem was plastered across her face and visible to the world; the only thing containing the secret was a stifled giggle. But like a tight fitting lid atop a boiling pot of stew, the giggle slipped around on her face and dripped happiness down her cheeks like gravy on a biscuit. She was alone. There was no reason to stifle the giggle. Yet she found herself unable to giggle aloud.

The delight that she felt made her feel giddy, childlike and warm inside. Her cheeks blushed. She realized that she felt guilty for feeling so joyful and concluded that it was not humanly possible for her to be any happier than she was at that very moment.

She wished that there were a way for her to quantify her happiness. To measure it like you measured your temperature, blood pressure and cholesterol. She wanted to capture and remember exactly how happy she was feeling so that she could read it and be reminded of this feeling in the future. A cuff that you placed on your bicep at the drugstore could determine your level of delight, and a happiness remedy shared to help you measure and maximize your happiness level. "Your sugar level is low. You could be made happier by eating more chocolate" the display could read. Or, "go for a 2.5 mile run and release some endorphins. That will help elevate your happiness level." In her case, her happiness reading would state, "you have a perfect happiness score. You are flourishing in a state of bliss that is extremely unusual and without equal. Relish in this time of joy, while it lasts." She knew it would be important to include the "while it lasts" statement at the end of the happiness reading so as not to fool anyone into thinking that a perfect state of bliss was easily attained or maintained.

Grace chuckled to herself, wondering if some erudite student sequestered in a University of Illinois chemistry laboratory were hard at work on such a device, a tool to measure happiness and dole out happiness prescriptions and remedies.

It had been a gradual progress, but she found herself celebrating life in a way that she'd never felt possible before. As she crouched her way through the corridors of River North High School, slouched like a giraffe grazing from a short tree, she now celebrated her statuesque frame. After prom, she'd given her pastel heels to Goodwill claiming that at six feet tall, she didn't need to be any taller. But now that she embraced her height, she'd purchased a pair of two inch wedge sandals that she wore with pride. She'd practiced walking in them with a book on her head as Teenie and Maria had suggested, and now she could glide in them with three books balanced atop her head. Her posture perfect, and her heel walking gait described as flawless, by her new friend.

Noticing a flyer taped to the dormitory vestibule for an intramural, co-ed, recreational volleyball team that would compete against other student dormitory teams on campus, Grace decided to attend the informational meeting even though she'd never participated in organized athletics before and had only received average grades in physical education as a student. It was the promise of home made salsa and chips that really lured her into the meeting. Her plan was to slip in quietly, help herself to the chips and salsa that would be set-up on the table in the back of the room near the door and then sneak out unnoticed, but when Grace walked into the informational meeting, her dorm mates applauded wildly, led by Tomoko, her Japanese friend. Grace looked behind her with a puzzled expression.

"Grace, I'm so glad you're here! I was hoping that you would come out for volleyball," Tomoko squealed.

"I've never played volleyball before. Don't let my height fool you. I just thought that I'd come and get some information. I could stand to get some regular exercise," she stammered nervously, too embarrassed to admit that it was the salsa that had her attention.

"Don't worry, we'll teach you how to play. You can't coach height!" Tomoko squealed again. "If you hadn't shown up, I was going to knock on your door and beg you to play!"

"But I've really never played volleyball before, Tomoko. I've played in P.E. class, but that's it. And I wasn't very good. I'm not that coordinated."

"I'm a great coach. In high school I coached the junior varsity team and middle school girls. You're in good hands," Tomoko assured. "I will have you looking like you won the state tournament with your high school in a few weeks. Trust me, I know what I'm doing," she winked.

The group decided to schedule early morning practices before breakfast. Not really a morning person, Grace wanted to object, but the other players nodded in agreement at the practicality of scheduling an early practice that would not interfere with their class and work schedules. She decided that she could sacrifice a few winks for exercise. She'd gained ten pounds already.

The practice gymnasium was located directly across the street from their dorm. And each practice began with a brisk half mile jog around the indoor track. Grace understood the rules of the game and listened intently as her teammates coached her through the strategy of using all hits before sending the ball back over the net.

Tomoko was a player coach and had a remedy for Grace's problem. At the next day's practice, she handed Grace a rubber ball and told her that she wanted her to practice tossing the ball into the air and catching it ten times in a row. If she missed, she had to start over until she could do it ten consecutive times. Grace felt foolish standing on the sidelines tossing the small rubber ball into the air while her dorm mates worked on their volleyball drills. The assignment felt like some odd sorority rush hazing ritual and she wondered if she were being hazed. But as she tossed the ball into the air and chased it, no one paid her any attention. She found herself starting over until she finally caught the ball ten consecutive times in a row.

"Let's see what you got," Tomoko said. "Give me ten consecutive tosses. What time is your first class?"

"Nine o'clock," Grace replied.

"So is mine. So we have time. Go for it."

Grace tossed the ball into the air and completed the drill.

"I knew you'd be a quick study. Sometimes it takes my students two days to master this drill." Tomoko reached into her duffel bag and handed Grace a bag of small, plastic jacks. "Have you ever played jacks before?"

Grace nodded her head no.

Tomoko took the ball from Grace's hand and sat on the rubberized track floor. "You need to play this on a hard surface, but I can play it on the rubberized surface. You have to toss the ball into the air in a controlled fashion, scoop one jack without touching any of the other jacks and catch the ball in the same hand," she demonstrated. "Your other hand cannot touch anything. Once you can pick up one jack at a time, move on to scooping two jacks at a time." Tomoko demonstrated this trick effortlessly. "You try it," she encouraged.

Grace sat on the floor and tried to imitate Tomoko's technique. The ball bounced and rolled away from her.

"It's much harder to play on this rubber surface. Practice on your kitchen floor. Your hands are pretty big, so you should be able to scoop all of the jacks and the ball in one hand, but for right now, I just want you to work on twosies. This will help you with your hand eye coordination. Toss the ball into the air in a controlled fashion so you know where it is. It'll make sense once you get the hang of it. Once you master this, you can work on the drills we're practicing."

The game had frustrated her initially, and she cursed as she chased the ball across the kitchen floor, but she kept at it, wondering how she'd not learned to play the game as a child. She didn't have any early memories of her elderly parents playing with her on the floor, and by the time she met her friends at Battle Creek Junior High School, they were past the "jacks" stage of life. Tomoko had played competitive volleyball in high school and told her that their coach used jacks to help the girls work on their fine motor skills and hand eye coordination. It also relaxed the team between matches. Grace laughed when Tomoko told her that the coach also brought coloring books and crayons with him to tournaments as a distraction to relax his players. It must have worked. Tomoko's volleyball team won their state championship tournament her junior and senior year in high school.

At only five foot six, Tomoko could spike the ball over the net, boasting a two foot vertical leap.

At first, the bruises to her forearms were purple and painful, but like a trooper, Grace iced her arms and forged on. At practices, they worked with her on mastering the fundamentals of the game including the overhand serve. Her biggest challenge proved to be her hand eye coordination and hitting the ball with too much force and not enough finesse.

The team entrusted Tomoko to teach Grace how to spike. Her first attempts were gangly and awkward resulting in whistles by the student referee as her long lithe body leaned into the net time and time again. Repeated attempts weren't much better.

"Your chi isn't strong enough," Tomoko observed.

"My what isn't strong enough? My chi?" she repeated.

Tomoko placed her small hand on Grace's abdomen just below her breasts. "Your chi, your core, your stomach. You need to develop more core strength."

"What's my chi?"

"It's your center." Tomoko patted Grace's abdomen firmly. "An athlete's power comes from her chi, her core. That's why athletes always have amazing abdominal muscles with six packs. Because when your center is strong, your balance and coordination are improved. You get your power from your core. I do at least two hundred sit-ups every day. Three hundred if I can fit it in. And I also practice yoga."

Grace frowned at the petite Tomoko. "How do you have time to do that many sit-ups?"

"It's easy," Tomoko shrugged. "When I'm studying, I bang out fifty or seventy-five before switching from one subject to the next. And if I'm watching television, I do my sit-ups during the commercials. I can usually do almost one hundred and fifty during the commercial breaks. I switch from lower ab focus to upper abs."

Her hand wrapped around her waist, Grace felt her doughy mid-section, draped in a bright orange oversized Illini tee-shirt. She'd purchased the tee-shirt in an extra large on purpose to camouflage the freshman weight that she'd gained. Her gaze shifted to Tomoko who always wore a sports bra to their volleyball practices and private coaching sessions. Today's sports bra was electric green, her abdominal muscles tight and pronounced.

"You need to do sit-ups," Tomoko stated flatly. "Better yet. You need to hold the plank."

"What's that?"

"It's a yoga term. It's primarily core work, but it also tones your arms because you have to hold your own body weight. Let me show you."

Tomoko dropped to her knees and extended her feet into a push-up position. "The key is that your body should be flat like the plank on a pirate's ship. Your touchie or rear end shouldn't be up in the air like this," she demonstrated by protruding her gluteus maximus into the air. "That's cheating. It should be flat and parallel to the ground." Grace watched as Tomoko adjusted her body weight. "Start with trying to hold the plank for one minute." Grace was amazed that Tomoko could hold a conversation while lying in a suspended push-up position. "My personal best is about thirteen minutes." Tomoko stood to her feet. "Now you try it."

Grace kneeled on the mat. "Now get in position like you're going to do a push-up. I'll correct your form. Lean on your forearms and clasp your hands together." Grace did as instructed. "Now drop your butt down a little. Perfect! I'll clock you and see how long you last."

Without warning, Grace felt her arms trembling. "This is hurting my back," she complained.

"It's hurting your back because your core isn't strong enough to do all of the work by itself yet. Try to lift up one arm. It'll take some of the pressure off of your back."

"Grace lifted one arm and collapsed in a heap on the mat. That's hard!" she groaned.

"It'll get easier. Try it again."

She glanced around the gym to see if anyone was watching her. They weren't. Under Tomoko's patient gaze, Grace dropped to the mock push-up position once again.

"Now lower your butt. If your form isn't perfect, it will hurt your back. And remember with any type of exercise you will only reap what you sow. You won't get the full benefit of the exercise if your form isn't correct. You're only cheating yourself so learn and practice good form."

This time, Grace felt her toes cramping and her arms trembling simultaneously. A bead of sweat dangled from the tip of her pointy nose, and her arms felt like noodles. She dropped to her knees.

"Not bad. You held it for almost one minute that time. Not bad at all. But you can do much better than that so your assignment is to be able to hold the plank for two minutes. I'll test you this Friday."

"You mean five days from now Friday?"

"Yup."

"I have to hold it for two minutes in five days! I can't even hold it for one minute now. That's impossible."

"No it isn't. Just follow my practice schedule. Plank whenever you switch subjects or during commercials. Even if you're in the library, just drop and plank."

"You're kidding, right?"

"Actually, I'm not. In high school, my coach made my teammates hold the plank for a minimum of three minutes. If you couldn't hold a three minute plank, you got cut from the team. Period. This is college. No one is really paying attention to you. They'll just think that it's your stress reliever. Trust me."

"How in the heck can you hold the plank for thirteen minutes?"

"I could have held it longer. They stopped me at thirteen minutes."

"Why? Why'd they stop you?"

"They thought I was showing off. But I wasn't. I just have amazing core strength."

"Hmph! And you only weigh about ninety pounds, so you're not holding as much weight as I am," Grace grunted.

"Actually, I weigh one hundred and two pounds now. Muscle weighs more than fat. And yes, I weigh less than you do, but your arms should be stronger than mine so you should be able to plank your own body weight for at least three minutes."

"Three minutes? You said two minutes a few seconds ago."

"Three minutes will be the goal for two weeks from now."

That night, she forced herself to follow Tomoko's training schedule. She switched on the seldom watched small television in her dorm room and watched an episode of Diff'rent Strokes, forcing herself to plank during the commercials. As instructed, she rested during the program and planked on commercials. One minute forty-five seconds had been her personal best. The next day, she alternated sit-ups into her routine, her stomach knotting in pain at the unfamiliar workout. She'd not been bold enough to exercise in the library like Tomoko suggested, but she'd passed the two minute and three minute plank test with relative ease.

"Ace!" Tomoko squealed. "Grace, you just got your first ace!"

At the serve line, Grace watched as her teammates performed a clapping ritual on their thighs and between their legs and ended with a shout of 'Ace!' "Just like in tennis, if your opponent can't return your serve, that's called an ace," Tomoko explained. "Way to go, Ace!" she screamed from the sidelines. Grace was greeted with the ace routine two more times that day. She awkwardly faked her way through the ace chant when two of her teammates scored their own ace serve points. Her teammates had nicknamed her "Grace-the ace!"

Grace was really enjoying being part of the volleyball team. Under Tomoko's coaching, she'd mastered the overhead serve and was a force at the net. She sometimes still leaned into the net on her spike attempts, but so did many other players; however, her blocking and her powerful overhead serve had become the team's secret weapon. The dorm team was undefeated. She laughed when she realized that she'd never sampled the salsa that lured her to the informational meeting.

The knock at the door startled her. Grace peeked through the peephole and smiled.

"Hey, Tomoko, come on in," Grace smiled, suddenly self conscious about her untidy apartment even though Tomoko often stopped by unannounced and had seen the place in worse shape than it was now. "I was just doing my sit-ups before I clean up my apartment. Girl, I'm so glad that you gave me that commercial sit-up tip. I've been doing them during the commercials when I'm watching television, and I've already lost seven pounds of the ten that I gained," she boasted. "These commercials are always so loud.

And I can even run a ten minute mile now. I was going to surprise you with my new pace on our next run," she boasted.

Grace hurriedly stacked the scattered papers on the table in search of the remote control. Not finding it, she walked over to turn down the volume on the television set. "I think they deliberately turn up the volume on commercials because they know that people leave the room when the commercials come...." Her voice trailed as she stared at her friend for the first time.

"Are you crying, Tomoko?"

Distracted by her own clutter, Grace hadn't noticed Tomoko's tears when she opened the door. "Are you okay?" she asked, wishing she could take the words back. Her eyes swollen with fresh tears, clearly she was not okay.

One hand shielding her eyes, Tomoko plopped on the sofa and wiped her tears with the back of her other hand. Not sure what to do next, Grace spotted a box of tissue on the small dining room table. She quietly retrieved it and placed it in front of her friend.

Her mother's voice ringing in her head, "Grace, sometimes silence is the best thing you can give someone who's hurting. Just sit still until they're ready to share their pain." Grace sat motionless and stared at her volleyball coach.

Without looking up, Tomoko pulled four tissues from the box in rapid succession and rubbed her eyes. "I don't know what I'm going to do. I just don't know what I'm going to do," Tomoko finally mumbled almost to herself.

Grace wondered if someone had died.

Tomoko reached for more tissues. The silence was making Grace uncomfortable. She almost felt like she should leave and give Tomoko some privacy, but then she remembered that Tomoko had knocked on her door.

"I'm going to have to quit school."

Now Grace wondered if Tomoko's parents had died or if Tomoko had somehow lost her scholarship. Ignoring her mother's advice, Grace asked the question that was burning in her chest. "What happened, Tomoko?"

Startled, Tomoko's dark eyes stared at Grace as though she were surprised by her presence, her expression distant and vacant. Staring at Grace again, the tears flowed down her cheeks matched with heavy sobs. This time, Grace decided to heed her mother's advice and sat in the chair across from her friend and stared at her silently.

"I'm sorry. I just can't believe that this is happening to me," Tomoko blurted. "I really trusted her, but I guess I should have known better."

Like a statue, Grace sat quietly and listened as a horn sounded from the street. The horn made her think of her car. It was dirty and needed to be washed. She wondered who had betrayed Tomoko's trust, but she was afraid that another question from her might trigger another round of sobs.

Tomoko smiled at Grace. "You probably think that I'm crazy. I'm sitting here balling my eyes out and you have no idea what my problem is."

Grace returned the smile. She could hear Tomoko's deep inhale.

"I told my sister a secret that she swore she wouldn't tell anyone, but she did," Tomoko sniffled. "And now my life is being turned upside down," she trembled.

The horn sounded again. Grace wondered what type of car was blowing the horn. She wondered if real car aficionados could discern car makes and models by the sound of the horn. She made a mental note to blow the horn on her BMW to see if it sounded different from the horn that she now heard. Curious, she wondered if it would be rude to peek out the window and stare at the car.

"My parents have said that they will stop paying my tuition effective immediately if I don't stop it."

"Stop what?" Grace blurted unexpectedly. She braced herself for another round of Tomoko's tears.

Tomoko stared at the floor. Grace wished that she could retrieve the words and just listen as her mother advised. But it was too late. The question was now in the universe.

"My parents said that they will disown me unless I stop being gay."

This time, it was Grace who cried.

Chapter 5

It's Cheaper to Keep Her

The law school library was chilly, and her toes felt like popsicles. She wiggled them around and squeezed them together, wishing that she'd placed a pair of thicker socks inside her backpack. She made a mental note to upgrade to wool socks for next time. The last time she'd studied in the law school stacks, she feared that her pink, pinky toe would need to be severed, it was so numb. Once safely back in her dorm room, he'd helped her wrap her feet in layers of socks and made her drink hot tea, stopping just short of carrying her to the student health center for a frost bite examination.

Maria was glad that her popsicle toes hadn't warranted a visit to student health. She'd heard medical misdiagnosis horror stories from the upperclassmen about that place. Staffed by medical students and loosely supervised by interns, the word on campus was to steer clear of the student health center unless it was absolutely unavoidable. Within an hour of the warm sock, hot tea therapy, she could move her toes without grimacing, and the tingling, itchy sensation that she felt in her feet had subsided. She vowed to keep a tube of socks in her backpack just in case their next date involved a study trip to the law library.

Ironically, the student health center had been the catalyst for a civil exchange between Maria and her roommate, Shelby, but nicknamed "Thick Thigh Stinky Tights" by Maria.

A chubby girl from Shelby, Tennessee, her parents had decided to name their only daughter, Shelby. "Hi, I'm Shelby from Shelby, Tennessee!" she announced to any stranger she encountered. The announcement was accompanied by a school girl giggle that Maria found almost as annoying as the eight by ten glossy that Shelby inserted in between the desks that separated their small room. Besides, Shelby, there were three other girls in the photo whom Shelby described as her best friends. Each girl wore a pastel colored pinafore with a white Peter Pan collar blouse and black and white saddle shoes. Atop their heads sat a crown of daisies.

"This was our warm weather uniform," Shelby explained. "We each had a dress in yellow, pink, light blue and light green. Aren't they adorable? And they were so comfortable," she continued. Maria stared at the picture wondering exactly how large the two gigantic pockets on either side of the frock was. To her, the dresses were fashion mistakes.

"I see," she said. "And you had to wear this every day?"

"Yes, ma'am. I loved it. It was so light and comfortable. And the pockets really came in handy."

"You look like candy stripers," Maria observed.

"That's what everybody always says," Shelby replied. "But my mama and grandmama went to the same school, and they wore the same uniform. It's tradition."

"What about the saddle shoes? Did you have to wear saddle shoes every day too?"

"Of course! My mama and grandmama have a similar picture of them with their friends when they were Bishop girls. I hope when I get married I can move back to Shelby so that my daughter can go to Bishop. I'd hate to break the tradition."

Maria raised both eyebrows and stared at the photo. "What's with the crown of daisies?"

"It was our senior photo. It's how anyone looking at the yearbook could tell who the seniors were. The only other time that we wore the fresh daisy crown is graduation, but for graduation we wore white, tea length dresses. I wore my grand mama's dress and so did my mama."

Maria decided to change the subject. "Where did your friends go off to college?"

"Ole' Miss," Shelby said matter-of-factly.

"Ole' Miss in Mississippi?" Maria repeated. "All of them?"

"Well, two of them did." Shelby corrected, pointing to the photograph. "Sunday and Happy did. This is Sunday, and this is Happy," she clarified pointing to the girls wearing the light blue and light green frocks. "And I was Shelby, from Shelby," she giggled again. "We made quite an impression on folks with our names, let me tell 'ya! And this is Chris, but she wasn't really in our group, so I'm not sure what she's doing. I think she might be working at her family's business. We just needed another senior wearing the pink uniform for our photo since I had on the yellow dress."

"Why would you take a picture with a random girl?"

"It's tradition, Maria. My mama and grandmama both wore the yellow uniform on senior picture day and took a picture with girls wearing the other three uniform colors."

"Wait, when your grandmother and mother attended high school, weren't the photos in black and white?"

"You're quick!" Shelby grinned. "True, you can't see the colors in their photo, but they told me that they wore yellow and that I should take a photo like this, so I did," she shrugged. "We honor tradition in my family."

Maria stared at the photo and couldn't help thinking that the girls looked like they were posing for an Amish parade at Easter.

"Sunday's not a bad name, but is the other girl really named Happy?"

"Yup, that's her God given name. Her parents named her Happy because they wanted a happy child."

"Was she happy all the time?"

"Most of the time, she was."

"So why didn't you attend Ole' Miss with Sunday and Happy?" Maria giggled as the names rolled from her tongue.

"I wanted to broaden my horizon a little and live in a big city. I thought about attending Vanderbilt in Nashville, but then I realized that this might be my last chance to live outside of Tennessee, because I'm sure I'll marry and move back to Shelby or at least I hope I do."

Maria stared at Shelby like you stare at a museum artifact. She felt her eyes staring at the pastel colored pinafore photo.

"That's what my mama and my grand mama did. And Maria, I hope you're not offended, but where I come from, blacks and whites don't mix that much, so as soon as another room becomes available I'm going to move out. I think you're a nice girl, and all, but when my grand mama learned that my roommate was a colored girl, she had a fit. She said it was bad enough that I was living in Philadelphia, but having a black roommate was pushing it," Shelby said casually.

Maria slanted her eyes and glared at the pastel pinafore photo. "Well, at least those ugly, loose pinafore dresses covered up how round you and your friends are," she growled. "The four of you look like giant cupcakes at Easter," she laughed.

"Well, that was a mean thing to say," Shelby replied softly.

"And what you said wasn't mean?"

Shelby stared at Maria somberly. "I wasn't trying to be mean, I was just telling you how my grand mama felt. It's not personal."

"Well, if you don't see how your family's attitude is personal to me, then I don't have anything else to say to you."

And that was the last conversation that Maria and Shelby had. They never walked to the dining hall together, and only spoke to each other out of absolute necessity. "Did you move my shoes?" "Yes, I put them under your bed so that I could sweep my side of the room." Shelby spent her free time on the phone with the housing department demanding that another suitable room be sourced as quickly as possible.

Though offended by the comment about her girth, she must have sensed some semblance of truth in Maria's hateful remarks because she'd started to participate in a daily aerobics class. Maria found it strangely ironic and quite amusing that Shelby had managed to find pastel colored leotards complete with matching tights that made her round body look like a peanut M&M. After her workouts, she usually hung her damp, smelly, workout tights on her bedpost, and hence was born the nickname 'Thick Thigh Stinky Tights.'

Their war of silence had now entered its fourth week, and Maria had grown so accustomed to not speaking to her roommate, that she almost didn't comment on the crutches propped against Thick Thigh Stinky Tights' bed.

"What happened to you?" Maria found herself asking involuntarily.

Shelby glared at her roommate. "Well, if you must know, I twisted my foot in aerobics. I went to student health and they told me to just ice it and elevate it. I'll be fine. Not that you care," she replied tersely.

Maria wanted to share her opinion about the student health center, and caution Thick Thigh Stinky Tights to get a second opinion but decided to bite her tongue. She didn't want to appear overly concerned.

The following week, the crutches still propped against her bed, Maria noticed her roommate wincing when she put weight on her injured foot. "You're still not feeling better?" she found herself asking.

"No. It's actually worse," Thick Thigh Stinky Tights whined.

"Look, Shelby," Maria said, surprised that she'd remembered her roommate's proper name. "You should go back to the health center and demand that they take an X-ray and insist that they have an attending physician look at your foot. I've heard stories about the student health center misdiagnosing all the time. You shouldn't be wincing in pain by just putting weight on your foot. You might have a broken bone."

Shelby looked at Maria. "Get your jacket, I'll take you over there now," Maria offered. She half expected Shelby to reject her offer of assistance.

"It hurts when I touch it," Shelby confessed.

"Let's go," Maria insisted handing Shelby her crutches as her roommate hobbled to her feet She grabbed her purse and Shelby's purse and held the door open. "By the way, you are really slimming down," she smiled.

"You think so? The scale says that I've lost eight pounds."

Maria thought about apologizing for the porker remark, but decided that if Shelby was owed an apology, then she was due one for Shelby's desire to trade her in for a non-black roommate.

They walked the two blocks to the health center in silence. Miraculously, or as a result of their infamous reputation, the student health center was devoid of students. The attending physician agreed that a sprained foot should have healed by now and ordered an X-ray. Maria grinned, glad that they weren't being seen by a nervous medical student in an ill-fitting white jacket. The X-ray revealed that Shelby had a slight, hairline fracture in the bone connecting her third toe. The fracture was slight, but she was told to stay off her foot completely for the next six weeks to allow for total healing.

"Thanks, Maria," Shelby said when they returned to their room. "Thanks for going with me and suggesting that they do an X-ray. My aerobics instructor just thought it was a severe sprain. And so did the folks at student health the first time I went."

"Don't mention it," Maria smiled. "I'm glad that I could help. And at least you know what it is now, and they didn't have to cast it. With the crutches, you should avoid putting any weight on your foot at all." Her words were muffled by the ringing telephone on Shelby's desk. She snatched the phone up on the first ring.

"Finally!" Shelby squealed. "I'll start packing now. Good news, they found another room for me, so I'm outta here! My mama will be so excited."

Maria stared at Shelby, shaking her head in disbelief as Thick Thigh Stinky Tights dialed her Mama in Shelby, Tennessee. Maria grabbed her backpack and left the room without saying goodbye. When she returned from the library, Shelby was gone. Maria quickly hung a photo of her and her mother in the spot now vacated by the pastel colored portrait in case a newly assigned roommate wanted to hang another pastel colored pinafore portrait.

But so far, three weeks later, she still hadn't been assigned a new roommate. She smiled at the thought and could feel his breath in her hair.

"Boo!" he whispered.

"I heard you coming," she lied.

"I sneaked in a hot chocolate and a pair of tube socks that rolled out of my gym bag. Put these on. I'm sure your toes are turning into little icicles."

"How'd you know?" she smiled reaching for the gently worn socks and placing them over her own thin pair.

"Because your feet are always cold."

"How'd you sneak the hot chocolate in?" she asked.

"I have my ways," he teased tracing the outline of the sorority letters on her sweater with his finger. The gesture gave her chills.

His name was John Wardell Prentiss, and Maria was in love with him.

"What's so funny? What are you giggling about?" John asked.

"I was just thinking about how I found out your last name."

"When you stalked me at the church?"

The hot chocolate scalded her tongue. "I didn't stalk you," she protested.

"Yeah, you did."

"Did not!"

"Did too!" he laughed.

Almost in unison, the law students scowled at the undergraduate love birds, many of them also cradled cups of warm beverages, their bodies nestled under jackets and blankets in the frigid library.

"Tell me again why we are studying in the law library?" Maria asked, her eyes staring at a sign above the non working fireplace that read "No Food or Beverages Allowed." Almost every student cradled a beverage.

"Because I think it's good juju for me to prepare for my LSAT in this environment," John whispered. "Now stop talking or you're going to get us kicked out."

Maria watched as John sipped from her hot chocolate, not wincing as the steaming liquid entered his throat. She marveled at his tongue's tolerance for heat.

ৡৎ

"Boo!" John blurted. "What are you doing out here?"

His voice startled her. Shocked to see the person that she'd been daydreaming about standing right before her, she found herself speechless, her tongue tangled in her mouth.

Without waiting for a reply, John thrust a bag into her hands. "You forgot this at the church."

Reaching for the bag, she found her voice. "Wow! Thank you," she squeaked. "How did you know that this was mine?" Maria asked, clearing her throat with a slight cough that was more theatrical than necessary.

"I didn't, but Miss Lily saw you carrying it when you came in. And then she saw me talking to you. When Bible study started, she saw the bag sitting by the cookies," he explained. "She looked inside and realized that it was something that you probably needed tonight." His hands raised in the surrender pose, he took a step back and continued. "Now, I didn't look inside, so if it's something really personal like some feminine hygiene stuff don't be embarrassed. Miss Lily just insisted that I take it to you as soon as possible. She actually gave me permission to miss Bible study which is very unlike Miss Lily. But she wanted me to find you and give you your package. And for the record, you never disobey an order given by Miss Lily."

"Thanks for the warning," Maria smiled. "Miss Lily has a keen eye to notice that out of all of the people that were at service tonight, I was carrying this tiny bag."

John nodded in agreement. "Yes, Miss Lily has quite the eagle eye for someone her age. She notices everything from her little perch in the church vestibule. I bet if we asked her, she could probably describe in exact detail, exactly what every person in church was wearing tonight," he chuckled. "Oh, and she loves the Blues. Before her husband died, they chaired the married couples ministry and provided one on one counsel to engaged couples. Whenever someone asked them how they managed to stay married for over fifty-two years they would laugh and say that it was Johnny Taylor's song, "It's Cheaper to Keep Her" that kept them together.

"I know that song," Maria admitted. "That's an odd thing for the pastor and the first lady to admit."

"I know, right? They were both really down to earth. Sometimes I'll catch Miss Lily humming that song. The funny thing is that my mother loves that song too, so when I heard that story about Miss Lily, I knew she'd be good people. And she is. Miss Lily is really good people."

Maria smiled again and gripped the brown paper bag. "You have quite the death grip on that bag," John observed.

Glancing at her hands, she noticed that she had tangled the bag into a tight knot. "It's just a special antiseptic that I use to gargle with. I have a sore throat," she explained, clutching her throat for emphasis.

"Let me guess. It must be Dr. Tichener's?" John asked.

"How'd you know? You looked inside the bag didn't you?"

"Nope. I swear, I didn't look in your bag. Scout's honor!" John held up the index and middle finger from his right hand.

"Let me guess, you were an Eagle Scout?" Maria asked.

"Uh, no. I just thought I saw someone do this on television," he laughed. "But everybody knows that Dr. Tichener's is the best gargle remedy for a sore throat. Or at least everybody in the black neighborhood knows that."

"Exactly," Maria nodded in agreement.

"Now you didn't answer me. What are you doing standing out here at this time of night?"

She could feel her cheeks blushing. "Well, actually, I was thinking about walking back to the church to get my bag," she confessed.

"Are you serious? At this time of night? Do you know how dangerous it is to be off campus in that neighborhood at night?" John scolded. "Have you not read the crime blotter that we list in the paper, freshman?"

"I know, I know, I read the crime blotter, that's why I didn't take my purse with me when I walked to the pharmacy. I remember the tip about putting your identification and your cash in your pocket if you venture off campus, but my throat is really killing me," she whined.

John stared at her and shook his head from side to side in an obvious sign of disapproval. "But I also thought about calling the church and asking them to give you my bag to bring to me," she offered quickly. "But I didn't know your last name."

"Well, that would have made more sense."

"I was just standing here considering my options when you came up behind me," she continued.

"And for the record, walking back to the church at this time of night, should not have even been one of your options, little lady. And it's Prentiss. My last name is Prentiss."

"John Prentiss," she repeated.

"And if you had called the church and just said, 'give the bag to John, the Penn student who was sweeping the basement tonight,' the person in the office would have known who I was. Everybody knows me there."

"Well, I didn't know that, and since John is a pretty common name," she corrected. "I thought I would sound foolish asking them to give it to a guy named, John."

"My full name is John Wardell Prentiss."

"Well, if it makes you feel any better, if I had decided to walk back to the church I was going to stay for Bible study and bum a ride back to campus with you," she added.

"Okay, at least you're not completely crazy. Penn's campus is pretty safe at night because of the campus police and there are usually students walking around until midnight, but when you go off campus, it's a whole 'nother world out there. It's really not that safe to walk alone on campus after ten o'clock. Remember that, okay?"

"Duly noted," Maria saluted. "By the way, how did you know where I lived?"

This time it was John who seemed at a loss for words. "When I did that piece on you for the paper, you mentioned your dorm," he stammered.

"Funny, I don't remember mentioning my dorm to you, especially since the incident happened in the dining hall, and my dorm doesn't have a dining hall," she pondered. John chewed his lip and stuffed his hands in his pocket, his foot toeing a small pebble on the sidewalk. "So how is it that you were able to remember my dorm, but you didn't remember my name?" she quizzed.

"I remembered your name," John corrected.

"No, you didn't. At church tonight, you asked me what my name was."

"I did not."

"Yes, you did!"

"Did not!"

"Did too!"

I have a memory like an elephant. Your name is Maria Chantal Wesley, you're from Newberry East, Illinois. Your brother Neal played hockey. And you are allergic to dogs," he finished.

Maria stared at him suspiciously. "Why did you act like you didn't remember my name earlier?"

"I just wanted you to think that I'd forgotten your name," he offered in a soft baritone voice.

Maria tilted her head to the side. "Why?"

With his hands buried deep into his pockets, John's hazel eyes bore into hers.

"Why'd you pretend like you'd forgotten my name?" she asked again.

"Because you have a three carat ring on your finger given to you by the NFL's latest superstar, and I drive my grandfather's old Buick," he said softly.

"I don't get it? How does that make you forget my name?"

John's face turned serious, his brows knit together. Maria couldn't determine if the pensive look was a scowl or a frown.

"I will probably regret saying this, but I'm going to say it anyway. I pretended to forget your name because I wanted to knock you from your pedestal."

Maria stared at John in disbelief. "'You wanted to knock me from my pedestal?'" she repeated. "What is that supposed to mean?" she frowned.

Maria felt her grip on the brown bag tightening as she braced herself for his reply.

"What did I do to make you think that I was on a pedestal?" she demanded.

"Nothing. You didn't do anything. It's just that when I heard the story about you and that big diamond ring, I painted a picture of who I thought you were before I met you at the Black House, and then when I met you, you were nothing like what I expected you to be. And that really surprised me. And tonight, when I saw you at Shiloh talking to my girl, Lucy, that shocked me too because girls that look like you are usually mean to Lucy because she's overweight," he rambled quickly. "So then I thought that maybe you were just sucking up to Lucy because you are interested in pledging and that pissed me off, because that's what my ex-girlfriend did. She used Lucy to sponsor her into the sorority and then she stopped being friends with her as soon as she crossed and also turned out to be a two timing troll. When I saw her at the church with her new boyfriend, and I saw you with Lucy, I told myself that you were a stuck up sorority girl wannabe that was going to hurt Lucy again so you needed to be knocked from your pedestal," he paused to catch his breath. "So I decided to pretend like I forgot your name."

A look of confusion plastered across her face, Maria exhaled slowly. "Alrighty then. That was probably more information than I needed to hear." She stared at John as though expecting him to modify his comments or apologize for his hurtful tirade. John merely stared at her blankly, his hands still buried deep in his pockets.

She slowly shook her head from side to side. "You know, people say that journalists are supposed to be unbiased and impartial. Well, clearly that's not true," she chuckled sarcastically. "I'm disappointed in you, John. You're the editor of the student newspaper, and you've formulated an opinion about me based on absolutely no factual data," she said calmly. "I've been tried and convicted in the court of John. Well, you don't know anything about me. Just because someone gave me a big ring, that doesn't mean that I think that I'm on a pedestal. I'm not going to apologize for who my friends are, or for the gifts that I'm given. You're no different than the white sorority girls who offend and judge me every time I wear that ring. And for your information, I am interested in pledging, but I wasn't sucking up to Lucy. Lucy didn't even remember who I was when I walked up to her. I walked up to her because I wanted her to know that I thought her testimony was really touching. And I wanted to see if she wanted to walk back to campus together. See, I do read the crime blotter, and I do understand that it's dangerous to walk off campus at night," she finished. She stared at John expecting him to say something. His jaws remained clenched, his hands hidden.

"Well, thanks for bringing me my bag. Goodnight." she offered softly before brushing past him and walking toward her dorm.

She heard the deep voice and felt the soft, yet firm, grip on her shoulder simultaneously.

"I just don't think that I'm good enough for you."

And with that, Maria Wesley knew that she was in love with John Wardell Prentiss.

Chapter 6

Tanisha's Snowflakes

She knew she was in trouble when he woke her up. Accustomed to being double teamed by her brothers, Byron and Allen's pranks were usually harmless, yet annoyingly effective. The cleverest stunt proved to be the time they short sheeted her bed and lined her shower cap with lotion, forcing her to wash and rinse her freshly styled hair. But this time was different.

"I'm really tired, Byron. I'm going out with my friends later, and I need a nap. I'm not in the mood for another fake fire drill so beat it!" She rolled over on the sofa, her back towards him so that her face snuggled into one of the decorative pillows. Within seconds, she had drifted back to sleep.

"Tanisha! " Byron repeated. "Wake up, Tanisha." This time he shook her shoulder lightly.

"What? What time is it?" Tanisha groaned, still groggy from waking up early and joining her friends for a marathon Black Friday shopping excursion where her only purchase was a new pair of jeans.

"I need you to come with me to get Allen," Byron whispered.

"What? Why? Where is he?"

"Just come with me. I'll tell you in the car."

Tanisha ran her fingers through her hair and squinted to focus her eyes.

"Dad, Tanisha and I are going to drive to the store. We'll be right back."

"Sounds good," Jackie offered from behind his newspaper. "See if your mother needs anything."

"Where's Mom?"

"She's in our bedroom studying. She has a test on Monday. I can't believe he missed that shot! This is going to be a long season if they don't get better coaching. I don't know why they kept him on in the first place," Jackie mumbled to himself.

"Who's winning, Dad?" Tanisha heard Byron ask.

"Not the Bulls."

"We'll be right back. I wanna see the second half," Byron offered.

"Don't forget to see if your mother needs anything."

Byron step skipped up the six steps to the second level of the split level house. Billie Mae was twelve credit hours away from earning her Bachelor's degree in early childhood education. She planned to become a teacher.

Tanisha could smell food simmering as she entered the empty kitchen. She lifted the lid and inhaled the aroma of corned beef and cabbage, slowly cooking in the crock pot. She was tempted to reach in and sample her father's favorite dish, but knew that the meat would scald her sensitive tongue. For as long as Tanisha could remember, the day after Thanksgiving, her mother had always cooked corned beef and cabbage, Jackie's favorite dish. Even when her parents had separated and divorced, Billie still cooked corned beef and cabbage the day after Thanksgiving, often crying as she prepared it. The Carlson family enjoyed Thanksgiving leftovers again on Saturday and Sunday. Tanisha paused and opened a few cabinets in search of the snacks that Billie kept on hand to satisfy the grazing habits of Byron and Allen. She opened three cabinets before she found the snack stash, making a mental note to familiarize herself with her parents' new kitchen. "You'll have to give me directions to get to your parents' new house," David reminded. Tanisha grinned just thinking about it. "This is my parents' new house." She grabbed a large bag of potato chips as Byron pulled her through the back door, guiding her toward the car parked on the driveway.

His hand on her elbow, she was shocked when Byron opened her car door. *Well, I guess he is dating. I wonder if he places his girlfriend in the car.* She settled in and stuffed a handful of Jay's potato chips in her mouth, chewing hungrily.

"Does Mom need anything from the store?" Tanisha asked.

"No, thank God. Because we're not really going to the store, dingy."

Her hand shoving handful number two into her mouth, she chewed quickly and swallowed most of the chips before speaking. "Where are we going, Byron? What's going on?"

"We have to help Allen. He's in trouble."

"Trouble? What kind of trouble?" She released her grip on the third fistful of chips and tossed the bag into the backseat.

"He's at Jason's house. Apparently, they took Jason's mother's new car for a joy ride and didn't know how to parallel park it, so he called me."

"You're kidding, right? They're fourteen! What were they doing driving?"

"I know. That's what I said."

"Do you even know how to parallel park?"

"No. That's why I woke you up," Byron explained.

"Where's Jason's mother?"

"She's taking a nap. She has the flu or a cold or something, so she should be asleep for a little while."

"Those chuckleheads," Tanisha giggled. "They're still as simple as a penny. Where'd they take the car?"

"To the McDonald's drive thru."

"I was going to guess that. Wait. Why are you getting on the expressway. Did Jason and his mom move?"

"She moved a couple of years ago. Where've you been?"

"That makes sense. If they live in the city now they have to parallel park on the street. What if her parking spot is taken? Won't she remember where she parked her car?"

"They at least thought of that, so Allen is standing in the street guarding the spot, and Jason is circling the block," Byron laughed. "It's really something out of a Saturday Night Live skit when you think about it."

"Those two together are too much."

She watched as her younger brother navigated the car on to the expressway, checking the blind spot over his shoulder before merging into traffic. Tanisha wondered when men lost the instinct to check their blind spot before switching lanes, remembering that she'd never seen her dad, Jack, Jr., Glen, Brian or David check their blind spot or perhaps she just hadn't noticed it when they did.

Glen. Tanisha hadn't thought about Glen Horton in several weeks. As her mind wandered to how he was spending the holidays, Byron pulled off the exit ramp.

"That was fast," she noticed.

"It's not that far once you jump on I-57. Let's just hope his mother is still asleep."

Tanisha could hear the genuine concern in her brother's voice. Byron and Allen were clearly still the dynamic duo, the nickname that she'd given them when they learned that they could pool their sinister forces to double team her. Their super powers were now slightly diminished by the added dose of testosterone that now occupied their fiefdom. With their dad now living in the house again, their shenanigans and wrestling matches weren't as intense.

Tanisha saw the flailing hands first. "There he is," she grinned.

Byron pulled the car alongside Allen, and Tanisha rolled down her window.

"Hey, Tanisha!" Allen smiled leaning on the window. "What took y'all so long?"

"Man! You need to chill and be glad we came."

"Jason should be driving back around the block any second," Allen shivered.

"Where's your jacket, Blockhead? It's freezing out here."

"It's in the house. The house has an alarm charm on the door, and we didn't want to risk waking up JoAnn by opening the door. We were just trying to get to Mickey D's and get some grub. No harm no foul."

"There is a foul. Fourteen plus fourteen is twenty-eight, chucklehead, but you can't drive a car at fourteen. You could have killed somebody or killed yourselves! Where'd you learn how to drive anyway?" she scolded.

"I been driving, Tanisha. Grow up. Byron let's me push the car sometimes. But I wasn't driving. Jason was."

His hands in the surrender pose, Byron stepped away from his sister's swat. "I only let him drive in the grocery store parking lot at night."

"I'm a man. I need to know how to drive."

"You're fourteen!"

The black BMW cruised beside them on the street.

"Jason's mom is pushing a BMW now? You two are really clowns, you know that?" Tanisha opened her door and hugged her younger brother. He smelled like he needed a shower.

Looking guilty and sheepish, Jason jumped out of the car and hugged Tanisha around the waist. "Hey, Sis!" he squealed lifting her from her feet.

"Don't hey Sis me!" she said as she punched him in the chest. "Give me the keys before JoAnn wakes up and peels all of our heads. I am not taking the fall for you two."

"I left it running, and I let the window down so the car wouldn't smell like french fries, so let me show you how to close the window. It's tricky."

"Step aside, rookie. I know how to handle a BMW."

"Excuse me, sugar britches," Jason grinned.

Climbing into the seat, she shook her head when she realized that Jason had reclined the seat as far back as it would go. She looked on the panel and hit the button to place the seat and mirrors back to that of the primary driver. Pulling up alongside the car in front of her, she waved the boys out of the awaiting parking spot as Byron moved his car. She lined the passenger side mirror with the driver's side mirror of the car parked directly in front of her. One hand over the backseat, she slowly backed the car into the spot, turning the steering wheel in a counterclockwise motion. Once in the spot, she placed the car in drive and slowly adjusted the wheels so that the the vehicle was parallel with the curb. With the car in park, she turned on the radio and shook her head as the radio volume blared loud rock music. She pushed a few buttons until she heard smooth jazz emanating from the speakers. Lastly, she hit the center console to close the windows, checking to see if there were any McDonald's wrappers lying on the floor of the new car. She flicked a french fry into the street as she exited the vehicle.

"You two are clowns, you do realize that, right?" she asked as she handed Jason the key.

"You parked that like a pro!" Jason squealed. "I mean you really handled that like Mario Andretti! My mother always has to pull up and out and adjust three or four times when she parks in between cars."

"Thanks, Sis" Allen bowed at the waist.

"You must have aced your driver's education class," Jason smiled. He'd been Allen's best friend since kindergarten and had had a crush on Tanisha since he was in fourth grade.

"I did. And if you two geniuses live to see sixteen, and you pass your driving test on the first try, they'll teach you how to parallel park."

"I kept trying to pull into the spot," Jason confessed. "How'd you learn how to back in like that? That's how my mother does it too, but she makes it look so hard that I was scared to try and back it in so I thought I could pull it in."

"Because I have a driver's license and I know how to drive, Chuckles! And that's really the only way you can get your car into a tight spot like that. You can't maneuver the angles pulling into a spot that tight. The secret is in the mirror alignment." She paused. "I'm not telling you how to parallel park because you may try this stunt again, and next time I won't be home to bail your butts out!"

Tanisha noticed Allen shivering again. "If you were too scared to go in the house to get your jacket, how'd you call home?"

"We used the pay phone at the gas station."

"What if I hadn't been home? Huh? Byron doesn't know how to parallel park. What would you have done then? And by the way, here's a free tip. If you're gonna be dumb enough to take your mother's brand new BMW for a joyride, at least be smart enough to turn down the radio volume, place the radio back on her favorite station and hit the button to adjust the seats to the primary driver!"

"Word! I wouldn't have even thought to do that," Jason confessed.

"Me neither."

"Rookies. She's the only person driving this car, so you would have been busted. Live and learn fellas, live and learn. If you're gonna be a criminal, be a smooth criminal!" Tanisha glanced at her watch. "We've got to get back. I didn't realize it was this late. David is coming over tonight to meet Mom and Dad. Jason, I have to use the bathroom, will the chime wake up your mother?"

"Naaah, I don't care if she wakes up now. We're out of the woods. She's probably up now anyway. Besides, we have to go inside and get Allen's jacket," Jason remembered. "Who's David?"

⤜∾⤝

Tanisha adjusted her seat forward to accommodate her brother's long legs. She hadn't laid eyes on him in two months, and he appeared two inches taller.

"I can't believe you wouldn't let me ride shotgun! You know I'm too tall to be crammed back here," Allen grumbled. "So you're finally bringing boyfriend to meet Mom and Dad, huh?"

"Is this the white dude that you're kicking it with?" Byron asked.

"No. This is my friend David Barton. He graduated from Homer Glen, and he's not my boyfriend."

"Oh, this is the dude that's in medical school, right?"

"Right. How'd you remember that?"

"Mom was telling Dad about him. They thought they'd be home to meet him after he picked you up from the airport, but we had to go into the city and check on Grandma Bootsy."

"How's Grandma Bootsy doing?" Tanisha asked.

"She's fine. She just needed help moving some furniture, and she threatened to move it herself, so Dad made us all go and it took longer than we thought. I think it was a trick to get us to come over for dinner because when we got there she was already cooking a big meal."

"Did she fry chicken?"

"Of course she did. Fried chicken, mashed potatoes, fried corn, steamed cabbage and a chocolate cake."

"I love Grandma Bootsy's chicken and fried corn. I'm so jealous! I understand now, but I was so irritated when no one was home when David dropped me off, but I'm glad that you guys left the back door open so I could get in."

"That was my idea," Allen offered from the backseat. "I'm the only one who remembered that you probably wouldn't have a key. See how I look out for you? Next time let a brother ride shotgun."

"Mom was trying to get back so we were home when you got home, but you know you can't leave Grandma Bootsy's house without eating," Byron added.

"Slow down, you're riding too close to the car in front of you. You should be at least one car length behind the car ahead of you for every ten miles of your speed."

"I am not going to be five car lengths behind the car in front of me, Tanisha. Ain't gonna happen. Just chill and stop back seat driving."

"Well, I'm just saying. I'm precious cargo. Tell me what she said again."

"What did who say again?" Byron asked.

"Mom. What did Mom say about David?"

"Oh, we're back on that topic. She just told Dad that you were bringing a friend over to meet them."

Tanisha's stomach growled. "Allen, pass me the chips on the backseat. I'm starving."

"Uh, the chips are history. I just finished the bag off."

"I can't believe that you just wolfed down a whole bag of chips! That bag was more than half full. I tossed them in the car because I'm starving."

"Then why were they on the backseat? If you'd let me sit in the front seat where I belong, you'd still have your chips. It serves you right!"

Tanisha rolled her eyes at Allen as Byron exited the expressway "Did she say anything else?" Tanisha asked.

"Say anything else about what?"

"Did Mom say anything else to Dad about David?"

"Nooooo," Byron said slowly. "What's with the third degree?"

"Did Dad ask any questions?"

"He just frowned and said he didn't feel like having dinner with some random boyfriend. And Mom said that it wasn't your boyfriend, that he was just a friend. And Dad said that if he is a boy and he's your friend, then as far as he's concerned he's a boyfriend. And then Dad farted and we laughed."

"Okay, that's really gross!" Tanisha frowned.

"Well, you're asking me for every little detail so I wanted to make sure that I didn't leave anything out."

Byron turned on to the driveway and pulled behind a black Corvette.

"Does boyfriend drive a Corvette?" Allen screamed.

"He's not my boyfriend!" Tanisha groaned glancing at her watch. "He is always right on time! See, going to help you out of your little felony I wasn't home when he got here. There's no telling what's going on in there!"

Tanisha jumped out of the car before Byron placed it in park and walked through the kitchen door. She heard laughter in the living room and walked towards the voices.

Jackie was seated in his favorite chair, and Billie was sitting on the arm of the sofa nearest Jackie. David sat in the chair facing Jackie's chair. David stood up when she walked in.

"Hey, David," she smiled. "You're early."

"Not really. I just got here about five minutes ago."

"You are a stickler for being punctual."

"That's a noble trait, Tanisha. You should try it some time," her father offered.

"I'm on time, Dad."

"If you're on time, you're late. You should be ten minutes early."

"My dad says the same thing, Mr. Carlson. He was in the military."

"As was I, David. In the armed services, punctuality is demanded."

Tanisha was impressed that her father remembered David's name. And that he was smiling. "I see you've met my parents," she smiled weakly. "Well, I need about fifteen minutes to shower and change. I had to go to the store with my brother, and then we had to pick up my other brother."

"Where are frick and frack?" Billie asked. "What did Byron get at the store?"

"Oh, they're in the driveway. Byron just wanted to get some gum, and I just went with him for the ride, and then we remembered that we had to pick up Allen. I think they're fawning over your car, David," she added quickly, desperate to change the subject from the fake errand to the store.

"Oh yeah, what kind of car do you drive?" Jackie asked peering out the window.

"It's a Corvette, sir."

"A Corvette? My brother, Nathan, who lives in Detroit just bought himself a red Corvette. He's having a mid-life crisis," Jackie added. "He's in the middle of a divorce."

"If you'd like, you can take it for a spin around the block, sir."

"I might take you up on that, young man. I've always wanted to drive a Corvette. Let me take a look at it." Jackie rose from his chair and grabbed his jacket from the coat rack in the hallway.

David followed Jackie to the foyer and handed him the keys. "Take it for a spin around the block." Tanisha admired David's slim physique and noticed that he wore dark blue Levi jeans with a thick cable knit sweater that was the color of steel wool, with flecks of black and gray in the yarn. As was his custom, he wore black loafers without socks.

"Well, Tanisha does need to get ready, and that's going to take at least ten minutes longer than she told you that it would."

"No, it's not, Dad! I already know what I'm going to wear, I just need to take a quick shower."

"I would like to take it for a spin, but only if you accompany me, David."

"I'd be happy to, sir," David grinned.

Tanisha didn't like the idea of Jackie riding in the car with David. David winked at her and followed Jackie out the front door. Byron and Allen were peering through the windows trying to get a better look at the dashboard as the sun disappeared over the horizon.

"I'm David Barton. You must be Byron and Allen. I've heard a lot about you."

"These are my sons," Jackie added unnecessarily.

"And your other son is Jack, Jr. and he's still at college because he is a resident hall administrator and he had to stay in the dorms this weekend, right?"

"That's right," Jackie nodded.

"Nice car!" Byron beamed.

"Thanks, man! Your dad and I are going to take it for a spin while your sister gets ready. I'd let you guys come along, but you're too big to fit in the back seat."

"Take your time getting back because it's gonna take Tanisha hours to transform her face," Allen giggled.

"I told my mom we'd be back in an hour, Teenie," David laughed before climbing into the passenger seat.

Billie and Tanisha stood in the doorway as Jackie backed the car on to the street.

"He seems nice, Tanisha."

"He is."

"So why isn't he your boyfriend?"

"Mom!" Tanisha struggled for words, shocked at her mother's directness.

"Well? He's handsome, he's in medical school, and he seems to adore you. I can tell by the way he lit up when you walked into the room."

"What's the problem?"

"There's no problem." Tanisha thought about their New Year's Eve pact, realizing that in six weeks she would have to choose between Brian Kraft and David Barton. "David is cool. It's just really complicated, and I don't have time to go into it. I'm gonna take a quick shower."

The hot steam felt good on her neck. She scrubbed herself as quickly as she could, towel dried and applied lotion and perfume before slipping on fresh panties and the new jeans she'd bought shopping that afternoon. She pulled her Yale sweatshirt over her head, and inhaled the sweet smell of fabric softener, glad that her mother had washed the sweatshirt for her. Brushing her hair, she remembered that she'd left her purse and make-up bag on the kitchen table. She slipped down the stairs unnoticed and grabbed her purse. She was shocked that David and her dad were back so soon. But when she looked at her watch, she realized that she'd been in the bathroom showering and changing for over twenty minutes.

"How many tickets have you received driving that car, David?" Jackie asked.

"Well, I've actually only received one. And I deserved it. I was speeding. My parents wouldn't let me drive the car for a month after that. I learned my lesson, and I haven't gotten a ticket since."

"That's good. Now what are your intentions with my daughter?" Jackie blurted.

"Excuse me, sir?"

"You heard me. What are your intentions with Tanisha?"

Startled, Tanisha stepped into the living room. "Dad! Why are you giving him the third degree? This is so embarrassing!"

"I meant his intentions tonight, Tanisha. Calm down. Not his intentions for the rest of his life," Jackie chuckled.

"Oh, I see," David grinned sheepishly. "Well, my parents invited Tanisha over for dinner. We're just having takeout pizza and salad. My grandmother wanted to see her again."

"So Tanisha has met your parents and your grandmother and we're just now meeting you?" Jackie questioned. "Interesting."

David turned to Tanisha. "His grandmother lives with his parents, Dad," Tanisha explained.

"She's in her eighties."

"How long have you and Tanisha been friends?"

Tanisha feared this question. But she knew that if she tried to lie, her parents would see right through any lie, especially her mother.

"David and I met about five years ago. Maria dated one of David's friends and so that's how we met."

"So you've been friends for five years, and we're just now meeting you?"

Tanisha had anticipated this response as well.

"Dad, you don't meet all of my friends," she whined. "And there was a lot of stuff going on in my life. David went off to college, and then Lori died," she shifted hoping that this sad memory would stifle her dad's interrogation.

"Well, why are we meeting him now?" Jackie asked boldly, not phased in the least by his daughter's attempt at distraction.

"Because David brought me home from the airport, and you said you wanted to meet him, remember?" Tanisha noticed her mom place her hand on Jackie's shoulder, and shake her head softly from side to side. She watched as Jackie practically swallowed his next question.

"I'm ready whenever you are, David." Tanisha offered, forgetting that she planned to apply make-up.

"Not so fast. What are you doing after dinner?" Jackie quizzed as Billie covered her face and shook her head in defeat.

Again, David looked toward Tanisha for direction, but this time, Jackie stared at David and raised one eyebrow as though daring Tanisha to speak for him.

"Well, Teenie is going to the college party at the Illinois Institute of Technology tonight, right, Teenie?" David stammered.

"Maria is picking me up at David's tonight at about nine o'clock," she sighed.

"Nine o'clock? You're going to a party at nine o'clock?" Jackie asked.

"The party doesn't start until nine o'clock. We're trying to get there by nine thirty."

"Are you going to the party, David?"

"Uh, no sir. I'm a little old for that scene."

"So what are you doing tonight?"

"Well, I hadn't really thought of that. I might try and hang out with some of my friends who are home for Thanksgiving weekend. But I'm actually tired, and I have some studying to do, so after Teenie leaves

I was going to study for a few hours and then hit the hay."

"Good answer. Now drive carefully with Tanisha in the car. She's precious cargo, and I know how boys like to drive fast. I was young once too you know."

Tanisha slanted her eyes at her father. "We'd better get going, David."

"I will be careful, sir. It was nice to meet you, Mr. Carlson. Mrs. Carlson."

"You too, David," Billie replied.

"Thanks for letting me take your car for a spin, David. And thanks for bringing my daughter home from the airport. I was prepared to pick her up, but she told me that you would be picking her up."

"No problem, sir. Anytime."

"That won't be necessary. I'm perfectly able to pick up my daughter from the airport," he added defensively. "How did you fit Maria and Tanisha in that Corvette anyway?"

"Oh, I drove my mother's car to the airport. She has a BMW."

"What do your parents do, David?"

"They're both physicians," David offered as Tanisha tugged on his elbow.

"Let's go this way," Tanisha suggested walking toward the kitchen door and grabbing the jacket that she draped across the back of a chair.

Glancing back at the house, Tanisha could see Jackie and Billie staring out the window.

Per his custom, David opened Tanisha's door and closed it once she was seated.

Buckling his seatbelt, she could hear David's audible exhale.

"Your parents are cool, Tanisha," David offered as he maneuvered the car in reverse and spun into the street. "I don't know what I was expecting, but they're cool. Your old man knows how to handle a stick shift too."

"My dad is having his own little mid-life crisis, but he can't afford to buy a sports car. What did you guys talk about on your little drive?"

"Nothing really. Sports, mostly football and how the Bears might actually have a chance this season. He knows a lot about cars. I thought he was going to grill me about our relationship, but I see he waited to do that in front of you."

"I'm so sorry about that. He gives that 'Tanisha is precious cargo' speech to anybody who picks me up," she offered carelessly. "Not that I have a lot of guys picking me up, that's not what I meant," she added. "David, pull into that parking lot so I can put on my make-up. I don't want to meet your sister looking like I just woke up from a nap. I didn't want to stay and let my dad ask twenty more questions, but I can't apply eye make-up while you're driving."

David pulled the car into a grocery store parking lot and watched as Tanisha fumbled through her small make-up bag. His fingers tapped on the steering wheel column as she quickly applied eyeliner, mascara and light pink lipstick.

"Voila!" she grinned. "Much better don't you think?"

"You look the same to me," David smiled softly. "You don't really need make-up if you ask me."

"That's why I don't ask you," she smiled. "I'm all set. We can go now. Oh look, it's starting to snow. Did you know that it was going to snow tonight? I'm glad I wore my boots. But I forgot to bring a hat. Can I borrow a hat when we get to your house?"

"Yeah, sure," David mumbled, his fingers still tapping on the steering wheel. "Teenie, I need to tell you something," David said softly, as he removed his foot from the clutch and applied the parking brake.

"What's up?" she asked turning to face him.

"I know we are going to discuss our relationship on New Year's

Eve, but I feel like we need to talk about something now." David leaned into the driver's side door, his head against the window. "I really enjoyed meeting your parents, and you know how I feel about you," he paused.

"David, we have a deal, remember? Let's not get into this right now."

"Teenie, I've been seeing someone. She's not a student, but she lives in D.C. She works at the mall."

"What else is new? You've always seen someone, David. What's the big deal?"

"She's white," he said slowly.

"Okay, and so is Brian Kraft. You're an equal opportunity dater, and so am I. The world would be a better place if people stopped judging others based on race and skin color and just followed their heart. What's her name?"

"Teenie, she's five months pregnant."

Her gaze shifted to the windshield and fixated on a perfectly formed snowflake that landed on the windshield. She watched closely, expecting the snowflake to evaporate on the warm window, but the snowflake just sat there. Following her eyes, David turned on the wipers.

"Did you hear me, Teenie?"

"I think you said that your girlfriend is pregnant?" Teenie repeated in the form of a question. She inhaled and exhaled loudly through her nose. Her breathing sounded like an ocean wave.

"Her name is Rachel. She's twenty-two. We met at the mall. We were just hanging out. It wasn't anything serious."

"Well, it's clearly serious now. How long have you known about the baby?"

"She told me as soon as she found out. I've known for a few months."

"You've known for a few months," she repeated. "Do your parents know?"

"Not yet. I was going to tell them after the holidays."

"Why are you telling me now if you haven't even told your parents?"

"Because it's the right thing to do, and I felt dishonest keeping this from you, especially knowing that I've given you an ultimatum about our relationship. You've always been honest with me about your boyfriends, or at least for the most part. You kept your prom date from me for a few months," he snickered nervously. "But I just felt like I should tell you what was going on. I'm going to be a father, and I wanted you to know that before you made your decision about our relationship."

"I think you and Rachel just made the decision for me, David," she spat.

"Teenie, you and I could still work. I've been on pins and needles wondering if you were going to even choose me or not. If you tell me that you want to be with me, we'll figure out a way to make it work."

"Do you love her?" she asked.

This time David stared out the window. "I have strong feelings for her, but I have strong feelings for you too, Teenie. And we have history together."

"Do you love her, David? It's okay if you do. I hope you do."

This time, David stared at the snowflakes that spattered the windshield.

"You should marry her," Teenie blurted. "She's pregnant with your child, you have strong feelings for her so you should marry her."

"I'm so sorry, Teenie. I feel like I deceived you."

"I'm glad you told me."

"I don't know what to do. Tell me how you feel about me, Teenie."

"How I feel doesn't matter, David. Your girlfriend is pregnant so you should do the honorable thing and marry her."

"That's what my parents will say."

"Exactly. And I wouldn't want to be the girl who stood between you and your child's mother," Tanisha covered her face with her hands, accidentally smudging her freshly applied mascara. The sobs took her breath away. She noticed the stains on her hands and reached in the glove compartment for a napkin, wishing she had applied waterproof mascara.

"I'm so sorry, Teenie," David pleaded, placing his hand on her shoulder. She wiped a tear and smiled at him. "I didn't mean to hurt you. I didn't know if you would even care. Please don't cry."

"I just wasn't expecting that one," she stammered through her tears. "But I guess I almost deserve it. I've been stringing our friendship along for over five years, so something like this was bound to happen."

"It's not your fault, Teenie. I did this to myself, and now I feel like I've lost you. Damn!" he slammed his palm into the dashboard. "So now what do we do?" he asked. "Do you want me to take you home?"

Teenie shook her head left to right. "If I go home now, I'll have to answer twenty questions from my parents, so let's keep it moving. But first, I need to reapply my make-up. And we have ten minutes to get to your parents before we're officially late for dinner. I guess there's really no need for me to meet your sister now," she sniffled. "But I certainly don't want her thinking that I'm not punctual. Besides, I'm starving, and I want to see Gramsey and Mr. Belvedere," she forced herself to smile.

"I'm so sorry," he repeated. "I feel like such a jerk."

"I'll be fine. And you're not a jerk, David. You're a great guy. Congratulations, by the way. You're going to be a father, and I'm going to be Auntie Teenie. I want to meet Rachel to make sure she's worthy," she grinned as she reapplied her smudged make-up.

"Are you serious? Do you really want to meet her?"

"Sure. Why not. We're still friends, right?"

"Of course, we're still friends," David smiled.

So maybe that's what the dream meant. And the white girl on the Amtrak wearing a Howard sweatshirt was a foreshadowing of this drama. I wonder if Monica will agree with that dream analysis.

Tanisha giggled to herself.

"What's so funny?" David asked.

"Nothing. I was just thinking about a dream that I had," she said. "By the way, you know that you're going to have a translucent baby, right? As light as you are, and marrying a white girl, your baby is going to be damn near invisible." Tanisha smirked.

"You have some nerve! He laughed. Your dad is even lighter than I am, and you're banana yellow, so our child would be pretty light too."

"We'll never know now will we?" she smiled. "Can you do me one favor, David?" she asked.

"Of course. Anything Teenie."

"Can I be there when you tell your perfect parents that you got Suzy Snowflake, the uneducated mall worker pregnant?" she laughed loudly, but the laughter was fake as her heart was shred into a thousand tiny snowflake shards.

Chapter 7

Purple Haze

The east side of the crowded side street littered with double parked squad cars, the small corner coffee shop overflowed with uniformed police officers, most sipping from white coffee mugs and eating hungrily from blue plates brimming with pancakes at eleven o'clock at night.

On the weekends, the Blue Plate Special was a favored dining spot for Chicago Police Officers, college students and the gay and lesbian crowd that strolled Halsted Street. The twenty-four hour diner had a limited menu that included buttermilk or blueberry pancakes, eggs made to order, bacon, sausage and grilled cheese with french fries served with a dill pickle on the side. The modest menu was printed on small laminated index cards tucked inside placeholders in the center of the table that looked as though they were the original menus after twenty years in business. Now a man in his early seventies, Mr. Leiberman, the owner, still greeted many of the regulars by name as he strolled through the restaurant wiping tables and refilling water glasses. If a patron didn't finish his meal, Mr. Leiberman would box the leftovers and take them through the kitchen to a waiting line of homeless who gathered in the alley, always inserting a paper napkin and cutlery packet with the food.

Just three blocks from Kendal's apartment, he had mentioned the Blue Plate Special to Justine, and promised to take her there one evening. But tonight, it was AM who escorted her into the tiny diner at Kendal's insistence.

❦

"Chile, we have been worried sick about you! Where have you been?" Kendal squealed. "I know your simple tale did not cheap out on me and get on no CTA bus at this time of night. Kendal just knows that you are not that stupid, fish! I know you are broke as hell, but Kendal knows he raised you better than that!" His finger waving inches from her nose.

Speechless, Justine's eyes were locked on AM's.

Killer and Teapot squeezed past Justine on the landing and laughed at Kendal's antics. "Kleo, you know you are being too hard on our new friend. You need to cut her some slack. I saw her get out of a taxi while Killer was having his smoke," Teapot offered.

"Well, all right then," Kendal calmed. "That's more like it. But we have been worried sick about you."

Her eyes glued to AM's, "The taxi got lost," was all she could offer.

"Teapot, you need to whip up another batch of our signature cocktail, we are running low. And Killer, that trash needs tending to," Kendal ordered.

"Yes, maam," they both said in unison.

As party hostess, Kendal insisted that his friends provide whatever co-host duties needed doing, from cleaning up the bathroom behind an over served guest, emptying the trash, refilling the snacks or cleaning up a spill. The guests knew that a denied request made by Kendal would result in being black balled from the

Chapter Member guest list.

AM walked into the stairwell. "Hi, Justine."

"What are you doing here, AM?" she asked.

The soprano agitation now removed from Kendal's voice, it appeared baritone. "I invited him, fish," Kendal said softly.

Justine stared at Kendal curiously. "Why? Is he gay?"

AM laughed loudly.

"I don't know, is he?" Kendal replied. "Some of my friends inside were checking him out."

AM slanted his eyes at Kendal.

"I invited him because you two need to talk."

"You came all the way from Boston so that we could talk?"

"Well, not exactly," AM answered.

Kendal placed one arm around Justine's shoulders and the other around AM's. "You two need to talk, and it's way too loud in my apartment to have a conversation. Now, you're welcome to hang out in this stairwell, but you won't have any privacy. You look adorable by the way, fish. I love that tiara. I'm glad you embraced my denim and diamonds theme," he paused. "Now where was I? Oh, you two need privacy. There's a diner a few blocks down the street that's open twenty-four hours."

"The Blue Plate Special?" AM asked.

"How do you know about the Blue Plate?" Kendal asked.

"My parents are friends with the owner, Mr. Lieberman. I haven't been there in years."

"You're Jewish?" Kendal asked.

"Uh, huh."

"Well, that explains the nose," Kendal smirked. "I'm just kidding, dude. I knew you were Jewish. Now go on and take Miss Justine to the Blue Plate so you two can talk. I need to get back to my party."

"Kendal, how did you even know how to get in touch with AM?" Justine asked.

"Chile, he goes to Harvard Medical School. It really wasn't that hard. It's not like he's in the C.I.A. And even if he was, Kendal knows people. Chile, Puh-lease. Challenge a sister!"

"Andrea gave him my number, Justine," AM offered.

"You mean Andrea, my mother? You called my mother to get his number?"

"Okay, you could have played along with Kendal's little ruse for a minute, Clock," Kendal snarled, rolling his eyes and snapping his finger in an arc formation. Justine correctly assumed that "Clock" was Kendal's pet name for AM. Kendal turned his full attention to Justine and gently grabbed both of her hands. "I had to, fish. When I realized that you were really serious about moving to Texas, I knew I had to do something. Desperate times call for desperate measures. It's too hot in Texas for Kendal. I can't be visiting you in humid Texas. Besides, you're a city mouse, Justine. You're not a Texas girl."

Justine smiled hearing Kendal use her proper name for the first time in months. "Did you tell my mother that I was thinking about moving to Texas?"

"No. Of course not. I would not tell your business to Andrea. I do not "out" people, fish. You know that. I just told her that I wanted to surprise you and invite AM to a party, which I did," he shrugged. "So now you're here, he's here and you two need to talk. Go to the Blue Plate. Have some pancakes. Talk. I have a party to host." Kendal walked into the hallway and closed the stairwell door.

"It's good to see you, Justine," AM smiled. "You've lost weight. It looks good. Not that you needed to lose weight, you looked fine before," he added quickly.

"Thanks."

"Do you want to go somewhere so we can talk?" AM asked as a party-goer stumbled into the stairwell.

"Sure."

Justine turned on the landing and walked down the stairs. She could feel the familiar smell of AM's breath on her neck. At the bottom of the stairs, he reached and opened the door for her, doing the same with the lobby door. Once outside, he placed her hand in his. She didn't resist.

The florescent street lights and moonlight created a purple haze in the sky. The chilled night air felt good against her skin and cooled her blushing cheeks. Feeling as though she had been holding her breath in the stairwell, she gulped air hungrily, sucking it in through her nostrils, enjoying the cool sensation. As they walked along hand in hand, Justine felt AM's fingers tighten around hers. She smiled as he repositioned himself so that he was on the curbside of the street, a posture he always assumed in case a car swerved on to the curb, claiming that he could push her to safety if he were curbside. Once repositioned, he gripped her hand again. Justine wanted to say something, but didn't know where to begin. She breathed and waited for him to speak. The street noise proved louder than she remembered when she exited the taxi in front of Kendal's house. Now late night partygoers and diners laughed and bumped into them on the crowded street.

"So, why are you here, AM?" she felt herself ask involuntarily.

"Let's not talk now. Let's wait until we get to the restaurant. It's right there," he pointed.

Mr. Lieberman himself greeted them as they entered. "Welcome, welcome!" he beckoned. "There's a booth open right over there. I just wiped the table." AM tilted his head to the side.

"Uncle Morty, it's me."

Mr. Lieberman stared into AM's eyes. "Jacob? Jacob Wahlberg? Is that you Mr. Wahlberg? I thought you were at Harvard? What are you doing back in Chicago? I don't have on my glasses, I almost didn't recognize you. You've packed on a few pounds, huh?" he asked pulling Jacob into a tight bear hug. With his hand around AM's shoulders he snapped his fingers loudly. "Attention! Attention everybody! I need your attention! This young man is the grandson of my best friend in the world. His grandfather and I immigrated from Germany together in the forties. Saul Wahlberg and I were like brothers. This is his grandson, Jacob. He's going to be a doctor like his grandfather." The restaurant erupted in applause as though Mr. Lieberman routinely interrupted their meal for grand introductions. Seconds later the chatter resumed and the fork and plate clanking continued.

"And you look just like old Saul in his prime too! I tell you! Looking at you takes me back thirty years. Oh, I miss my buddy Saul. You're like a walking fountain of youth! What brings you here tonight? And at this hour?" Mr. Lieberman rattled his questions and statements without pausing for a reply. Following AM's gaze, he noticed Justine for the first time. He grabbed her hand and air kissed it. "Hello, my dear. I'm Mr. Lieberman. Or you can call me Uncle Morty."

"Hi, I'm Justine Wellington," she smiled.

"Princess Justine, it's nice to meet you," Uncle Morty bowed.

Justine looked at AM with a puzzled expression.

AM pointed to her head. She still wore her diamond tiara.

"We were at a costume party, and I forgot I still had this on," she explained.

"No explanation necessary. I work in Boys' Town. I've seen more characters coming in here dressed in drag and costumes. Ooooh, the stories I could tell. I might write a book. If I can ever get away from this restaurant, I am going to write a book on the things that I've seen and heard."

"Uncle Morty, why are you still wiping down tables? Mom and Dad said that you retired and that you were a silent investor now."

"That's hogwash. This is my baby. I don't cook anymore, but I enjoy seeing my old friends. I worked in here for over twenty years. People missed me, and I missed them. And after Sarah died I didn't have anything to do at home."

"But don't you still own that jewelry store on Wabash?"

"I do. But they don't need me down there. I still do repairs occasionally, but my sons run that now. It's doing quite well I might add. Very well indeed. I just bought a place in West Palm Beach, and I sold my house in Highland Park and moved downtown."

"That's what Dad mentioned. He said that you live on the Gold Coast," AM whistled. "In the high rent district."

"Shhh. I don't want people to know all of that. But I did get a nice little place with a Lake Michigan view. I like it, and I'm not reminded of Sarah when I walk in every room. That big Highland Park house had too many memories. A lovely family bought it too. They have three kids, just like me and Sarah. It was time to turn over that big house to a young family."

"Little? You're being modest, Uncle Morty. Dad said that your apartment is next door to the Drake Hotel and you have five bedrooms and five bathrooms. Dad said it's huge."

Uncle Morty laughed. "It's nice. It is a little bigger than I thought I wanted, but I wanted to have plenty of room so that when the kids and the grandkids want to come into the city they can stay with me, and we're not all over each other. And it works too," Uncle Morty chuckled. "Seems like I have a houseguest almost every weekend. It's my sons' personal in-towner. But I don't mind. I'm glad to have the company. And Stella moved down with me, so she helps me keep the place tidy, and she still makes the best peach cobbler I've ever tasted."

"You should put that on the menu, Uncle Morty," AM suggested.

"No can do. I haven't changed the menu in over twenty years. If it ain't broke don't fix it. My limited menu is my trademark."

"Why do you only offer a few things, Uncle Morty?" Justine asked. "I've never been here, but a guy that I work with told me about the Blue Plate and said that the food is really good."

"Well, Princess Justine, I opened this restaurant as a hobby, when my sons took a more active role in our jewelry business. People always told me that they liked my pancakes, eggs and grilled cheese sandwiches. So I decided to feature those items. I added bacon and sausage and fries to balance it out," he explained. "I planned to add more things to the menu, but word got out that we only offered these items so people would come just to see if it was true, and soon we had people lined up out the door, so I decided that I didn't need to add to the menu," he shrugged. "Now over twenty years later people are still coming to the Blue Plate Special to sample our limited menu. And they always come back too," he grinned. "People don't know this, but it was Stella who taught me how to make those pancakes. It's really her secret recipe. In fact, when I die, I'm leaving the restaurant to her. It's in my will. And it's also in my will that she can't alter the menu," he chuckled.

"Because if it ain't broke," he paused and pointed at AM.

"Don't fix it," AM finished.

"Who's Stella?" Justine asked.

"She was Uncle Morty's housekeeper and cook."

"She's family now," Uncle Morty corrected. "Stella was and is family. Her skin is a sweet brown caramel like yours too," Uncle Morty smiled. "It's late. I better get going so Stella doesn't worry. She stays awake until I come home, and I always make it home before midnight. Now you two order whatever you want, and it's on the house. Carlos, this is my family, so this one is on me. Do not take money from him, you hear me, Carlos?" Uncle Morty said loudly.

Carlos nodded and smiled. "Yes, sir."

"It was good to see you, Uncle Morty," AM smiled as he hugged Uncle Morty.

Uncle Morty reached to hug Justine too. "Just seeing you tonight added ten years to my life. I'm back with my buddy, Saul. I'm going to smile all the way home. Now wait, you still didn't tell me why you're here. Is it Princess Justine's birthday? Tell me you know to take her to a better restaurant than the Blue Plate Special for her birthday, Jacob. Your grandfather Saul would not be pleased."

AM laughed. "No. That's not it. It's not her birthday," he paused.

"Well what brings you here? I remember when your grandfather was in medical school, he barely had time to sleep let alone travel," Uncle Morty chuckled. "Why are you in Chicago?"

"Well, the truth is," he sighed slowly.

Justine stared, awaiting AM's explanation.

"I've decided to transfer to Northwestern to finish medical school."

Chapter 8

Fashion Mistake

Her freshly painted toes peeking beneath the layer of blankets, she was glad that she'd treated herself to a pedicure at the beauty school earlier in the week. Staring down at her swollen feet, at least her toes were polished a bubblegum pink. Teenie and Maria would be proud. Rashanda was exhausted from ten hours of hard labor, including two hours of active aerobic pushing where her long nails clawed into the flesh of her thin thighs. She now cooled her backside on soothing bags of ice that the young labor and delivery nurses replaced every fifteen minutes. She wondered if there was a timer set at the nurse's station. The older nurses checked her vital signs every hour, and the younger nurses replaced her ice bag and laid extra blankets across her legs to balance the chill that she felt with the ice bottom blanket. When she worried about the fresh scars on her thighs, an older nurse assured her that cocoa butter and vitamin E oil would heal the self imposed scratch marks on her thighs.

She waddled to the bathroom to change the pad that seemed to need replacing every fifteen minutes. "The heavy bleeding should subside in about a week," Nurse Betty had explained. The television was turned on, but she had muted the volume to try and follow Nurse Betty and her mother's advice. "For the next few weeks, you need to learn to sleep when the baby sleeps or you won't get your proper rest." But Rashanda was far too anxious to sleep. With Ian asleep in the chair beside her bed, and the baby sleeping in the bassinet on her other side, she thought about the last twenty four hours.

Everything had happened so fast. From the attempted burglary in the dorm, to Mrs. Hall chugging beer and burping as she described how she kicked the intruder in the nuts. It all seemed surreal. Rashanda felt like it had been a dream, but as the ice on her posterior shifted, she knew that it had been real.

ço௸

The police escort had been Barbara Ann's idea. "These children have been through enough this afternoon, the least you can do is help them get to the hospital as quickly as possible." The officers obliged without protest. Ian's mother also instructed two of the girls in the dorm to mop up the amniotic fluid and tidy up the apartment. "Now Ian, is your bag packed?" his mother asked matter of factly.

"Is my bag packed? Why do I need a bag?" Ian questioned.

"Because you will be spending the night at the hospital with your wife and new baby, son." Rashanda beamed when Barbara Ann referred to her as Ian's wife for the first time. "You might want to brush your teeth and change your clothes."

"I didn't think of that," Ian admitted, scurrying into the bedroom.

There was a calm sense of urgency about everything that was happening. Ian rushed around tossing things into a backpack, but his mother had a warm calmness about her that Rashanda had never seen. She wondered if it was the beers that had mellowed Ian's mother out.

"Your parents are on their way, Rashanda. They are going to meet us at the hospital. I just called them," Ian shared.

"What's going on?" Tiffany asked standing in the doorway. "Why are the police here? Is Shanda okay?"

Hearing her sister call her by her pet name, Rashanda started to cry, reaching for her sister's hand.

"Tif! What are you doing here? You left over an hour ago."

"I left my bag in the closet. I remembered it when I got downtown, so I just decided to ride back up here and get it so you wouldn't have to mail it to me," she explained quickly. "What's going on?"

"My water broke. I'm so glad that you're here," Rashanda sobbed softly.

"You mean the baby is coming today?"

"That's right, young lady. The baby is coming today," Barbara Ann repeated. "I'm Mrs. Hall. I'm Ian's mother."

"I remember you from the wedding," Tiffany smiled. "I'm Rashanda's sister Tiffany."

Without a hint of recognition, Barbara Ann smiled and continued to calmly give orders to the students gathering in the hallway. "Now which one of you is the resident assistant or RA?" she asked.

A short young man wearing a Northwestern sweatshirt stepped forward. "I am. I'm Bob."

"Well, Bob, since Ian is going to be otherwise engaged for a few days, you need to step up and make sure that the dorm runs smoothly. The first thing you need to do is file a report with the housing office telling them about the attempted break-in. Include a copy of the police report and also suggest that they hire a retiree to sit in the lobby during the day since this dorm is so remote and off campus. Having a student in the lobby at night is fine, but they clearly need someone in the lobby during the daytime too. Now you make sure and give my son credit for that idea, you understand?"

"Yes, maam," the RA replied.

Ian walked over and resumed control. "Mom, I can take over from here. Bob has been an RA for a few years. He knows the ropes. Why don't you get your purse so you can follow us to the hospital."

"Well, okay," Barbara Ann said. "Does Rashanda need to pack her bag?"

"My bag is in the car, Mrs. Hall. I packed it a few weeks ago and left it in the trunk."

"Smart thinking, Rashanda. And call me Barbara Ann," she reminded. "Well, let's get this party started. I'm going to be a grandmother!" she grinned.

"Ma'am, since we've seen you drink two beers, as an officer of the law, I cannot allow you to operate a motorized vehicle," one of the officers stated softly. "I could get suspended from the force if I watched you do that."

"You've got to be kidding me. I have been drinking beer since before you were born. I am perfectly able to drive."

"I'm sure you are, Ma'am, but I'm just doing my job."

"Mom. Tiffany has her license. She can ride with you and drive your car," Ian suggested.

Barbara Ann exhaled loudly, her nostrils flaring like a bull. "Have you ever driven a Mercedes Benz, Tiffany?" she asked.

"In fact, I have. My dad just bought one for my mother. It's the E320 station wagon."

"Oh well, I guess I have no other choice. Ian did you call your father and tell him to meet us at the hospital?"

"Yes, Mom. I called Dad after I called Rashanda's parents. He wasn't home, so I left a message on the machine."

"Are you feeling okay, Rashanda?" Ian asked noticing his bride's tear stained face. "Have the contractions started?

"I'm fine. I'm not in too much pain, but I feel the contractions that I felt that time we went to the hospital and it was a false alarm. I just can't believe that the baby is coming today," she smiled.

"Those are probably the Braxton-Hicks contractions," Ian nodded. "I also called Dr. McKnight at home, and he's meeting us at the hospital, so we'd better get going."

The rest of the labor experience seemed to happen in slow motion. Dr. McKnight and Nurse Betty entered her room as the admitting nurse was leaving.

"Well, look who's having a baby today," Dr. McKnight beamed. "My two favorite patients, Dr. and Judge Hall. How are you feeling Mrs. Hall?"

"I feel fine Dr. McKnight. I really do," she smiled.

"You're definitely not in active labor yet," Dr. McKnight explained, his hand in hers. "But since your water broke, I want you in the hospital. The nurse told me that you are about four centimeters dilated so Ian I want you to walk her around the hospital to help speed up the contractions."

"Yes, sir," Ian replied.

Barbara Ann and Tiffany entered the room at the same time. "Dr. McKnight!" Barbara Ann beamed like a cheerleader. "I haven't seen you in ages."

"Well if it isn't my favorite patient of all time," Dr. McKnight grinned walking over and kissing her once on each cheek. "You are just as beautiful as ever, Barbara. Where's that old husband of yours?"

"He's on his way now."

"Why didn't you come together?"

"I was already in Evanston visiting the kids when Rashanda's water broke," she paused, placing her perfectly manicured hand on Dr. McKnight's shoulder. "Excuse me, I'm forgetting my manners. Dr. McKnight, this is Rashanda's sister, Tiffany Jordan. Tiffany, this is Dr. McKnight. He's been our family doctor since forever. He delivered Ian." Rashanda watched as the beer swigging Barbara Ann put on her prim and proper hat for Dr. McKnight.

"I sure did," Dr. McKnight smiled. "Nice to meet you, Tiffany. I see that you're just as pretty as your sister. Are you going to be a lawyer too?"

"No. I'm going to be a teacher," Tiffany replied.

"Good for you. The world needs more good teachers."

"Barbara, Rashanda is my only delivery today, and she's several hours from delivering, so let's go down to the cafeteria and have a cup of coffee so we can catch up," he suggested. "Now, Mrs. Ian Hall, I want you to walk around for about fifteen minutes every hour, and when you're not walking around, try and take a nap. You're going to be a mother today, and you will need your rest," he smiled.

"How can you tell that I'm several hours from delivering, Dr. McKnight?" Rashanda asked.

"Mrs. Hall, I've been delivering babies for over forty years. I'll know when you're in active labor, trust me," Dr. McKnight winked.

"You're in good hands, Rashanda. He knows what he's doing." Barbara Ann patted Dr. McKnight on the back. "Now take me to the cafeteria, I need a cup of coffee. And you're buying, Dr. McKnight. I have a beer buzz, and I want to tell you how I kicked a would be robber in the nuts earlier today!" Barbara Ann boasted.

Dr. McKnight stopped in his tracks and shook his head from left to right. "You kicked a would be robber in the nuts today? And now you're hours away from being a grandmother? Barbara, you never cease to amaze me. I can't wait to hear this story. Ian, walk your bride around the corridor. And when your father gets here send him to the cafeteria to join us."

"Yes, sir," Ian said. Rashanda thought Ian might salute as his medical hero walked out arm in arm with his mother.

Tiffany had already nestled into the window seat bed and laid down for a nap. Following doctor's orders, Ian walked Rashanda around the labor and delivery floor before crawling in the bed with her and taking a nap next to his wife. Rashanda smiled at how quickly her husband could fall asleep. She knew that this quality would serve him well in medical school. She was too excited to sleep, but felt herself nodding in and out as nurses walked in to check her monitor periodically.

She was more hungry than tired.

"But I'm starving," Rashanda whined. "Why can't I eat?"

Nurse Betty smiled. "You don't want anything heavy in your system right before you deliver a baby. Trust me."

"Why not? I'm so hungry." She almost confessed to walking back to her dorm from campus, but feared that Ian might overhear and scold her. "I ate a really late lunch today," she added.

"I'll have the nutritionist send in some chicken broth for you."

"Chicken broth? Can't I have a cheeseburger or at least some pizza?"

Nurse Betty laughed. "If you eat a cheeseburger, you'll regret it later, you really will," Nurse Betty grinned. "I'll have them bring you some chicken broth, ice chips and a tonic water," Nurse Betty said firmly before leaving the room with her clipboard chart.

Rashanda was outraged. "Ian! Wake up, Ian!"

"Is it time?" he asked, jumping from the bed.

"No. That mean nurse won't let me eat anything, and I'm starving. Why can't I eat something other than chicken broth?"

Ian yawned and stretched. "Chicken broth? Is that what she told you?"

"Yes. Chicken broth. I want some meat!"

Ian snuggled on his side in the small hospital bed. "Rashanda, I'm sure the nurse has her reasons. How are you feeling?"

"Hungry."

"Well, try to take a nap like Dr. McKnight suggested."

"I can't. I've got to wait and eat my chicken broth. I'll save you some," she said glibly.

ॐ

"But you don't understand, I never vomit," she pleaded. "Ever-never-ever-never! Something's wrong with the baby," she cried.

"No. The baby's heart rate monitor is fine, your monitor is fine. Everything is fine," Nurse Betty assured calmly.

"I'm going to throw up again. Oh my God," Rashanda growled as her mother held a cold compress against her forehead while Tiffany massaged her feet.

"Remember to breathe, Rashanda. You're breathing for the baby," her mother coaxed.

Rashanda pulled her feet away from Tiffany's grasp and slowly tried to stand. "Mom, when was the last time that I threw up?"

"As if Mom tracks that, Shanda. You're tripping."

"Shut up, Tiffany!" Rashanda screamed, gripping the edge of the bed.

Mrs. Jordan cut her eyes at Tiffany to silence her.

"Where's Ian? And what is that smell?" she shrieked. "Who's eating salt and sour potato chips? That smell is making me sick!"

"But you like salt and sour potato chips," Mrs. Jordan reminded.

"That smell is making me throw up!" Rashanda gagged again, dragging her IV unit with her into the bathroom.

Tiffany backed towards the door, quietly removing the half eaten bag of potato chips as she left the room.

Rashanda cupped water in her hand and rinsed her mouth. "I feel like I'm going to die," she cried.

"You're having a baby, honey. You're in labor," her mother reminded.

"Rashanda, you are clearly in active labor now, so I'm going to reconnect your baby monitor, and you won't be allowed to get up from the bed anymore, okay?" Nurse Betty said cheerfully.

"What if I have to pee or throw up again? That yummy liquid lunch that you served me is running right through me."

"We can insert a catheter into your bladder to drain your urine, and if you have to throw up, you can do it in this little pail," she waved a mustard colored pail that sat on the nightstand.

"Oh, that's gonna be cute," Rashanda growled.

"Have you had a bowel movement today?" Nurse Betty asked.

"I don't remember. I've been a little busy," she snapped.

"Well, if you feel like you have to have a bowel movement, don't bear down or push. Contractions feel like a bowel movement."

"Okey dokey, duly noted...." her voice trailed. "Oh, my God! Mom, this hurts!" Rashanda screamed.

"Breathe, Rashanda!" her mother coached.

"This is a big one," Nurse Betty nodded studying the baby

monitor.

"Where's Ian?" Rashanda shrieked as Ian walked in laughing with Dr. McKnight.

"Now, you look like a woman in active labor!" Dr. McKnight observed just as Rashanda threw up into the pail.

It was six o'clock in the morning, and Rashanda had been pushing since four a.m. but the pushing seemed to be in vain as no progress was being made. The baby's heart rate monitor was now beginning to trouble Nurse Betty who whispered something to Dr. McKnight. Rashanda heard Dr. McKnight order the neonatal intensive care unit to the delivery room. Delirious and in pain, Rashanda was now afraid as Dr. McKnight grabbed her hand and said, "I think we should prep for surgery."

"But I don't want to have a C-section," she cried. "Please let me try again."

"You're exhausted. I think that your hips are just too narrow to push the baby through the birth canal." Ian rubbed her hand and kissed her forehead.

"I think we should do a C-section, Rashanda."

"Please, Ian. Let me try one more time."

"We don't want the baby to be in distress. The important thing is that you have a healthy baby," Dr. McKnight said sternly. "I think we should prep for surgery."

"Here comes another contraction," Nurse Betty announced.

Inhaling deeply, Rashanda closed her eyes, and gripped Ian's hand tightly.

Ian looked at Dr. McKnight. "Dr. McKnight, with all do respect, let's give her one more chance to try and push more effectively."

"Let's push through this series of contractions and see what happens," Dr. McKnight encouraged.

Her epidural had worn off, and she was now feeling every labor pain intensely. Dripping in sweat, her hair a wet mass of string, her agony was being witnessed up close and personal by a swat team of medical students wearing ill-fitting white medical coats. The sleep deprived students hedged bets on the gender of the baby once they learned that the couple had chosen not to find out the sex. Rashanda cursed the day when Ian had eagerly convinced her to sign the release waiver allowing the medical students to witness her delivery. "It's a teaching hospital, Rashanda. It's a learning experience for the students."

Rashanda had noticed the medical students' sad looking white polyester jackets as she strolled the maternity ward that afternoon, thinking that the medical students were required to wear the ugly jackets with the too short sleeves as part of a hazing ritual imposed by the interns and attending physicians.

Though crowded to capacity with the nurses, medical students, her mother and Tiffany, Rashanda didn't hear any of their voices, hearing only that of Dr. McKnight who announced that her pushing was "more effective" this time! "I see the baby's head. Keep pushing just like that Rashanda, the baby is crowning now."

"You can do this, Rashanda!" Ian encouraged.

Her nails dug deeply into the flesh of her thighs as she bared down with all of her might.

ﻌ৵৶

"Christine Marie," Tiffany repeated. "That's a pretty name. Will you call her Chris or Chrissy?"

"No. Her name will be Christine Marie."

"You know her friends are going to call her Chris or Chrissy.

And you know that Maria is going to swear up and down that you named your baby after her."

"I know. But we used our grandmother's middle names, so it's a family name."

"That's so special," Justine smiled. "Hi, Christine Marie. I'm your Aunt Justine. Everybody is going to be so jealous that I got to see her first," Justine grinned snapping another photo of the sleeping baby, bundled like a burrito.

"Well, you live the closest. Just send them lots of photos. But don't take any photos of me until Tiffany fixes my hair. I look like death sucking a pickle, and this robe is a fashion mistake."

"You look like a woman who just had a baby. But you know who looks like fashion mistakes are those medical students walking around with those little white jackets on. Almost all of their jackets are at least one size too small."

"I noticed the same thing. They look like they're pledging a fraternity," Rashanda laughed. "They look like sleep walking zombies wearing their little brother's laboratory jackets. I'm too embarrassed to face any of them now that they've seen me push out a baby and poop on the delivery table. I told you that an army of them witnessed me giving birth, right?"

"Yeah, you told me that you had an audience, but why'd you poop on the delivery table? That's disgusting."

"When you're pushing out a baby, everything gets pushed out. So I had little pebbles that kept squeezing out," Rashanda explained.

"Okay, see, that's way too much information. That's just not right."

"They offered to give me an enema to clean out my colon, but I didn't want that," Rashanda continued. "I really didn't have anything on my stomach, but what I did have in there came out."

"That's an image that I could have done without. New topic please!" Justine pleaded.

"Fair. Let's see. Oh, Grace called right before you got here and told me that she's going to drive up to see us next weekend. She sent that huge baby bouquet in the corner. And she insists on buying the baby's crib and dresser."

"That girl has more money than she knows what to do with."

"Truth. You know the executor told her that the people who bought her grandparents' estate in Wilmette are ready to sell because they are moving to France next year, so Grace is planning to buy it. She's going to come up to sign some papers next week."

"She mentioned that to me too. What in the world is she going to do with a big house like that?"

"When I toured that place with her I couldn't believe how gigantic that house is."

"I think it's kind of sweet that she's going to own the house where her mother grew up," Rashanda offered. "Most people who have money like that keep the estates in the family anyway. She said that her parents are going to live in it for now. They miss being near the water, and they're looking forward to living in the house that they lived in when they first got married. Isn't that sweet?"

"I guess. Are they going to live in the servant's quarters or the main house?"

"That's a good question. I think they're going to live in the main house, but we'll have to ask Grace."

"Was Ian surprised that you didn't curse and shout obscenities at him like he'd seen pregnant women do in the movies?" Justine asked.

"No. Or at least he didn't say that to me. Truthfully, I really don't remember him being there. When my hands weren't gripping my swollen thighs, I do remember gripping someone's hand tightly, but I told myself that it was God's."

"Were you hallucinating?"

"I wouldn't say that I was hallucinating, but I was having an out of body experience, praying and breathing through the pain, talking to God and asking for strength to get through the delivery, reminding myself that I was breathing for my baby, and that if I held my breath, my baby wouldn't get oxygen."

"You must have really not wanted to have a C-section."

"I really didn't. You know how scared I am of needles. I did not want to be sliced open. Plus, after all of that labor intensity, I really didn't want to have surgery too. Having an unplanned emergency C-section is like gaining two pounds because you ate a warm chocolate brownie crowned with vanilla ice cream and drizzled with chocolate sauce after a bad break-up. It's just not fair. Everyone knows that a brownie eaten after a bad break-up should be calorie free. It's a rule."

Justine laughed at her friend's analogy. "Everything with you is about food! So that motivated you to heave that baby out, huh?"

"It worked. Plus, I was hungry! And I knew that if I had a C-section the recovery period would be longer."

"How much time are you going to take off from school?"

"None."

"None? Did you say none?"

"None. The doctor said that as long as I don't over do it, there's no reason that I can't go back to class next week."

"But Christine Marie is so tiny and little," Justine cooed peering into the lucite bassinet. "I can't believe that skinny old you pushed out an eight pound baby. That's amazing to me."

"Believe it. I'm sitting on the ice packs to prove it. And I'd do it all over again," Rashanda grinned. "I am so hungry."

"You just ate a cheeseburger and fries."

"And I just pushed out an eight pound baby, don't judge me," Rashanda laughed. "I wish Ian would come back with my Garrett's popcorn."

"Did you send him on a Garrett's run?"

"I sure did! Maria told me that Richard gave her mother a Cartier watch as a push present when she had her daughter, so since we can't afford a gift like that now...."

"What do you mean 'since you guys can't afford a gift like that now?' You guys can't afford a Timex watch," Justine laughed.

"Shut up, Justine! I figured he could get me some Garrett's popcorn. He's bringing me the caramel corn cheese corn mix that we like."

"Yum, I'm sticking around so I can have some of that too."

"So who's going to watch the baby so you can go to class?"

"Well, there are only two days when Ian and I both have classes around the same time in the morning and in the afternoon, so the cafeteria worker's mother is going to come to the dorm and watch her on those two days."

"That's going to be so hard, Rashanda. Aren't you going to be sad leaving your baby with a stranger?"

"I'm sure it won't be the best day of my life, but I want to finish school on time so I can stay on track for law school. Besides, she's not really a stranger. She reminds me of my grandmother, Big Momma. She worked as a cook, housekeeper, and nanny for a family that lived in Highland Park. The wife died a few years ago, but she still works as a housekeeper and cook for the husband. Her name is Stella. But enough about me. Tell me about you and AM!"

Justine tilted her head to the side. "Did you say, Stella?"

Chapter 9

School of Service

Her legs measured thirty six inches from hip to toe. Shocked, the girl measured her twice. "Wow! Your legs are freakishly long for a woman!" Grace rolled her eyes at the insensitive medical assistant. "Your chart says that you're seventy-four inches tall. That's six feet two inches! My dad isn't even that tall," she chuckled.

Accustomed to height comments and jokes, Grace slipped on her shoes and stood to her feet. "And you still wear heels too?" she noticed.

"It's only a one inch pump," Grace replied. "I wouldn't really call that a heel. I have three inch heels in my closet."

"Three inch heels? Your posture is really good too. Most tall girls that I know slouch so they can appear shorter. But your posture is perfect like a gymnast or dancer. Are your parents tall?"

"Not really. My dad is tall, but he's not extraordinarily tall for a man. And my biological mother wasn't very tall at all. Actually, I really don't know where my height comes from."

"Were you adopted?"

"Huh?"

"You said your biological mother wasn't very tall. Were you adopted?"

"Uh, yes. Technically, I was adopted."

"So you were raised with your biological father, but not your biological mother, huh? That's odd."

"Well, yes, but not exactly," Grace trailed.

"I see so many girls on campus slouching. Part of it is the heavy backpacks that they carry," the medical assistant rambled. "And sometimes I think they slouch because they think that it's cute. It's not cute."

"You're right. It's not cute. I used to slouch when I was in middle school and high school, because I was taller than most of the boys, but then I realized that slouching just made me look like a tall, slouchy girl. It didn't hide my height, so my friends made me practice walking with books on my head."

"Well, it worked. You have perfect posture. Do you play basketball?"

"No. I couldn't master the running while dribbling concept, which is pretty essential for a basketball player."

"Not necessarily. A lot of good basketball players never run with the ball. They could have just had you play center or power forward, blocking shots and getting rebounds. You would have been an unstoppable defender. What a waste."

"Excuse me," Grace replied.

"No offense," the medical assistant offered. "I played basketball in high school, and I was pretty good. I played point guard, and was good enough to get a scholarship to go to school here, but if I had your height, I'd be playing basketball at Stanford, Tennessee or Duke. Did you play volleyball?"

"I didn't play volleyball in high school, but I play on an intramural team now. I'm the team's secret weapon," she smiled, hoping this redeemed her in the eyes of the medical assistant.

"Whew! At least you're using that height now. I can't get over how straight you stand. I need to improve my posture. I'm going to practice walking with books on my head."

"That's what did it for me. I'm telling you, a few years ago, I would have been one of those slouchy girls that you described. By the way, I also just started practicing yoga."

"Yoga? Do you need to be tall to practice yoga?"

Grace stared at the medical assistant. "No. You don't need to be tall to practice yoga, but yoga helps with your posture."

"How?"

"Well, by building core strength, or abdominal strength," she amended. "Because when your abdomen is engaged, your posture is improved. Try it. Suck in your stomach."

Grace watched as the medical assistant sucked in her stomach. "You're right. I felt my spine straighten when I did that."

"That's right. When your abdominal muscles are not engaged, your back tends to curve over into a C shape like this," she demonstrated, relaxing her abdominal muscles and watching as her shoulders dipped and her spine relaxed. "Try to remember that you always want to keep your chi engaged, even when you're sitting."

"My what?"

"I'm sorry. Your chi is your core or your abdomen. It's your power center. You always want to keep your power center engaged. I learned that in yoga too. And I also learned that once you begin to relax through the postures and master your breathing, you sleep better at night."

"Really? I suffer from insomnia sometimes. I wake up in the middle of the night and have trouble going back to sleep."

"Do you drink caffeine? That might have something to do with it."

"I don't drink that much caffeine."

"You should try limiting your caffeine intake and try yoga. In fact, a friend of mine just opened a new yoga studio on campus. It's on Pennsylvania Avenue just across from the Pennsylvania Avenue Residence Hall. It's in that space that used to be a barber shop."

"I think I know where that is. There are a bunch of restaurants on that street. What's the studio called?"

"God's Grace Yoga."

"Grace? Isn't that your name? Your friend named her yoga studio after you?"

"The studio is called 'God's Grace Yoga' which speaks to the mercy, grace and favor that only God can bestow," she explained. "It's not really named after me."

"It sure sounds like it. Shoot, I would just tell people that the studio was named after me."

"Well, I am a silent partner in the studio," Grace admitted. "But I didn't have anything to do with the name. My partner chose the name."

"Well, you must be a pretty important partner to have the studio named after you."

"Are you a student here?"

"Well, I was. I'm on academic probation this semester because I failed an Economics class. So I'm taking classes at Parker Junior College to make up that credit."

"That's fine. As long as you have a valid student identification card, you can register for the reduced student rate. Come by. Your first five sessions will be on the house."

"That's cool. Thanks, Grace."

"We offer that deal to everyone. My partner and I are really trying to get more students interested in the practice of yoga, so tell your friends. After your first five sessions, it's only five dollars per class for students. The yoga studio at the student health center charges twenty dollars per class, and that's their discounted rate."

"How are you going to make any money with your fees so low?"

"It's not really about the money. It's about the service. We want to offer yoga as a service for the students. Yoga has been practiced in the Asian cultures and around the world for over five thousand years, but it's still just gaining ground in the United States. The God's Grace Yoga studio is our service project. A way of giving back to the community."

"Most students that I know are trying to make a profit. And your studio is in a high rent district. How are you even able to pay the rent only charging five dollars per class?"

"Let's just say that God is good," Grace smiled. "Are we finished here?"

"Yes. You're all set. And here's your physical form. Why do you need a physical form filled out anyway?"

"I need it for a project that I'm working on."

"Are you trying to find your biological mother?"

Grace decided that she had shared enough information with the inquisitive medical assistant, remembering what her mother Ethel Dudley had taught her; "Grace, as you get older, you will learn that you don't have to answer every stupid question that someone asks you," she explained, pronouncing asks like axes. "Lawd knows, you will encounter stupid questions for the rest of your natural life, but you can choose not to answer them. Just smile with grace and keep it moving," Ethel continued, laughing at her play on her daughter's name.

"I hope to see you at the yoga studio one day," Grace smiled gracefully.

❦

She had mastered warrior one, two and three, and could now hold a bind in both pigeon and eagle postures, but her long legs and tight hips made the lotus pose an impossible challenge. She inhaled deeply through one nostril, closing it with her thumb before releasing her index finger and exhaling through her other nostril.

"As you wiggle your fingers and toes, and slowly become aware of the room, please come to a comfortable seated position." Grace used this as permission to extend her legs straight out in front of her.

"Place your hands at heart center," Tomoko instructed softly. "Rolling out your mat and coming to class takes courage. Showing up, taking the first step and getting started is the hardest part of any journey. The light in me salutes the light in each and every one of you," she articulated softly. "May you go back into the world and let others see the light that is in you. A light that God has placed in you to draw others closer to him through you. I honor you as you have honored me with your presence today. And I thank you for allowing me to share in your yoga practice. Namaste." Her voice was soft, just above a whisper as she bent at the waist, her legs crossed in the lotus position, her nose touching the tip of her mat. In return, Grace bowed at the waist and almost touched her nose to her knee this time.

Theirs was a God centered yoga practice. Each class began with a different scripture meditation or mantra, usually taken from the Bible. Students were encouraged to meditate on scripture during the meditation portion of the class, as soft music played through the portable stereo system.

"There are spray bottles and towels here for you to wipe down the mats, so please do so," Tomoko announced as a group of yogis approached her.

Grace stretched her long legs and rotated her neck. From her perch in the back of the room, she watched as the students, mostly women, cleaned their mats and whispered softly to themselves. She counted thirteen in class today. Their largest class yet.

"I can't believe that this class is only five dollars per class after the introductory period," one student whispered to another.

"I know. That was so much fun. The poses were harder than I expected them to be, but I feel like I did something good for my body."

"What's the teacher's name again?"

"I don't remember," her friend replied.

"Tomoko," Grace offered. "Her name is Tomoko."

"Thanks," the girl smiled at Grace. "Tomoko said that she's going to offer a Hatha yoga class, another Vinyasa class and an athletic yoga class too."

"What's Vinyasa?"

"It's where we move from pose to pose quickly. It's more intense than the Hatha class that we did today. I actually broke a sweat when I did my first Vinyasa class on campus."

"Oh, I'll have to try that and see if I like it. I really like the schedule of this studio."

"I like the schedule of this studio too. There are only two classes each day right now, but she's planning to add more when she hires a few more instructors. I love how she has the early morning class and then the late night class."

"She calls it the sunrise sunset schedule," Grace offered, catching herself from saying "we call it."

"Do you know how she can afford to only charge five dollars per class?" the student asked Grace. Surprised by the question, Grace inhaled slowly, searching for a reply.

"I heard her explain to another student that teaching yoga is her community service; her way of giving back to the university community," her friend answered.

Satisfied with that response, Grace exhaled and smiled. "That's what I heard too," she added.

"I'm just scared that I'm going to get hooked on her classes at the cheap rate and then she's going to raise the price."

"I hope she doesn't do that."

"She won't do that," Grace added quickly "I know that for a fact."

"How can you be so sure?"

"We're friends," Grace added. "In fact, I think she's going to run a special for her regular students and allow them to practice in the studio for free if they come at least three times each week."

"Are you serious?" both girls asked in unison.

"That's what she mentioned. But don't quote me until she rolls that deal out."

"Her parents must be really wealthy."

Grace watched as Tomoko exited the yoga studio and walked into the lobby with some of the students.

"Actually, I don't think her parents are involved with God's Grace Yoga," Grace smiled. "Tomoko is just trying to share her gifts and be of service to others."

"But how can she afford it? I mean, who pays for this studio space and her salary?" the girl whispered.

"I don't know all of those details, but I know that there is at least one angel investor involved in God's Grace Yoga."

"I've heard of those. It's where a wealthy person anonymously donates money for a worthy cause or invests in various businesses and projects, but they don't want anyone to know who they are, right?"

"That's right. I guess some people just like to give anonymously," Grace added.

"My dad said that's what the super rich do. They angel invest," the girl added. "They don't want people knowing who they are. A lot of rich people get satisfaction helping people without any acknowledgement."

"Not me," her friend offered. "I'd want people to know if I was writing big checks and making big donations."

"Why?" Grace asked.

"So they could look up to me and feel jealous," the co-ed giggled as she wiped down her yoga mat, rolling it up into a tight cylinder and placing it in the cubby with the other mats.

"I think God smiles down on us when we do things from our heart, even if we don't get public praise for them," Grace replied softly. "At least that's what my parents raised me to believe."

"You're right. I was just kidding," the girl smiled. "Have a nice day."

"See you next time," her friend waved at Grace.

"You too." Grace was glad that the girls hadn't asked her name. She watched as the last group of yoga practitioners left the studio, commenting to each other on how beautiful the recently renovated space was. Hearing the compliments, her chest puffed with pride.

Grace and Tomoko had conceived the design together.

"Truth be told. I don't even know if I want to be a doctor," Tomoko sobbed. "My parents have encouraged me to be a doctor since I was a child, and I've always just gone along with the idea," she sniffled. "I know they wouldn't approve of what I really want to do. They'd disown me. Well, they're going to disown me anyway, so I may as well make myself happy," she said to herself, staring into a fresh tissue. Grace wasn't sure if Tomoko was even aware that she was still in the room.

The pause was exaggerated as though priming Grace to ask a follow-up question. "What do you really want to do, Tomoko?" Grace asked.

"I want to be a yoga instructor," she replied confidently. "I've been practicing yoga since I was ten years old. My mother is a yoga instructor, and I became a certified instructor when I turned sixteen. I've always wanted to open a yoga studio. After finishing medical school, I plan to open a yoga studio and maybe start an alternative health care practice specializing in acupuncture and Asian healing techniques," Tomoko paused. "My parents are going to have a field day if they find out that their daughter wants to lead an alternative lifestyle and practice alternative healing. In our culture, they won't have any alternative but to disown me. Way too many alternatives," she laughed loudly, fresh tears streaming down her face.

Glad to see her new friend laughing, Grace laughed too.

"I don't understand, if your mother is a yoga instructor, why doesn't she want you to become one?"

"Because it doesn't pay very much, and my mother wants me to have a better life than she did. She doesn't own a studio, and has no desire to own a studio. She's content teaching at the parks and recreation department in our hometown. Her students are mostly housewives and senior citizens."

"Oh," was all Grace could think to say.

Tomoko blew her nose loudly in a fresh tissue. "So opening a yoga studio is not gonna happen anytime soon because that takes money my friend, and I'm broke. My parents are ready to disown me now that they know that I'm gay, and if I don't become a doctor, how am I going to get the money to open a yoga studio? I was just venting." Tomoko grabbed the soiled tissues and walked into the kitchen. Grace heard her open the cabinet under the sink and toss the tissues into the trash. "Can I have a glass of water?" she asked.

"Sure, help yourself."

Tomoko entered the living room sipping a glass of water without ice. "Since they think that I'm choosing to be gay, I'm just going to have to tell my parents that I will stop being gay," she paused. "I will let them pay for my school, and then once I get my medical degree and don't need their financial support anymore, I will come out of the closet. They will disown me then, but at least it buys me more time and gets me through school."

"That's so sad," Grace said, wondering how her parents would feel about her sexuality secret and briefly wondering when she would tell them. "I feel so sorry for you."

"Don't. Half the kids on campus that I know who have come out, haven't come out to their parents, so I'm just another Illini statistic. I'll lead my real life at school, and fake it when I go home like the other gay students on campus." Another pregnant pause ensued. Tomoko took a long swig of water. "Thanks for listening to me, Grace. I should get going so you can get back to your studying. I'll drop off a brand new box of tissue for you since I've practically wiped this one out," she smiled.

"Tomoko, I think I can help you," Grace said softly. "In fact, I have two things to share with you, and both of them might help you."

The yoga studio had Brazilian cherry floors and floor to ceiling mirrors on every wall. Tomoko had fallen in love with the red Brazilian cherry floors, but decided that the less expensive oak planks were more practical. Grace had surprised Tomoko, contacted the general contractor and changed the order. The exterior wall at the back of the studio had two windows that were covered in bamboo blinds that softened the room. Tomoko insisted that the blinds remain open during class in order to allow natural light to filter into the studio. The windows were located near the ceiling which prevented anyone in the alley from peering into the class. Located so high in the ceiling, window coverings weren't really necessary, but they did make the windows look better as Tomoko assured that they would.

Below the windows were wide mouth cubbies that stored the yoga mats, styrofoam blocks and blankets used by the students. Centered at the front of the room, a narrow shelf housed the portable radio and a cabinet that contained yoga mat disinfectant spray and a stack of white cotton towels. Entering from Pennsylvania Avenue, students were welcomed into the studio by a large mahogany writing desk and two executive desk chairs. A row of high back chairs upholstered in a soft mint green with yellow flecks lined up along the window facing the desk. Grace noticed that the students never sat down to remove their sneakers, boots or clogs. The chairs served as place holders for the students' backpacks.

Yoga literature was scattered on top of the desk and faced a wall of shoe cubbies which contained more yoga literature, and copies of the God's Grace Yoga schedule printed on bright yellow paper. The cubby installer had informed the ladies that the unit was capable of storing up to forty-eight shoes, if each cubby was stuffed with two pair. A wicker basket of white hand towels sat next to the cubby cabinet which was adjacent to a large blue water dispenser with cylinder shaped paper cups ready to quench the students' thirst. The water dispenser gurgled as though belching every five minutes. When the studio was quiet, the dispenser generated white noise that Grace found soothing. A simple analog clock, that reminded Grace of the kitchen clock at her parents' house, was the only wall adornment. Tomoko had wanted to purchase a digital clock, but Grace had insisted on the analog clock. A small bamboo plant sat on the corner of the large desk, a gift presented to Tomoko by one of her Asian students as a symbol of luck and good fortune.

Grace gladly deferred to Tomoko's design expertise since, as a certified yoga instructor, she was more familiar with yoga studio layout. The entire space had been gutted and rehabbed to their specifications, and Grace had spared no expense. Tomoko had squealed when she saw the Brazilian cherry floors and other upgrades that Grace had added behind her friend's back: granite countertops and bamboo flooring in the bathrooms, slate tile in the kitchen conference room and upgraded Kohler faucets. The bathrooms were the crown jewel of the space. Each marked with the male and female symbol denoting unisex usage, visits to the bathroom often brought a squeal from the surprised students who wandered in to relieve themselves before or after class, creating a parade of curious students. "You've got to see the bathroom!" they would squeal.

There was a third door marked Staff Only that was actually a conference room that contained a refrigerator, kitchen sink and counter, washer, dryer, conference room table with six comfortable chairs, lockers and a private water closet. The water closet contained a private sink and was next door to a private shower and dressing area that allowed the space to be gender neutral.

Grace's trust administrator was pleased when she contacted him with her idea to invest in a yoga studio. Although not a yogi himself, his wife had recently started practicing yoga, so he viewed Grace's idea as a promising new trend and a shrewd business decision. In fact, so pleased was he to help her negotiate her first business transaction that he advised that she purchase the space instead of leasing it as she had originally proposed. Calls were made, and when they learned that the vacant storefront adjacent to the studio was owned by the same person, a deal was brokered for the purchase of both spaces to allow for possible expansion or to be leased as a commercial rental property. An all cash deal, Grace owned the property five days after placing the phone call to her trust fund administrator.

Tomoko had no idea how vast Grace's wealth was. "Please allow me to help you open a yoga studio," Grace had offered that night. "Let's just say that I have money, and I need to invest it. I'll explain more later, but for now, just let me help you." The net worth numbers were still too staggering for Grace to truly grasp, and the actual amount made her uncomfortable.

Initially, the local banker was hesitant, but when he received the wire transfer from The Northern Trust Bank, where Grace's trust was held, he knew that it was a serious project. The banker recommended a general contractor as well as an architect to handle the design. Both would be paid directly through the bank. Still skeptical, Tomoko realized that Grace really was in a position to help her when they toured the space with the architect and general contractor just ten days after she had cried on Grace's sofa.

"How much is this going to cost?" Tomoko asked quietly. "Are you sure you can afford this, Grace?"

The general contractor replied, "We were instructed by the

bank not to discuss cost with either of you. We were advised that Miss Dudley's account would be covering all of the expenses and that we were not to discuss pricing at all. This project has what's called an "infinity" budget, so you just tell us what you would like done, and we will accommodate your request."

"As long as your requests are structurally feasible," the architect added. "So design the yoga studio of your dreams," he smiled. "Pretend you're at a five star restaurant that doesn't have any prices on the menu. Just order what you want, regardless of the cost," he grinned. "This is going to be fun!" he finished, practically licking his chops.

Tomoko smiled at her friend as she realized that Grace's offer to help was more than a casual platitude offered to comfort a desperate friend. As they walked through the empty space, Tomoko suggested that the heating and air conditioning system be reconfigured to allow the yoga studio space to be zoned separate from the rest of the building's heating and air conditioning system, explaining that because yoga is best practiced in a warm room, the ability to heat and cool the yoga studio separate from the rest of the space would be ideal. But when she whispered this idea to Grace, Grace insisted that she repeat the idea to the general contractor.

"We can definitely do that. We will create zoned heating and air conditioning. Ladies, the best way to ensure that we design your ideal space is to imagine this studio as a blank canvas. Recommend whatever your heart's desire. If you think it, say it." The girls giggled and sketched what Tomoko described as a class A yoga studio. Within three weeks of purchasing the space, construction was under way.

Weeks later, when Grace returned from the Bursar's office, a receipt in hand showing that she had paid Tomoko's tuition and housing for the remainder of the year, Tomoko almost fainted.

"And I set it up so that when you register for classes next semester, they will send a bill to my bank, and my banker will take care of your tuition," she explained.

"I don't understand," Tomoko said. "Why are you doing this? Why are you being so kind to me?"

"Because I can, and we're friends. I don't want you to have to live a life that's a lie just because you need your parents to pay for your schooling, Tomoko."

"I'm going to pay you back, Grace. I don't know how I'm going to do it, but I will pay you back. I promise."

"God gave me this money to help people. You're my friend, you need my help, so I'm helping you," Grace smiled. "It's a gift. Don't pay me back, just pay it forward."

❧

"You did really well today, Grace," Tomoko complimented. "I don't know why you hide in the back of the studio. You're becoming one of my better students."

"I felt like I did better today, but I still can't sit with my legs criss crossed like a pretzel like some of the other students can, so I just prefer to be in the back. Plus, I'm tall, so I feel like I'd be blocking someone's view of you if I sat in the front."

"Oh yeah, how'd your physical go?"

"Great. I've gained two pounds, but other than that, no surprises."

"Are you sure you really want to go through with this, Grace?"

"I've been praying about it. She saved my life. It's the least that I can do."

"But you're giving her one of your kidneys. What if you need it later?"

"Well, Chip, said that there's no history of kidney disease on his side of the family."

"And Chip is your biological dad, right?"

"Right. His real name is Charles Lovett, but I call him Chip like everybody else."

"And my mother said that the Moores didn't have a history of kidney disease either, so I should be fine."

"And your mother was Lydia Moore, right? I remember that name because I love the name Lydia. You have such a complicated family tree," Tomoko smiled. "But I think I'm keeping all of the names straight."

"You're doing great. Lydia Moore was my birth mother, and she died when I was two. But Ethel Dudley is the mother who raised me, and I don't want her to have to go through dialysis. She doesn't want me to donate my kidney, but I'm doing it anyway. I think the fact that she's not my biological mother but I'm still a donor match for her is God's way of telling me that I was born to help her."

"You are such an angel," Tomoko smiled.

"I'm really not. I'm just not ready to lose my mother yet," Grace sighed. "Or I should say I don't want to lose another mother yet." She juggled the car keys in her hand. "We'd better lock up, I have a paper due tomorrow, and I'm starving. Did you notice what's for dinner tonight?"

Chapter 10

Love Is

The day had gone better than expected. In her letter, she described it as a perfect day despite the cold temperatures and gray skies that the forecast predicted. By mid afternoon, the sun shone brightly and the temperatures were balmy, with birds chirping and flowers threatening to bud as though mocking the meteorologists and their technology. She viewed the unexpected false start to spring as a private smile from God, a nod that he was pleased with their "rain or shine" pact. That evening, with the pseudo smell of spring in the air, the meteorologist warned of one final weekend frost, reminding viewers that it was unwise to plant annuals in late March.

Even Mama Kaye had warned her against getting married on April Fool's Day. "Now, I am not a superstitious woman," Mama Kaye cautioned. "I don't believe in the horoscopes or none of that other foolishness that my Mama and 'dem used to warn us about when I was a young gal. 'Don't sweep your dust over the threshold of your door or you'll be sweeping out your essence and another woman might take your man.' 'Don't walk under a ladder or open an umbrella inside the house,'" she continued. "No siree, I don't believe in none of that nonsense. And I most certainly don't believe that the number thirteen is unlucky. I was born on the thirteenth of the month, and so was my Mama, and I lived on the thirteenth floor when we first got married.

Now I do follow the advice to not place my purse on the floor. But I just think that's a good practice anyhow."

"Tell me again what happens if you place your purse on the floor, Mama Kaye? I don't remember," Maria pretended, testing Mama Kaye to see if she would repeat the same folklore that she had learned from her mother.

"Well, you won't have any money in your purse. Everybody knows that, sugar. And don't go forgetting that neither. My mama taught me that you should always place something between your purse and the floor, even if it's just a tissue. I know Lizzy taught you that? I'm gonna skin that girl's hide if she hasn't passed that on to you."

"No, Mom taught me that too, I just didn't know if you kept your purse off the floor for the same reason."

"Well, where do you think she learned that from? Me that's who. I practically raised your mama after her mama died. So keep your purse off the floor. Plus, I don't like to get the bottom of my purse dirty no how," she offered, her tone obvious and firm. "Now where was I? Oh, we were talking about this wedding date. I'm happy that you have found a nice fella to marry, Lawd knows I am, but I just don't know that I would encourage you to get married on April Fool's Day, especially if it's not a Saturday."

"But we want to get married before he has to take the bar, and neither one of us wants a big wedding so we just picked April first," she stammered, glad that she wasn't sitting in Mama Kaye's face so she couldn't smell the lie on her tongue.

"What does your mama have to say about it?"

"Mom thinks it's fine. She's just happy that I'm finally over Todd."

"Who?" Mama Kaye asked loudly.

"Todd. You remember him. He's the boy that I had a crush on all through high school."

"Was he the football player that gave you the big ring?"

"No ma'am," Maria giggled. "That was Dante. "Todd was the guy that Mom never liked."

"Oh, the pretty boy who broke up with you on the phone and had the theme music playing in the background. I remember that clown now."

Maria sighed and shook her head. *She can't remember his name, but she remembers the painful details of how he dumped me.* "Yes. That's the one, Mama Kaye."

"What did you ever do with that big ring?"

She had grown accustomed to how quickly Mama Kaye could switch from one topic to another and back again. She called it her 'random Randy routine.'

"I tried to give it back to Dante," she said softly, hoping that Mama Kaye remembered that it was Dante that had given her the ring and not Todd. "But he told me that it was a gift, and that since it was a friendship ring, he wouldn't take it back. So Mom and Richard put it in a safe deposit box, and told me to try and give it back again, and if he still won't take it back, I can sell it back to the jeweler and use the money to pay for graduate school."

"I kept all of the rings that my fellas gave me too. What's that other boy doing these days anyhow?"

From experience, Maria knew that Mama Kaye's 'that other boy' referred to Todd and not Dante. "Todd is working at his parent's dry cleaning business."

"And he didn't finish college did he?"

"No ma'am. He didn't."

"Tsk, tsk. I bet you're glad he dumped you now aren't you?"

"I wouldn't say it quite like that, but everything worked out for a reason," Maria smiled. "Just like you told me it would."

"How's my little Jeni Kaye? What's she doing?"

"She's fine. She's trying to teach herself to read. She holds the book upside down and pretends like she's reading."

"That's my girl. She's a smart one that one. Her little thick thighs are going to slim down now that she's running around. She's moving on out of the way for the next one."

"I hope not," Maria groaned. "Mom is forty now. That's too old to be having babies."

"It certainly is not. She's probably got at least one baby left in her," Mama Kaye said. "She won't go through the change for another ten years or so. She could have another baby or maybe two, especially with the shots and what not that they give these ladies to help have their babies nowadays. My mama had her last baby at forty-five. She had it the good old fashioned way. They called my brother her change of life baby because she was going through the change. Heck, I think she was having hot flashes and nursing my brother at the same time. And he turned out just fine, he sure did."

Maria shuddered at the thought of her mother having another baby.

"So this is the fella that you told me about at the hospital when Jeni Kaye was born. The one that you weren't sure liked you. Well, I guess he liked you, huh?" Mama Kaye chuckled without waiting for a reply. "Your mama told me that she met him, and that he's a nice young man. What's your last name going to be?"

"Prentiss. His name is John Wardell Prentiss."

"Maria Wesley-Prentiss. That has a nice ring to it. It's a strong name. You can name one of your sons Wesley."

"That's exactly what we're planning to do. How did you know that I was going to hyphenate my name, Mama Kaye?"

"Because your mama hyphenated hers, and all of the ladies do that now. They didn't so much do it in my day, but I had a few friends who did. It's a choice."

"John's mother hyphenated her name, so he's cool with it. Rashanda didn't hyphenate her name when she got married. She's just Rashanda Hall now."

"I see. So when are you do, Maria?" Mama Kaye asked casually.

Surprised by Mama Kaye's question, Maria laughed nervously. "What do you mean? When am I do what?" she stammered slowly.

"Maria, I was born on a Tuesday, but I wasn't born last Tuesday. The only reason a twenty-one year old college girl rushes down to the justice of the peace and gets married on a Tuesday is because she is in the family way. Now, how far along are you, sugar?"

∽∾

The plane trip back to Yale had been a teary one. Without saying a word, the flight attendants supplied her with fresh tissues, finally leaving the small box with her as she sobbed quietly in her window seat. Passing on the beverage and snack being offered, she was just glad that the people sitting next to her slept the entire flight and spared her the need to make idle chatter. The flight attendants waved and smiled at her as she deplaned, one touched her shoulder softly, but no words were spoken. She wished that she could tip them for their kindness.

Like a zombie, she walked through the terminal, glad that she didn't have to deal with the hassle of baggage claim. Glancing at her watch, she quickened her pace, praying that she could catch the earlier Amtrak back to Connecticut. She followed the herd through the security area, barely paying attention to the signage in the unfamiliar airport. She slipped into the restroom to pee and splashed cold water on her naked face.

Her head and ears clogged from crying, and her eyes puffy with tears, she walked right into his chest as he stepped into her path.

"Hey pretty lady, can I have your number?" he asked in a false baritone.

A look of irritation on her face, Teenie lifted her head, her jaws ajar. Like a knight in shining armor, Brian Kraft smiled at her, his blue eyes twinkling. Her hand clutched her heart as she smiled widely. "Brian? What are you doing here?" she stammered, her own eyes brimming with fresh tears at the sight of him.

With one gesture, he removed the carry on bag from her shoulder, and wrapped her in his arms, his nose tickling her neck as he inhaled her scent before peppering her lips with a passionate kiss. His mouth tasted like peppermint. The intensity of his kiss and embrace caused her backpack to slip from her shoulder as she wrapped her arms around her boyfriend's neck.

"I missed you, and I wanted to surprise you," he smiled. "I'm going to drive you back to Yale so you don't have to take the train. I didn't want you on the train at night. My neighbor let me borrow his car. By the way, my parents would love to see you if you want to swing by the apartment first. They're not heading back to Lake Forest until tomorrow morning."

She touched his face to make sure that he was real. She had missed him. "You are the most thoughtful man," she smiled, as a passenger bumped into Brian's shoulder roughly.

"Hey! Watch where you are going," Brian barked at the man who didn't bother to look over his shoulder. "I'm not invisible."

Cupping his cheek, Teenie gently turned Brian's face toward her, his scowl replaced with a soft smile as he covered her hand with his. "Oh, I'd love to see your parents, but I'm really tired, and I have an early class tomorrow morning."

Suddenly aware that they'd violated her 'no public displays of affection' rule, Teenie pulled her hand away from his cheek, wondering if the passenger had bumped Brian intentionally.

"Let's get out of here before we get trampled," Brian suggested, lifting her backpack with one arm and her carry on with the other. "Are you okay? Your eyes look swollen like you've been crying," he noticed returning his full attention to Teenie, She sighed strongly without answering his question. His arm around her waist, Teenie looped her arm through his and leaned her head against his arm as they maneuvered through the crowded airport. She decided that it was time for full disclosure.

The ride to New Haven, Connecticut was intense. The traffic on Interstate 95 was at a stand still due to an accident and lane blockage. The delay added thirty more minutes to the ninety minute journey. Like a skilled trial lawyer, Brian used each additional minute to interrogate Teenie like a witness on trial.

"So let me get this straight, he gave you an ultimatum that you had to pick me or him by New Year's Eve, but now he's having a baby, so now you're going to pick me?" Brian asked softly.

"No, that's not what I said at all. He didn't say that I had to pick you or him. He just wanted me to make a decision about my friendship with him."

"But since you're currently in a relationship with me, if you decided to start a relationship with him, you're in essence ending the relationship with me; thereby picking him or me."

Teenie knew that it was futile to argue with his logic. "David and I were always just friends. We've been friends since I was in eighth grade. He has always wanted to be in a relationship with me, but I wasn't ready for that. He's almost four years older than I am, so I didn't think it was a good idea for us to be more than friends. And then I met you," she added softly. "So technically, I've already picked you." She hoped that her twist worked. "And you've always known about David," she reminded, watching as he furrowed his brow, trying to absorb her explanation or preparing his rebuttal, she couldn't tell which.

"You've told me about him as your friend, but you didn't tell me that he was in love with you, Teenie."

"I didn't say that he was in love with me, Brian."

"Any man who gives a woman an ultimatum on their relationship is in love with the woman. Why did the news that he is marrying his pregnant girlfriend make you so upset? Why were you crying your eyes out?"

"I wasn't crying my eyes out," she defended crossing her arms over her chest.

Brian tilted his head sideways and stared at Teenie knowingly.

"Why are you looking at me like that? I admit I was a little upset. But I was surprised that he hadn't told me about Rachel or the baby before. She's over five months pregnant, and I talk to him at least once a week. We've been friends for a long time, and now he's getting married and having a baby," she paused. "It was a lot of information to take in all at once. And it made me sad to think that our friendship is probably going to be different."

"Okay, that's fair, but weren't you just a little jealous that he is moving on? That he won't be carrying a torch for you anymore? Let me rephrase that," he offered quickly. "What if he hadn't told you about Rachel or the baby until after you made a decision about your relationship? And let's say you decided to break up with me to be with him, and then he told you about his new family situation. What would you have done then?"

This was the one question that Teenie had not answered. She'd asked herself the question over and over, and hearing the question from someone else made her want to cry. Maria had asked the same question when she picked her up at David's parents that night. At the Illinois Institute of Technology party, Teenie had sat huddled in a corner with Maria, crying and thinking, refusing all offers to dance. That night, David's brilliant, beautiful, type A sister, Dr. Claire Elliot Barton-Bishop had described Teenie as "a keeper." "She's a keeper, David. I like this one. She's smart, pretty, funny, and she wants to pledge our sorority. Teenie's almost too good for you, chucklehead," Claire had stated loudly as Teenie helped clear the dinner dishes. David had smiled knowingly at Teenie, his eyes apologizing again for their shared secret. Teenie had excused herself to the powder room where she splashed water on her face to wash away the tears that wanted to pour down her cheeks like a waterfall. The rest of the evening she busied herself chatting with Gramsy and playing with Mr. Belvedere, wondering if this would be the last time that she saw either of them. After the Barton family learned that David's girlfriend was expecting his child, they would expect him to marry Rachel, and then Teenie's presence in their home would no longer be welcome or easily explained. When Maria finally rang the doorbell, Teenie exhaled. In the foyer, Mrs. Barton hugged Teenie and told her to come back when she came home for Christmas vacation. David walked her to the car and told her to call him the next day. He stood on the driveway and watched as the car drove away. Once safely in the car with Maria, the tears flowed freely as she shared the news with her best friend.

"Did you know that he was in love you with?" Brian continued snapping her from her trance.

"Of course not. He never said that he was in love with me. I knew he liked me, but I told him that it wasn't a good idea to start a relationship while he went off to college. I wanted him to enjoy college without feeling like he was cheating on me, and I wanted to be free to have a boyfriend in high school."

"And he bought that?"

"He had no choice. He had a girlfriend named Patty. And he knew about the guy that I dated before I started dating you. Besides, David and I never even kissed."

"You've known him since you were fourteen, and he's never tried to kiss you?"

"Never. We're friends. I keep telling you that."

"Oh."

"What does that 'oh' mean?"

"The fact that he's never kissed you makes me feel better," he grinned. "Does he know about me?"

"He knows all about you. When I told him that I bumped into you at prom, he remembered you as the boy that I kissed from camp."

"You told him about our little party in the poppy field?"

Teenie smiled at the memory, choosing not to share how she was forced to tell David about Brian once he discovered her hickey. "Yes. He knows all about you."

"Ok then," he grinned, looping his fingers through hers as the Interstate 95 traffic opened up. "You had me worried."

Looking through the windshield of the large sedan, Teenie noticed for the first time that they'd been driving without the radio.

"Thanks for coming to pick me up. That was a nice surprise," she said eager to change the subject before leaning over and kissing Brian on the cheek.

Brian smiled and squeezed her hand. "Our neighbor was just happy that someone wanted to drive this old Buick. He's the only guy in our building who still has a car. Most people who live in Manhattan don't own a car. It's too expensive to park a car in midtown Manhattan, and it's easy to rent one when you need to get out of the city. New

Yorkers take the subway or a taxi to get where they need to go."

"Why does your neighbor still have a car?"

"It was his wife's car. They had a house in Connecticut and only came into the city to go to the theatre. It reminds him of her."

Teenie fumbled with the radio buttons.

"The radio doesn't work. That's the one tragic flaw of this old car."

"Did his wife die?"

"She was hit by a car. A car swerved and hit her while she was crossing the street. It was really sad. He's never gotten over it. He still calls her his "bride." He was in Florida with his daughters for Thanksgiving, so he said we could use the car if we needed to," he smiled.

"Well, I'm glad that I could benefit from your neighbor's kindness. I was dreading taking that train tonight. I just want to get back on campus, take a shower to rinse the travel germs off my body, and chill for a minute before I have to study for my exam," she sighed settling into the headrest.

"Teenie, just so there's no confusion. You know that I love you, right?" Brian said firmly. "I love you," he said slowly, articulating each word. "I know I don't say it all of the time, but I do."

She squeezed his hand firmly in hers. "I know, and I love you too," she over articulated.

"I just wanted to get that out in the open so there's no confusion. Since you seem to be a little slow on the uptake when it comes to boys being in love with you," he teased.

Teenie swatted his shoulder with her free hand and gripped his fingers tighter.

As she feared would happen, Rachel's new status in David's life strained Teenie's relationship with him. She'd stopped writing him, and they hadn't spoken in several weeks. After sharing the baby news, David called her the following day, asking for permission to come by and see her before she went back to Yale. Still confused and angry, Teenie feigned busy. That afternoon, he had shown up at her doorstep anyway and found her relaxing on the sofa in the family room. With her parents and brothers home, he suggested that they go for a drive so that they could talk. She had refused. She heard her mother tell her dad that she believed they were having a lover's quarrel. Still undeterred, David made himself comfortable on the sofa where Teenie tried desperately to ignore him as they watched television in silence. Wanting to pummel her fists into his chest, and fearing that she might do it, she faked a headache and excused herself to her bedroom without walking David to the door. She stared out her bedroom window at his car, wondering how long he was going to sit in the family room and wait for her to return. Finally, listening through the heating vent, she heard her father address him with these words. "David, you are a nice young man, but it seems that Tanisha doesn't want company right now, so I think it's time for you to leave." Peering behind her draperies, she watched David walk outside, his shoulders slumped. He glanced at her bedroom window, which caused her to duck down. She sneaked one final glimpse as he slowly backed his car down the driveway. The next day, he called and offered to drive her to the airport. She thanked him politely but told him that her father would be taking her.

At Yale, she used the answering machine to screen her calls, only picking up the phone when it wasn't David. After several attempts to reach her, and no return calls, David stopped leaving messages. A few times, she would receive soft hang-ups on her machine, signaling that the person had listened to the entire message and then hung up just as the beep sounded. She theorized that the hang-ups were David, calling just to hear her voice on the answering machine. Maria confirmed her theory like any good friend and true narcissist would.

After one painfully long crying session with Monica and Laura, Monica suggested that Teenie confide in their residence hall assistant, Barbie, the psychology pre-med major. Barbie was not her real name, but a nickname that the girls had given her because she always wore pink. With nothing to lose, Teenie sat in Barbie's pink room and told her the story of David, from their initial meeting at the ski event in Wisconsin to the pact they made to just be friends and David's New Year's Eve relationship definition deadline. Taking notes in a pink notebook, and wearing a pink sweater, Barbie listened intently, asking clinical questions about Teenie's feelings that Teenie had never shared with anyone. Barbie helped her accept that in some small way, she felt betrayed by David's behavior, falling short of getting Teenie to acknowledge or admit that she was seriously considering the idea of ending her relationship with Brian Kraft to start a relationship with David Barton. On that point, Teenie would not concede. In her soft clinical voice, Barbie did explain to Teenie that ending any relationship or friendship is like a death, and the only way to manage through a loss is to allow for a grieving period. She encouraged Teenie to grieve the end of her relationship with David the way that you would grieve a death. This was something that Teenie knew how to do. Teenie decided to channel her sadness and anger into something positive, the same way she had done the summer that Lori Perkins died.

Teenie began visiting the campus gym with Laura who encouraged her to take up running. A cross country runner, Laura told Teenie that after running, her brain would begin to experience a runner's high where your endorphins kick in, your brain feels free and clear and your legs don't feel like they're moving, or so she described. Teenie hated running, but she ran around the indoor track, wondering how long it would take for her legs to enter the runner's high zone. Instead of feeling free and clear, her brain always pondered what decision she would have made had she not known about Rachel and the baby. After three weeks of daily runs, her thoughts were still tangled and unclear, and she felt just as confused as ever, but the daily runs gave her more energy to get through finals week, and she dropped five pounds.

Over Christmas break, David didn't call Teenie until the day before he was leaving. His phone call surprised her. Although she wanted to see him, her pride wouldn't allow her to invite him over. She told him that she had other plans. Before he hung up, she learned that he had told his family about Rachel. They had not received the pregnancy news well. But like he expected, they insisted that he marry Rachel. They were trading in his beloved Corvette for a Ford sedan since he would need room for a car seat. Hearing that, Teenie felt sad for him, knowing how much he loved that car. Before hanging up, he wished her a Happy New Year since he was returning to D.C. to spend New Year's Eve with his fiance. Hearing the word "fiance," the tears spilled from her face before she hung up the receiver.

Teenie spent New Year's Eve in Lake Forest with Brian Kraft, silently wondering what the night would have looked like had David not been expecting a child with a girl that he met at the mall.

When she returned to Connecticut after Christmas break, Teenie decided to stop screening her calls. But it proved unnecessary, her phone seldom rang, and when it did it was her parents or Brian, with the occasional call from Maria. Rashanda was busy in her new role as mom, Justine was busy with work, school, and AM, and she and Grace had never had much of a phone relationship. Even the hang-ups on her answering machine had stopped. When she shared with Barbie that she missed David's calls, Barbie encouraged her to study at the library so she wouldn't be in her room staring at the telephone. At the library, Teenie focussed on her studies and reviewed the historical material that she needed to learn in order to pledge Delta Sigma Theta Sorority. The pledge process proved a timely distraction from the David Barton drama, or the DBD as Maria had dubbed it. Teenie was glad that she had gotten ahead in her classes as the pledge activities kept her up until well past midnight most nights. Although over scheduled and exhausted, she enjoyed the process of getting to know her line sisters, nine African American girls that she had noticed on Yale's campus, but with whom she had seldom interacted as she was always in the presence of Monica and Laura.

Early in the pledge process, Teenie found herself becoming close with Micki, one of her pledge sisters. Micki was a bi-racial girl of Hawaiian heritage who lived in Edina, Minnesota. Embracing the true spirit of sisterhood, Teenie invited Micki to move into her dorm room during the pledge process because Micki's dorm was off campus and created a challenging and dangerous commute when the pledge meetings and library study hours concluded well past midnight each night. Teenie found that she enjoyed having a roommate.

"Are you biracial too?" Micki asked one night when they returned to Teenie's dorm.

"No. Both of my parents are black," Teenie said. "My dad is just really pale because his grandfather was white," Teenie explained as they prepared for bed.

"Oh. I thought you were biracial. You look like you could be mixed, and you have so many white friends, that Nicole and I had a bet going with Dominique that you were biracial. Dominique didn't think that you were, but Nicole and I did."

"Nope. I'm not. Is that why everyone was shocked that I won the double dutch contest tonight?"

"Exactly. Even the big sisters were shocked that you could jump rope that well," Mickie admitted. Each night after library hours, the Delta pledges had to learn Delta history and rehearse their songs and dance moves for the upcoming pledge show. Teenie and Micki's line sisters decided to incorporate a double dutch routine into their performance. The girls had a contest to see who was the most skilled jumper and should be featured in the routine. Only four of the girls knew how to jump double dutch, and Teenie won the contest easily.

"Really? Why? I grew up on the southside of Chicago. I've been jumping double dutch since I was six years old."

"But on campus, we only see you with those white girls, and your boyfriend is white too, so we all just thought you were one of those black girls who identified with whites better than blacks."

"Oh. Nope. I identify with everybody. I met Laura and Monica when we attended a leadership camp in eighth grade. We lost touch for a few years but reconnected junior or senior year, I can't remember which. Come to think of it, I met my boyfriend at that camp too," Teenie explained.

"You've been dating the same guy since you were in eighth grade?" Micki asked.

"No. We all reconnected in high school, so we've only been dating for a couple of years now. But my boyfriend before him was black, and all of my friends in high school are black," she offered, wondering why she felt the need to add that. "Not that it makes a difference," she mumbled.

"No, you're right. It doesn't matter."

"Then why did you guys make a wager on my ethnicity?" Teenie asked as she rolled her hair, with obvious irritation in her voice.

"Calm down, Teenie. We were just having fun. Really, no harm no foul. We were just trying to figure you out," Micki explained, her hands in the surrender pose. "To be honest, we weren't expecting you to be so connected to the black experience, and to be so edgy," Micki laughed.

"Edgy? That's a new one. You guys think I'm edgy?" Teenie smiled.

"You're not dashiki wearing edgy, but you're definitely edgier than we expected you to be. We didn't think you would win the double dutch contest," she laughed tossing a pillow at Teenie in the small room. "But seriously, now that I've gotten to know you, you just seem so comfortable around everybody, white or black. You just fit in."

"I'm not trying to, I'm just being who I am."

"And that's what's so cool about it. We didn't expect you to fit in so well with us because nobody knew anything about you, and you're always with Lauren and Monica."

"Laura and Monica," Teenie corrected softly.

"Yeah, them. It seems like you don't even see the color of someone's skin. Like it doesn't even matter to you."

"I guess it really doesn't now," she shrugged. "But it used to," she added quickly. "When I was younger, all I saw was skin color. The white girls never played with me, and since I was the only black girl at my elementary school, it was isolating and lonely. I would be the only girl in my class not invited to a birthday party, and I knew it was because I was black."

"Been there, done that," Mickie groaned. "It was humiliating. They would play with me at school, but never invite me to their homes, and when I invited them to mine, they would never come," Micki yawned softly.

"Exactly. I could help them with their homework, but we never interacted outside of school. So for a long time, I didn't want to have anything to do with the white girls at my school, but when I went away to camp and became roommates with Laura and Monica, they were so friendly and nice to me that it threw me for a loop, and then Brian and I clicked, so it all just fell into place," she exhaled catching her breath. "There was only one other black girl at the camp, but she treated me like dog poop, so that's when I realized that I shouldn't let a childhood experience rob me from being friends with people just because they didn't look like me. Well, that's not true. It took me a while to get comfortable having a white boyfriend," Teenie rambled. "But now I don't even think about it. My brother Jackie is still dating his white girlfriend from high school. And at first, that really bothered me, but she's actually very nice. You're biracial. Do people at Yale expect you to be different because your dad is black and your mom is Hawaiian?" Teenie asked. "Micki, do people expect you to act a certain way because your mom is Hawaiian and your dad is black?" Teenie repeated, but her pseudo-roommate was fast asleep and snoring softly.

Since he had pledged a fraternity two years before, Teenie was tempted to invite David to her neophyte pledge show. She knew that he would get a kick out of watching her perform, but when she picked up the phone to invite him, she feared that he might bring the pregnant Rachel. Teenie wasn't ready to meet her yet, so she invited Brian Kraft instead even though she had to explain what a pledge show was. Laura and Monica agreed to entertain Brian when he drove from Princeton since Teenie knew that she would be busy with the pledge process and would not be able to spend any time with him.

Her hair freshly washed and styled, and her make-up expertly applied by one of her line sisters, Teenie was ready for the mandatory pledge performance. As the girls marched into the room in height order, the tall Teenie was next to last in line. She blushed and winked when Brian blew her a kiss. Teenie's guests seemed oblivious to the fact that they were the only whites in the room. She watched as Laura and Monica seemed to flirt shamelessly with Brian's cute roommate who had driven with him. When the music started, Brian managed to maneuver to the front of the crowded room and snapped photo after photo of Teenie, cheering loudly when she performed her double dutch solo without a flaw. Pleased with their performance, the big sisters allowed the pledges a fifteen minute break to greet their guests and well wishers before scurrying them off to their next pledge activity.

"Hey pretty lady," Brian cooed when she walked over to him. "Can I hug you or is that against the pledge rule? I don't want you to get in trouble."

"You'd better hug me. I don't care what the stupid pledge rules are," she whispered as he pulled her into his arms and kissed her.

"I hope you don't get punished for having a white boyfriend," Brian whispered, his nose resting on hers.

"I'm not worried about it. A few of the big sisters have white boyfriends."

"You remember my roommate, Kyle," Brian announced, his arm around Teenie's waist.

"Hi, Kyle. Thanks for riding with him."

"Nice to see you again, Teenie," Kyle smiled. "I've never seen anyone jump two ropes like that. That was cool."

"It's called double dutch. It's really popular in the black community. You should get out more," she teased, her arms wrapped securely around Brian's waist.

Kyle tilted his head to the side, obviously confused.

"She's kidding, Kyle," Brian smiled. "I didn't know what double dutch was until she explained it to me either."

"I was just pulling your chain, Kyle," Teenie smiled. "I hate that you have to turn around and drive right back tonight," she whined to Brian, her lips in an exaggerated pout.

"Me too, but at least I got to see you," Brian smiled. "It looks like Laura and Monica are digging Kyle. Look," he nodded. Teenie watched as Laura and Monica seemed to be vying for his attention, their body language screaming, 'pick me, pick me!' "I have an idea. Since Monica and Laura are roommates, Kyle could crash in their room, and I could crash in your room, since you don't have a roommate," he whispered. "I am a little tired from the drive, and I did bring an overnight bag just in case."

Her arms around his waist, Teenie stared into Brian's eyes.

"That could work," she whispered. "We're not supposed to have any contact with boyfriends during the pledge process, but I could give you my key, and you could meet me in my room. I don't have any big sisters that live in my dorm, so no one would know," she continued.

"Hi, pseudo. Is this boyfriend?" Micki grinned. "Hi boyfriend, I'm Teenie's pseudo roommate, Micki."

"Hi, Micki. I'm Brian Kraft." Brian shook her hand firmly. "What's a pseudo roommate, Micki?"

"I completely forgot," Teenie blushed, smacking her hand against her forehead. "Micki is staying with me during the pledge process because her dorm room is really far off campus. So she's been bunking with me for the last couple of weeks."

"Oh, I get it. She's your kinda sorta roommate. Your pseudo roommate. That's cute."

"So we call each other, Pseudo," Micki grinned. "Pseudo, the dean told us to line up so we can get to study hours. I hate to steal her away, Brian, but the pledge process doesn't sleep."

"But it's Saturday night. They make you study on Saturday

night?"

"Yup. Nice to meet you, Brian."

"You too, Micki."

His arms around Teenie's waist again, this time, Brian poked out his bottom lip. "So it looks like I will be hitting the road after all, huh? Maybe I can just get a hotel room and you can meet me there so we can spend more time together or I can take you to breakfast in the morning," he suggested.

"We have church service at eight o'clock in the morning, and then we have a volunteer thing that we have to do at a senior citizen's home," she explained softly.

"Well, there goes that idea," he groaned.

"Maybe I can get Micki to stay in someone else's room tonight," she suggested.

"No. Because then she'll have to move all of her stuff. It's cool. I drove here, so Kyle is going to drive back. How long is the pledge process anyway?"

Teenie glanced over her shoulder before replying. "We're not supposed to know this, but I think it will be over next weekend."

"That's good. So I'll plan to come back the weekend after that. How does that work for you?"

"That works just fine, Mr. Kraft."

"Uh oh, your other pledge sisters are already lined up, so you'd better go get in line, Mrs. Kraft," Brian winked before kissing Teenie on the lips one last time.

Teenie blushed at his latest pet name for her. "Call me and leave a message so I know you made it back safely," she insisted. "Don't forget!"

The following week, all three of her aunts surprised her and attended the initiation ceremony and brunch. Wearing her aunt's sorority pin, and beaming with pride, Teenie thought about calling

David's mother and sister to tell them that she was now a member of their glorious sisterhood. Prepared to dial the Barton's number from memory, she hesitated, remembering that her role in the Barton family had changed. She placed the phone back in the cradle and stared at it before deciding to stroll to the basement of her dorm to check the mailbox that had been ignored for almost two weeks.

The pale green envelope had a small yellow duck in the corner beside the Teaneck, New Jersey return address. Teaneck, New Jersey? I don't know anyone who lives in Teaneck, New Jersey. Curious, Teenie ripped the envelope open as she walked back to her dorm room, carefully balancing her other mail underneath her armpit. Pulling out the large card, she stopped in the hallway. It was an invitation to Rachel's baby shower. As the mail tucked underneath her arm began to jostle and slip, the shower invitation envelope tipped and tiny pink and blue baby bottles the size of her thumbnail tumbled out. Teenie stared at the debris at her feet before slowly reading the oversized card.

Please join us as we shower our daughter
Rachel Ann
with love and gifts
to celebrate the birth of our first grandchild

Eric and Reese Bing
902715 Harbor Trail

She bent down and carefully placed the tiny baby bottles back inside the envelope as her euphoric pledge mood turned melancholy. Her good Teenie, bad Teenie voices raged in her head. He's not serious right? Does he really think that I want to attend his baby shower? But you're friends, Teenie. You've always been friends. Why wouldn't he invite you? If he hadn't invited you, your feelings would have been hurt. True. He probably wants you to meet Rachel. I hope the little mall worker looks like a troll doll! Be nice, Teenie.

As she trudged back to her room, she was glad that she hadn't called David's mother with her pledge news. Carelessly tossing the envelope on her desk, more baby bottles tumbled out. She stepped over them and decided to go for a run, still chasing the elusive runner's high that Laura promised she would one day experience, but hadn't yet.

The baby bottle tipped them off and gave away her secret. Teenie had not planned to attend the baby shower, but when Monica and Laura saw the telltale pink and blue miniature baby bottles stuck in her carpet, they knew that she'd received an invitation to the baby shower. Rifling through the stack of mail on her desk, Laura waved the invitation in the air triumphantly, like a pirate who had discovered a booty filled treasure chest. They both insisted that she go. Restless for a road trip, they invited themselves to go with her. While Laura and Monica coordinated the travel plans, Maria Wesley called and volunteered to take the train from Philadelphia to New Jersey to attend for moral support. Teenie knew that her friends were also curious to meet the girl that had turned her life topsy turvy, so she welcomed their company. Monica and Maria had even suggested that Teenie bring Brian along, a suggestion that Teenie refused to consider and didn't dignify with a response.

The invitation sat on her desk for almost two weeks, mocking her like a cruel joke. Finally, as the date approached, Teenie dialed the number to r.s.v.p. She was shocked when she learned that the voice on the phone belonged to Rachel.

"Hi, I'm calling to r.s.v.p. to Rachel's baby shower," Teenie heard herself saying.

"Well, you're in luck. This is Rachel. Who's this?" she asked.

Caught off guard, Teenie took a deep breath. "This is Tanisha Carlson. I'm a friend of David's," she said softly.

"Hi, Tanisha, did you say? I don't think I remember David mentioning you, but I'm glad you can come, and I look forward to meeting you."

He's never mentioned me? That weasel! "Well, David calls me, Teenie," she added hopefully.

"Oh, Teenie! Of course! David talks about you all the time. You're his play sister. I know who you are, but I've never heard him call you Tanisha."

Teenie smiled into the receiver, flipping the envelope over and realizing that the invitation had been addressed to Teenie Carlson.

"He's told me so much about you. I think it's sweet how he treats you like his little play sister. I can't wait to meet you."

Teenie returned the sentiment, visions of David's high school girlfriend, Patty, running through her head. Patty had gone so far as to introduce Teenie as David's play sister whenever they were together.

"I'll get to meet you and David's family at the same time. I'm so excited."

"His family is coming?"

"His parents are coming, but not his siblings. Claire just had her baby, so she can't travel yet. I'm so excited that our babies will be close in age," Rachel squealed.

Teenie decided that she did not want to receive Barton family updates from David's fiancé so she didn't bother to ask if Claire had a boy or a girl. "Rachel, is it okay if I bring three of my friends with me?" she asked quickly. "I don't have a car on campus, so I'll need a ride, and my friend Laura has a car," her voice said, but her head was thinking, "I don't care what she says. I'm bringing Laura, Monica and Maria. With David's parents there, this is going to be one awkward shower."

"Of course it is. That's perfectly fine," Rachel said. "The more the merrier."

The Teaneck neighborhood where Rachel's parents lived was very upscale, with large older homes on estate size lots. Long winding driveways, mostly circular ones, led to the grand homes that appeared to sit atop a hill peering down on the quiet street below. The neighborhood reminded Teenie of her Aunt Helen's neighborhood in Chicago.

On their drive from New Haven, to Teaneck, the girls picked Maria up at the New Jersey Amtrak station.

"Okay, I'm confused," Maria said. "If her parents live within a mile of here, they're clearly loaded. So why is girlfriend working at the mall?" Maria asked.

"I was thinking the same thing," Monica admitted. "These houses are huge."

"I don't have a clue," Teenie confessed.

"You said she is twenty two, right, Teenie?" Laura asked, as Teenie nodded.

"So maybe she's working to put herself through school."

"She's not in school," Teenie added. "I do know that much. When David told me about her, I asked him where she went to school, and he told me that she wasn't in school. She just worked at the mall."

"So David knocked up a townie," Maria whistled. "This oughta be good."

Teenie took another deep breath as Laura pulled in front of a house decorated with green and yellow balloons and a large stork perched in the front lawn.

Laura popped the trunk and retrieved the gift that Teenie purchased from Rachel's gift registry. It was a brown teddy bear that was used to soothe babies by simulating a heartbeat sound when turned on. She'd nicknamed it the 'womb bear.'

"I did not bring a gift," Maria boasted. "That Amtrak ticket was gift enough. Teenie, I hope you know that 'womb bear' or whatever you call that thing is from all of us."

As the girls giggled their way up the long driveway, David Barton came bounding down to greet them, as though he had been peering out the window awaiting her arrival.

"You must be Laura, and you're clearly Monica," he introduced, giving each girl a quick church hug. "Teenie described you both perfectly. And Maria, you look lovely as always. It's good to see you. All of you look like a bouquet of spring flowers," he admired, noticing their colorful ensembles. Monica had wanted to wear jeans, but Teenie and Laura had convinced her that it was inappropriate to wear jeans to a baby shower, especially since Teenie needed to make a good first impression and would most definitely need to wear something cute. Maria used the dress code as a reason to go shopping, and had coincidentally purchased the same identical sleeveless cashmere turtleneck twin set as Teenie, but in a pale blue to Teenie's lemon yellow. Maria wore black slacks and Teenie wore a khaki colored pencil skirt with loafers. Laura wore khaki slacks and a white green oxford and Monica wore a pink sweater with a denim skirt. "And Miss Tanisha Denise Carlson!" he laughed lifting Teenie into the air and twirling her in circles. "It's so good to see you, Teenie!"

The girls giggled as Teenie swatted his arms, demanding that he put her down.

"You feel like you've lost weight, Teenie," David noticed as he lowered her to the ground. "And you smell good. Is that a new perfume?"

She watched as Laura, Monica and Maria whispered to each other. "I've lost a few pounds. I've been running," she replied flatly, as she smoothed her skirt.

"She's been trotting," Laura corrected. "Running is what I do. Teenie trots. You cannot call a twelve minute mile a run."

"Shut up, Laura," Teenie teased. "I hate running, so I'm just glad that I'm moving."

"And that perfume she's wearing is the one her boyfriend, Brian, gave her for Christmas. He picked it up when he was in Paris with his parents," Laura emphasized. "What's it called, Teenie?"

Teenie clenched her jar and slanted her eyes at Laura. "I don't remember."

"Oh, well, it smells good," he offered. "And you look amazing, so lean and fit. Not that you weren't before," David amended, holding both of Teenie's hands in his. "Your timing is perfect. My parents were just asking about you."

"Are they inside already?"

"Yeah, they came up on, uh, Thursday, actually."

"Thursday? Why'd they come so early?" Teenie asked, her head slightly tilted to stare into David's eyes. "Well, I guess they wanted to spend more time getting to know Rachel and her parents. Duh," she smiled, answering her own question. "Are they staying in Manhattan? I remember your mom mentioning how much she enjoys going to the theatre when she's anywhere near New York City."

Still holding Teenie's hands in his, David smiled. "Ladies, why don't you go on inside and make yourselves at home. I need to tell Teenie something real quick," he said.

"Sounds good," Maria offered. "I'm starving. Are they serving mimosas at this shindig?"

"In fact, they are," David smiled. "Mimosas for the adults, and lemonade for those not quite twenty-one," he coughed. "Which would be all of you."

"What's a mimosa?" Monica asked.

"Champagne mixed with orange juice," Laura and Maria said simultaneously.

"I want a mimosa," Maria squealed. "Do you think they will trip that we're not twenty-one yet?" Maria asked.

"Yes. My mother will card each and every one of you," David emphasized, using his index finger he pointed at each girl. "Enjoy the lemonade. It's fresh squeezed."

"Take the gift inside for me," Teenie handed Maria the box wrapped in yellow and green paper.

"Just go inside. The door is open," David said as the girls walked toward the door. "You didn't have to bring a gift, Teenie."

"It's a baby shower, of course I had to bring a gift."

"But you're a poor college student, I don't want you spending your money on me."

"The gift is for the baby, not you. Everything is not about you, psycho," Teenie teased.

"I see your sense of humor is still in tact."

"Alive and kicking," she smiled. "And why didn't you tell me that Claire had her baby?" she asked, punching him in the arm.

"I thought I did."

"No, you didn't. Rachel mentioned it when I called to r.s.v.p. What did she have?"

"She had a boy. His name is Barton Bishop. Isn't that a great name?"

"It is. Well, at least your baby will have a cousin near the same age," Teenie added. "Are you guys going to find out if it's a boy or a girl?"

"We did."

"You did? Well? Is it a boy or a girl?"

"It's a girl. But we haven't picked out a name yet," he paused seeming eager to change the subject. "I'm just glad that you made it, Teenie. When Rachel told me that you were coming I was afraid that you would fake and not show up."

"Why'd you invite me if you were afraid that I wouldn't show up?"

"I just thought that you replied to be polite, but you weren't really going to come. It's really good to see you, Teenie. And I'm glad that you're not mad at me anymore," David paused as though awaiting a reply.

Teenie simply shrugged her shoulders. "It's good to see you too, tubby. Are you gaining sympathy weight?" she asked patting David's fuller mid-section.

"It looks like I gained the weight that you lost, not that you needed to lose any weight," he added quickly. "Maybe I should start trotting like you."

"Don't hate on the trot. It's obviously working because I look amazing, and you look, well, like that," she poked his belly.

"Teenie, I need to tell you something before you go inside," he said softly, gripping her hands once again.

"Okay, shoot," she sighed. "I have to pee."

"You and that bladder of yours," he paused, staring into her eyes. "Teenie, Rachel and I got married yesterday. We thought that since my parents were in town, we should go ahead and get married before the baby comes."

Teenie stared at David silently and swallowed. "Oh," she nodded softly searching for words. "I guess that makes sense. Congratulations."

"I didn't want you to notice the wedding bands and wonder what was going on. I wanted you to hear it from me. I tried to call you a few times to tell you, but I was afraid that if I told you, you might change your mind and not come to the shower, and I really wanted you to meet Rachel. We got married in the backyard. It was just her family and my parents. Very small."

"It's cool, David. I'm really happy for you," she smiled. "You have a wife now, and you're going to have a baby."

"I know, right? It's all happening so fast."

"I'm happy for you," Teenie smiled. "Now take me inside so I can meet Mrs. David Barton. Plus, I have to pee."

❧

The pact had been Maria's idea. "If we're still dating the same people in two years, let's elope and get married on April 1st."

"That's the dumbest thing that I've ever heard," Teenie groaned. "Maria, you always come up with these ridiculous schemes. Remember the one about prom night? I'm so glad we didn't heed that one."

"Okay, that was a dumb idea, but this time I'm serious."

"Why April 1st?"

"Because it's April Fool's Day, and no one gets married on purpose on April Fool's Day unless it's a Saturday, so people will think that we're kidding when we tell them that we got married. We can always have a ceremony with our families later, but by April 1st of junior year, we'll be twenty-one, and it will be fun to have the same wedding anniversary. Besides," she paused. "It's Lori's birthday, remember?"

"Oh, my God. How could I forget that?"

"If I were there I would punch you in the arm for speaking the Lord's name in vain," Maria scolded.

"My fault. I can't believe I spaced on her birthday. Okay, for kicks and giggles, let's say that we are still dating the same guys. What if they don't want to get married?"

"In one year, if I'm still dating John and you're still dating Brian," she paused. "Once we dangle the carrot in front of their faces, they'll sprint us down the aisle," Maria giggled. "Plus, John is getting tired of taking cold showers."

"Too much information," Teenie groaned.

"At least Brian is on a different campus, but I see John every day. It's harder for me," Maria sighed. "Do you and Brian talk about it?"

"Yeah, he's starting to hint about it more and more now. He's giving me the 'we've been dating for almost three years, you know I love you and we're going to get married one day' speech. In fact, he has a "special" friend at Princeton," she shared softly. "Did I tell you that? It's some chick that he canoodles with," Teenie giggled.

"Canoodles? I love that term! A girl who lives on my floor has the same situation with her boyfriend. Her name is Dora, and she's saving it for marriage like us, and her boyfriend goes to the University of Michigan, so he has someone there that he canoodles with," Maria giggled. "I'm going to give that term to Dora. A canoodler," she repeated.

"I'd hate to be the canoodling girl," Teenie groaned. "She knows what her role is, and she's okay with that. That wouldn't work for me."

"Me either. I knew Todd was dating other girls, and it used to make me crazy. I'm just so glad that I didn't give my virginity to him. Thank you, Jesus!"

"Amen! How does the canoodling relationship work with your friend?"

"When Dora goes to see him in Ann Arbor, Michigan, she wears the girlfriend tiara, and goes to all of the parties and stuff arm in arm with him. He plays on the football team. He's not a starter, but the fact that he's on the football team makes him a rock star on campus."

"So he basically has his pick of the yard," Teenie groaned.

"Exactly. Apparently his canoodler knows all about Dora," Maria sighed. "The canoodler probably isn't okay with it, but I"m sure she thinks that eventually Dora's boyfriend will choose her over Dora," her voice trailed. "But they never do."

"No, they don't. If canoodler knows he has a girlfriend and is still willing to canoodle with him, that makes her a desperate, stupid fool. And as simple as boys are, most of the good ones don't want to marry a desperate, stupid fool even if she's pretty."

"True. Especially a pretty fool with no standards. Listen to this, Dora said that before they finally get married, she's going to take his butt to the doctor and have tests run to make sure that he's disease free."

"Are you serious?"

"Her mother told her to do it. Her parents are going to insist that he receive a full spectrum of tests before they give their permission for him to marry their daughter."

"I love it. That's a really good idea. Cause if he's canoodling with someone, ain't no telling what he might have been exposed to."

"Exactly. He says he wraps it up, but the test won't lie."

"I'm going to remember that one."

"But seriously, Teenie, doesn't that make you mad when you think about it, that your boyfriend is canoodling with someone else?"

"Obviously I don't like it, but I try not to think about it. I knew that he had canoodled when we started dating, but he doesn't flaunt it in my face," Teenie sighed. "He knows that I'm waiting until marriage, and he respects that, so he's not pressuring me."

"How'd you find out about his canoodler then?"

"His roommate, Kyle, slipped and told me. He wasn't trying to be mean or anything, he just thought I knew. He slipped and said it like Brian was going to get a haircut," she laughed. "It was actually quite funny."

"What happened?" Maria pressed.

"When I called one night he told me that Brian was making a run to get some "protection" for his special meeting later."

"Eeeewwww! Gross!" Maria groaned.

"I know, right? And when I said what are you talking about he said 'you know tonight's the night that he sees his little stress reliever.'"

"He didn't! Is that what he calls her?"

"Yup! His little stress reliever."

"All righty. And what did you say?"

"I was just silent, and that's when Kyle realized that I didn't know. He felt really bad."

"Does Brian know that you know?"

"I'm not sure. I haven't said anything to him about it. He's been discreet up until this point, so there's no reason for me to throw it in his face. What about John? Is he stressing you out about doing the deed?"

"John is so focussed on becoming the next Thurgood Marshall that he hasn't brought it up in awhile. He views it as one would view a fast. When he gets hungry, he just refocusses his energy on other things."

"Aren't you curious to see what it will be like?"

"I am, but I don't want to be the one to break our deal. But I'm serious, let's elope and get married on the same day if we're still with our guys. You need to take the halo off your head and kick this 'goody two shoe, good girl always doing the right thing' image and do something shocking for once in your life!"

Teenie stared at her reflection in the mirror. I'm not a goody two shoes. I don't wear a halo. "Okay, deal," Teenie sighed.

"Pinky swear, Teenie," Maria pleaded.

"I pinky swear," Teenie groaned.

୨∾ଙ

After almost ten years of wacky, quirky, whimsical ideas and schemes, Maria Wesley had finally gotten one right. Maria's John had practically done a back flip when she presented her marriage idea to him. "If we're going to elope, let's just do it now," John suggested. "We can have a wedding next year, but let's just do it. In fact, let's get married in New York City!"

As though reading from the same play book, Brian had a similar proposal. "Let's do it now. Why should we wait until you're twenty-one?" Brian pleaded. "You're an adult now. The only thing that you'll be able to do at twenty-one that you can't do now is buy alcohol, and you don't even drink, Teenie."

"I just feel like I should wait until I'm completely and utterly legal in every sense of the word," Teenie protested. "My parents won't trip as much if I'm fully legal."

"What if we don't tell them?" Brian suggested. "Let's just get married and keep it a secret. I'll graduate next year, and you'll finish the year after that," he paused. "I'll apply to Yale Law School so we can be together for your senior year."

"But I thought you wanted to live in New York and go to Columbia Law School, not Yale."

"But that was before we started talking about getting married," he challenged. "Come on, Teenie. Your entire life you've always done exactly what was expected of you. Live on the wild side for a change. Let's do this. Let's get married."

Teenie chewed on her bottom lip searching for a reply.

Chapter 11

Genesis

Three years later...

With Lake Michigan as its backyard, the large home was neither as drafty nor as chilly as she feared it would be. Instead, the home's interior climate almost bordered on what she and her friends described as 'project heat' hot; the outrageously warm winter temperature that public housing dwellers often maintained when given the privilege of a self controlled thermostat in their unit, but absent the energy conservation responsibility that typically pairs with payment of the monthly utility bill as effortlessly as peanut butter pairs with grape jelly.

On her families infrequent visits with her cousins in the Cabrini O'Greene Housing Projects near downtown Chicago, Rashanda usually got a nosebleed from the stifling warm project heat temperatures in their unit. On one winter visit, she checked the thermostat and was shocked when it read eighty four degrees. That explained why her cousins lounged in shorts with a windchill factor of six degrees near the lake. It was project heat hot in their apartment, and as expected her nose began to bleed, prompting a perfect excuse to bid adieu to her distant relatives.

Rashanda's parents never allowed their thermostat to register above seventy degrees, and at night her dad turned the thermostat down to a blistery sixty-six while they slept. On those nights, when

Rashanda was awake studying, she could feel the chill in the air, rolling in like the San Francisco fog. If her parents were not home to adjust the temperature down, her father called with a reminder to do so. He finally installed a timer to regulate the heat control, but like a night watchman, her dad still inspected the thermostat daily during the winter months to ensure that the timer adjusted the heat control properly. Rashanda remembers cuddling with her sister, Tiffany, in an attempt to stay warm during the day, especially when her equally frugal mother refused to adjust the thermostat up even two degrees while her dad was at work. Rashanda learned to dress in layers in the house.

Even though she now held the same thermostat control as her less privileged project cousins, it never occurred to her to wield her scepter index finger as though entitled to eighty five degree temperatures in the middle of January.

"So that's how you and Aunt Teenie are related? You are best friend sisters?" Christine Marie asked carefully, enunciating each word slowly.

"That's right. Aunt Tiff is my sister, and Aunt Teenie is my pretend sister," Rashanda explained. "Aunt Teenie and I are like sisters but we don't have the same mother. We're 'framily' friends who are like family. Say framily."

"Framily," Christine repeated. "And Auntie Maria and Aunt Grace and Auntie Justine are framily too, right Mommy?"

"That's right, sweetie. You have a lot of aunties that love you. And don't forget Auntie Grace's friend, Auntie Tomoko. She's framily now too," she added.

Rashanda smiled, unable to recall how some of Christine's framily had been assigned the "aunt" title while others carried the "auntie" title before their name. She carefully brushed her daughter's thick, coarse hair, applying the pomade oil to her scalp and gently brushing the oil through to the ends of her hair. The hair combing had become their nightly bedtime ritual, the eight o'clock stroking that usually lasted fifteen minutes and allowed fifteen minutes for a bedtime story. The bedtime routine was followed with military precision so that Rashanda could read and prepare for school the next day.

As she stroked her daughter's hair before parting it in sections to braid and tie up with a scarf, she kissed the top of her daughter's head. "I love you, Chrissy," she smiled.

"I love you too, Mommy" came the reply.

The Hall family ran on a tight schedule. Now an orthopedic surgery resident, Ian spent most of his time at the hospital, usually making it home by eleven o'clock most nights. But even if he arrived home after eleven o'clock, he always awakened in order to have breakfast with Christine Marie before scooting back to the hospital to accompany the attending physicians on their hospital rounds. Twice each week, Rashanda and Christine joined him at the hospital for a quick dinner in the cafeteria. Christine loved the hospital cafeteria dinner outings, and Rashanda had grown accustomed to the hospital food.

Stella, their caregiver, had turned out to be a tremendous blessing to their young family and cared for Christine on Tuesdays and Thursdays. As planned, Grace's parents, Mr. and Mrs. Dudley, had moved into the Moore estate on Sheridan Road.

Mr. Dudley drove the ladies downtown for their twice weekly hospital dinner dates, casually reading the newspaper in the car while the ladies dined with Dr. Ian, as Mr. Dudley called him. Mr. Dudley would not allow Rashanda to drive his car, but always drove her wherever she needed to go. Often, when they returned to the large sedan, Mr. Dudley was dozing. With one gentle tap on the glass, he jumped up and opened their car door, this instinctive gesture always served to remind Rashanda that he had worked as a chauffeur for the Moore family. Mr. Dudley always insisted that Rashanda ride in the back so that she could entertain Christine.

Riding in the back of the large Buick Roadmaster, Rashanda felt like a member of the gilded privileged class. Watching as the elderly Mr. Dudley yawned, hummed and slowly drove down North Lake Shore Drive and Sheridan Road, it was on those evening hospital visits that she wished she had at least considered the car offer from her friend. But she felt greedy even thinking about accepting another generous gift from Grace; because, at Grace's insistence, Ian, Rashanda and Christine Marie had also moved into the estate that had once been owned and occupied by Grace's grandparents and her biological mother, Lydia Moore.

"Don't be silly, you have a baby now, and I own this big house that's practically on Northwestern's campus. It would be easier on Ian if he didn't have to work as a Residence Hall Coordinator and deal with the administrative stuff and student issues to pay for his housing."

Rashanda couldn't argue that point especially when, just weeks after bringing their new baby home from the hospital, one of the more introverted students in his dorm attempted suicide after a nasty break-up with his girlfriend. The paperwork and student resident counseling sessions that Ian helped facilitate had taken a toll on the new father. Plus, the guilt he felt for not recognizing the signs that the student was in distress only added to his angst. The faith based counseling sessions helped all of the students, including Ian, accept that a suicide attempt is often unpreventable. But even still, Ian carried a larger burden of guilt as the residence hall coordinator. Rashanda had to remind Ian that he was also a student as well as a father and a husband and he could not neglect his sleep, studies and other responsibilities even when dealing with dorm crises.

"Besides, you need more space now that Christine Marie is here. Please think about it, Rashanda. I'm really not going to take no for an answer. I'm going to pester you until you say yes," Grace insisted. "Besides, my parents are insisting that they want to live in the guest house, so there won't be anyone living in the main house except the housekeeper who will be in the maid's quarters, so she won't be in your way. Sol goes home on the weekends anyway. Consider it my wedding present to you. My trust pays all of the expenses, so it won't cost you anything to live there."

"If Ian agrees to do this, he will probably insist that we at least pay for the utilities," Rashanda pleaded.

"Absolutely not! My trust covers all of that."

"But that's a big house, Grace. It must cost a fortune to heat that thing, and you know how cold I get," Rashanda added.

"I know, popsicle toes, but I will make sure that Sol keeps the house heated to at least seventy-five degrees. In fact, I'm going to make that one of her daily responsibilities, to check the thermostat and make sure the temperature doesn't dip below seventy-five. Because I know you, you'll keep the heat down trying to save me money. You don't need to worry about the money, I have plenty of it, and I don't want my niece in their freezing," Grace said. "By the way, some stupid teenagers were trespassing and broke a couple of windows, and since they couldn't find the exact match, because the house is so old, my trust fund administrator advised that we have all of the windows replaced with ones that will be more energy efficient, or something like that. So the heat probably won't be that expensive anyway, not that I really care."

"I don't want Ian to feel like we're accepting charity and he can't support his family," Rashanda whispered.

"Tell him that staying in the house will help me out. You'll be keeping vandals at bay on the weekends when Sol goes home."

"But won't your parents be in the guest house? Can't they just move into the main house?"

"I suggested it, but they refused. They want to stay in the carriage house. It was either that or they were going to stay put in Newberry East."

"Grace, I don't know how we could ever repay you," Rashanda offered softly the night that they moved into the grand estate. The trust fund administrator had hired an interior designer who furnished every room in the house, down to the art work, knick knacks and kitchen ware. Tomoko and Grace had driven to the Merchandise Mart to select and weigh in on the larger furniture pieces, trusting the finer details to the interior designer's exquisite taste.

"Rashanda, there's no need to think about repaying me. One of the cool things about having all of this money is that I get to help people. And you are like a sister to me. What's mine is yours. I would give you a kidney if you needed one, but I only have one left," Grace chuckled.

The kidney transplant operation had gone extremely well. Grace was back on her feet and practicing yoga three weeks after her surgery. The nurses and surgeon said that her yoga practice and the conditioning that her volleyball exercise provided helped her heal quicker than expected. Four years post surgery, her mother's body had not shown any signs of rejecting Grace's kidney, but Grace had still hired a nurse to check on her aging mother weekly.

Initially, Ethel Dudley was a non-cooperative patient. She frowned through the weekly home physicals and felt especially violated when asked to provide a urine sample for analysis. Mrs. Dudley's demure insolence and quiet resistance changed when, months into their patient nurse relationship, the thin nurse finally accepted Ethel's offer to share in a cup of coffee. As was her custom, Mrs. Dudley served the coffee with a slice of the homemade dessert that she always had on hand to feed Mr. Dudley's sweet tooth. The dessert of choice on this particular week happened to be her famous pecan pie. Surprised by the slice of pie being handed to her on thin bone china, Mrs. Dudley grinned as the thin nurse polished off the pecan pie in five bites and asked for a second slice. Mrs. Dudley had met a new friend. And from that point forward, each week, Grace's mother always had a slice of home baked pie or cake waiting for the nurse, and each week the nurse consumed the delicacy while explaining that Mrs. Dudley's weekly treats caused her to add an extra day of yoga to help stave off the extra calories. Ethel Dudley now viewed her weekly check ups as social and not clinical, excusing herself politely to visit the ladies room where she would provide the urine sample without prompting, leaving it discreetly in the small foyer near the nurse's medical bag.

When the Dudleys moved back into the Moore estate and learned that Ian and Rashanda would be living in the main house, they were delighted. Mrs. Dudley offered to care for Christine on Monday, Wednesday and Friday, the days when Stella wasn't working. Christine had nicknamed Mrs. Dudley 'Mudley,' in her attempt to say Mrs. Dudley. The Dudleys drove Christine to her pre-school class at the exclusive and private Roycemore School in Evanston. The Roycemore tuition was yet another gift from Grace. "My mother attended Roycemore, so it'll be like I get to share in the experience through Christine Marie," Grace explained. "Please allow me to enroll her." Ian and Rashanda did not put up a fight on this one.

"This brings back so many memories," Mrs. Dudley exclaimed the first time she walked through the kitchen and assumed feeding responsibilities for Christine when she was a toddler. I remember feeding Grace's momma in this very kitchen. This is going to keep me young," she exclaimed. Mudley refused to accept money from Rashanda, stating that it would be like taking money from their own daughter.

On the weekends, Ian and Rashanda's mothers alternated every other Saturday caring for Christine so that the young couple could have time alone. Their couple time usually consisted of riding the train downtown to study at the Northwestern University law library so that Ian could be near the hospital in case he was required to return to review a case, and Rashanda could be near the law library stacks. While Rashanda studied, Ian usually reviewed medical journals or curled up on the sofa to nap, his head nestled snuggly in her lap, her book balanced squarely on his head. Once, when they tried to catch an afternoon matinee at the Water Tower Place movie theatre, they both fell asleep as soon as the lights were dimmed.

Returning home each afternoon after her law school classes, Rashanda was greeted by the smell of a home cooked meal courtesy of either Stella or Mrs. Dudley. Rashanda believed that the southern golden girls were having a silent cooking contest, each trying to win the hearts of the young family with her cooking skills. Ian and Rashanda were careful to lavish praise on both of the women equally. Rashanda cooked for her family on Sunday, which really wasn't necessary due to the leftovers that always spilled from the fridge.

"Things won't always be this busy and hectic, Shanda. I promise,"

Ian would whisper each night when he crawled into bed, half asleep before his head hit the soft pillow.

"We're blessed, and I wouldn't have things any other way," she would reply.

ৎ৯৵৶

"Are Aunt Teenie and Auntie Maria twins, Mom?" Christine asked.

"Huh? What did you say, sweetie? Mommy was daydreaming."

"Are Aunt Teenie twins with Auntie Maria?"

"It's 'are Aunt Teenie and Auntie Maria twins?' or you could say 'Is Aunt Teenie Auntie Maria's twin?'" she corrected.

"Are Aunt Teenie and Auntie Maria twins?" Christine repeated without prompting, familiar with the gentle grammatical corrections of her mother.

"And no, sweetie. They're not twins. Why do you ask?"

"Then why do they have the same birthday with their husbands?"

Rashanda tilted her head to the side. "They don't have the same birthday, and I don't think that their husbands have the same birthday either. But I could be wrong on that one. Where did you get that idea?"

"They do!" Christine insisted. "Mommy, they said that they have the same married day with their husbands, so doesn't that mean that they are twins? There's a twin set at my pre-school."

Rashanda smiled. "There's a set of twins at your pre-school," she corrected again. "Well, Aunt Teenie and Auntie Maria did get married on the same day, but that doesn't mean that they are twins. A twin is a brother or a sister who is in the mom's belly at the same time," Rashanda explained. "Aunt Teenie and Auntie Maria had the same wedding anniversary, not birthday," she paused. "But that was Aunt Teenie's first husband," she offered slowly.

"Aunt Teenie has two husbands?" Christine asked.

"No, not exactly," Rashanda paused. "Aunt Teenie and Auntie Maria got married on the same day a few years ago," she paused searching for the words to the question that she knew was waiting release on her inquisitive daughter's tongue.

"Well, what happened to her other husband?"

$$\wp \ll$$

"Old, New, Borrowed & Blue"

A great secret keeper, it had been a long time since Teenie kept a secret on herself. Throughout her youth and adolescence, she possessed several secrets that she worked to keep under wraps: her bed wetting shame, the decayed front fang that she managed to conceal from even her closest friends, the secret of her mother's mental illness, and later her dalliance at summer camp. Teenie was accustomed to keeping secrets on herself and others, and was still the key keeper for secrets entrusted to her safe keeping by Maria, Rashanda, Justine, Grace, and now Laura and Monica. A loyal friend, she prided herself on never betraying these confidences or discussing the secret with the other girls in the circle even when it appeared obvious that the secret was common knowledge. She often pretended not to know certain information when the girls discussed it, even when she had been made privy to the news long before it became public fodder in their girl circle. But this time was different, this time her secret made her smile and blush.

With similar tastes in fashion, the girls decided upon matching white dresses, simple sheaths with capped sleeves that they found at the Saks Fifth Avenue in New York. The dresses would be their something new. Both wore black patent leather pumps as their something old, Teenie's shoes the same ones that she wore for her sorority initiation to Delta Sigma Theta Sorority, Inc. Maria had worn similar shoes for her initiation to Alpha Kappa Alpha Sorority. Because of their new sorority girl status, the girls each owned a faux pair of pearls that they swapped that morning for their something borrowed. They decided that their something blue would be a small blue rhinestone hair comb that they found in the accessory department at Saks. As they giggled their way through the store, Maria and Teenie held hands and practically skipped the few short blocks to Brian's parents' apartment on Riverside Drive. Their fiances had agreed to vacate the apartment at a specified time and meet the girls at City Hall for the ceremony. The doorman smiled and bowed his head as he opened the door for the girls. The day before, the marriage license in his pocket, Brian had introduced Teenie to the doorman as his wife, and explained that she would have a key and should be treated the way other owners were treated.

"Welcome back, Mrs. Kraft," the doorman nodded and smiled as he held open the door.

"Thank you, Clyde," Teenie nodded as she stifled a nervous pre-wedding giggle.

Once upstairs, she fumbled to get her key to turn the old lock, and when she finally did, the smell of fresh flowers overwhelmed her. A vase filled with white roses and gardenias greeted her in the entry way. As she and Maria walked into the large apartment, she realized that every room contained a similar vase of flowers, each with a similar note perched inside its vase.

To Mrs. K, with love, Mr. K

"That is so freaking romantic!" Maria gushed.

Teenie simply smiled and nodded.   Hurrying into the bedroom, she rushed to gather her things so that she could shower in the master bedroom and allow Maria the privacy to freshen up in the bathroom adjacent to the bedroom that they had shared the night before. As Teenie scurried to gather her toiletries, she almost missed the small box in the center of the large bed, a blue Tiffany box with a note from Brian.

T,

I wanted your first Tiffany box to be your something blue.

Love B

Tears pooled in her eyes as she carefully removed the white satin ribbon and opened the tiny box. She took a deep breath when she saw what was inside. Nestled in a tiny velvet cushion was a small emerald cut sapphire ring in a tiny gold band. She quickly slipped the ring on her left hand, grateful that Maria had convinced her to get her nails professionally manicured the night before. She stared at the ring and stroked the stone before kissing the gem.

In the crowded courthouse, couples—young and old—waited for their names to be called as one would wait in a doctor's office or the department of motor vehicles. Young, dour faced expectant mothers with brooding men at their sides sat next to senior citizens gripping each others arthritic hands and kissing like teenagers. Their silver manes not withstanding, they appeared as giddy to be married as Teenie and Maria. The wedding day attire on display at the courthouse was as varied as the participants. One woman wore a full blown white wedding gown, and her groom wore a dark suit with a corsage pinned to his lapel. One man wore paint stained overalls and checked his watch nervously as though he were getting married on his lunch hour.

Teenie leaned her head on her friend's shoulder, glad that Maria had made the suggestion to get married together. Maria clutched John's hand in her left hand and squeezed Teenie's right hand. Teenie squeezed Brian's hand which prompted a peck on her forehead. Instinctively, she leaned from Maria's shoulder to Brian's and shifted her gaze from her beautiful new bauble to his freshly shaven face. She rubbed her nose against his chin.

"Don't you clean up nicely?" Teenie whispered.

"And so do you," he replied.

"I can't believe that you bought me a sapphire from Tiffany," Teenie whispered. "It's absolutely beautiful."

"I'm glad you like it. You wouldn't let me buy you an engagement ring, so consider this a promise ring."

"Okay. I hope your parents don't trip on how much it cost," Teenie whispered.

"Teenie, I have a discretionary account at my disposal. When my mother sees your ring, she's going to wonder why I didn't buy the larger stone," Brian smiled.

"Are you going to tell your parents that we're married tonight?" Teenie asked.

"Of course. There's no reason for me to keep it a secret from my parents. They love you. They are probably going to want us to start a family right away."

"Are you serious?" Teenie asked.

"I'm dead serious. I would have told them last night, but I was afraid you might get jittery and back out at the last minute.

You're the one who has kept me a secret from your parents," he reminded. "But now that I've met your father, I understand," Brian sighed. "I just hope that Jackie does not use that drop gun and kill me when he finds out that we've eloped."

"He won't kill you. He probably won't talk to you for awhile, but he won't kill you."

"I like your dad. He's like a black Archie Bunker."

"That's how I describe him to people all the time. But he wants me to be happy, so he'll be nice to you. You'll see."

"I just can't believe that you are going to marry someone that your parents have only met a couple of times. It's so Romeo and Juliet," he said. "And it's so unlike you, but I love it."

"And I love you," she sighed. "Oh I forgot to thank you for the flowers that you had sent to the apartment. They are so beautiful. And there were so many of them. How did you do that?"

"One of the perks and privileges of having a concierge in the building. The concierge has a key to all of the apartments, so when I told her what I wanted to do, she made it happen."

Teenie smiled at her fiance.

When they checked in at the court house, the non-responsive clerk allowed them to register as a dual ceremony. Barely glancing at the grinning couples, she checked a few boxes on each of their forms, stapled another sheet to their paperwork and pointed to the galley seating in the courthouse. Clearly, couples agreeing to speak their vows in unison was not a novel idea to the seasoned clerk. Once their names were called, the civil ceremony took less than three minutes.

"I now pronounce you husband and wife," the judge smiled, his grin suggesting that he at least appreciated the romantic significance of the girls' matching dresses.

"Teenie, that gold band looks perfect next to the sapphire. Just perfect," Maria gushed.

"Thanks, Mrs. Prentiss," Teenie replied. "Are you going to get an engagement ring?"

"I might eventually, but right now I don't want one," Maria nodded. "After wearing that big rock that Dante gave me, I don't even want that kind of attention. I might change my mind, but right now I just want a simple band," she smiled staring at her newly adorned ring finger.

"It was that big rock that brought us together," John added.

"It was, wasn't it?" Maria smiled. "If I hadn't worn that ring, the cafeteria drama wouldn't have started and I wouldn't have met you at the Black House to be interviewed for that article. Maybe I should wear it then."

"We're going to use that big rock as a down payment on a condo," John added.

"Are you really?" Brian asked.

"Absolutely. It was a gift, so we may as well enjoy it. She tried to return it and he told her to keep it. We'll tell Dante that it was his wedding gift to us," John smiled, his arms snugly around Maria's waist. Maria shrugged her shoulders. "I'll buy my bride a different ring when I finish law school."

"That's fine by me," Maria added.

"So we're going to tell Rashanda, Justine and Grace that we got married, but not our parents, right?" Maria confirmed.

"Right," Teenie agreed.

"Well, technically, I've already told my mother, and I've told Mama Kaye." Unlike Teenie, Maria was a horrible secret keeper.

"Maria, you still can't keep a secret. Did you tell your mother not to say anything to my mother."

"Of course. I told Liz that Billie did not know and that you weren't telling your parents for awhile, so she won't say anything. My mother and your mother don't talk anyway."

"What did Liz say?"

"She was shocked that you were being so sneaky. She said that I was corrupting you, and that she wasn't surprised that I would run off and get married, but she was shocked that you would do it."

Teenie grinned.

"She also said that she couldn't believe that we were getting married just to have sex," she leaned in and whispered as their husbands waited in line to have their marriage licenses signed and dated.

"That's not why we got married," Teenie whispered.

"Speak for yourself," Maria winked. "Liz said that she hopes I don't have a honeymoon baby and that I at least finish college so that I can bring home a diploma and not a birth certificate."

"Maria! People can hear you," Teenie blushed.

"Well, that's what she said," she snickered. "In fact, I might call her tonight and tell her that she's going to be a grandmother. It is April Fool's Day. That would be hilarious!"

"That's so mean," Teenie teased. "But that would be funny."

"I'm going to do it."

"You never told me what Mama Kaye said when you told her that we were getting married."

"Mama Kaye was fine with it. But she thinks that I'm already pregnant," Maria giggled. "Oh, and she also thinks that it's a bad idea to get married on April first," she paused. "Or maybe she thought it was a bad idea to get married on a Tuesday. Or both, I can't remember which. You know what? We should have taken a few of those flowers from the ones Brian sent you and made a little bouquet out of it."

"Why?"

"Because we didn't have a bouquet. The bride should have a bouquet, dingy."

"That's not what I meant."

"Why what then?" Maria asked.

"Why did Mama Kaye think that it was a bad idea to get married on a Tuesday or April first or both?"

"Oh. Who knows? Mama Kaye has all kinds of quirky things that she believes in like not putting your purse on the floor or you won't have any money," Maria added. "I know it's a wacky superstition, but I totally try not to put my purse on the floor and so does my mother."

"Me too," Teenie smiled. "And I learned that one from my mother too. Why did Mama Kaye think that you were pregnant?"

"Because she said that no one rushes off to get married on a Tuesday unless they are with child or in the "family way" as she put it."

Chapter 12

Infinity

"I'm pregnant," she said softly. "Actually, we're pregnant," she corrected, remembering to breathe. As good as she was at secret keeping, she knew that this would be one that she couldn't keep. She reminded herself to ask Rashanda how she had coped with morning sickness.

"It looks like the stork arrived a little early," she tried again, staring at her reflection in the bathroom mirror. "He's going to freak out," she sighed throwing her arms in the air in defeat. "He is going to freak all the way out. This is going to put a monkey wrench in everything. I don't even know how we're going to write this one into the playbook."

For the most part, the young couples' married life had been manageable. They each alternated travel between Princeton, New Jersey and New Haven, Connecticut every other weekend. Mr. and Mrs. Kraft had taken the nuptial news fairly well; although Brian did share that the day before he told his parents about his new bride, his older brother had announced that he had a drug habit, refused his parents offer to enter a rehabilitation clinic and shared that he was planning to work as a carnival stagehand. So, comparatively speaking, Brian's announcement that he had married his African American girlfriend didn't seem so bad. They did ask if Teenie were pregnant, and when he said that she was not, he didn't know if they were relieved or disappointed. As a wedding gift, and a gesture that she was now family, Brian's parents opened a joint bank account for the couple. Teenie smiled when her first bank statement appeared with her newly hyphenated name: Tanisha Denise Carlson-Kraft.

Brian's parents had not proved the challenge. But Teenie's parents had. At Brian's encouraging, Teenie decided to tell her parents that she had wed. But before calling them with the news, she enlisted advice from Rashanda, Justine and Grace. She knew Maria was in favor of full disclosure, so when she received independent unanimous votes from the other girls, Teenie decided to put on her big girl panties and call her parents. She was glad that Brian had been in the room with her.

"You did what?" her father asked.

"Brian and I got married, Dad," Teenie repeated. "We went to New York and eloped. Maria eloped with her boyfriend John. We got married on the same day."

She could hear heavy breathing and she clinched her toes.

"Brian's here with me now," she added, fearing that her father might say something unflattering about her new husband, she decided it would be best to let her father know that he was within earshot.

"Is he on the phone?" Jackie growled.

"Yes," Tanisha replied meekly.

"Let me tell you something, young man. I don't know where you get off thinking you can just marry my daughter without discussing it with me first..." his voice trailed.

"Dad, he wanted to call and ask your permission, but I stopped him because I knew that you would say no."

"Well, if you knew that I would say no, why did you go ahead and do it anyway? For that matter, why are you telling me now?"

"Because I love Brian, and I didn't want to keep it a secret from you guys," she said softly, the phone cradled between her shoulder and her husband's.

"Mr. Carlson, I didn't mean any disrespect, but I love Teenie, and she is over eighteen, so she's an adult."

"Her name is Tanisha!" Jackie barked. "And I don't need you to tell me how old my daughter is! You know what? I knew when I met you that there was something sneaky about you. I couldn't put my finger on it, but I just sensed it. Um, um, um. And now you've done run off and married my only daughter. I didn't even get a chance to walk her down the aisle."

"Sir, we were thinking we would have a small ceremony this summer so our family's could participate. And that way you can walk her down the aisle."

"What's the point now? I don't need to give her away. You already took her from me. Billie talk to your daughter."

Hearing the disappointment in her father's tone, the tears rolled down Teenie's cheeks.

"Tanisha, it's Mommy."

"Hi Mrs. Carlson. It's Brian. Tanisha is a little upset right now, so she's trying to get herself together."

"She's crying isn't she? I can hear her in the background. Well, tell her that her father will calm down. He's just surprised by this news. This is some big news, Brian," Billie said. "I don't know how you expected us to react, but we certainly weren't expecting this."

"I know. My parents were surprised too," he paused. "But they're happy for us."

"I think her father went outside," Billie whispered. "My husband is just worried that she's pregnant. She's not pregnant is she Brian?"

"No. She's not pregnant, Mrs. Carlson."

"Okay, good. Her father will calm down, it's going to take him some time. Tell Tanisha that I will call her later."

❧❧

"Who are you talking to?" Brian asked when he walked in.

"Oh, you scared me," Teenie blushed. "I was talking to myself. Trying to figure out how I'm going to tell my dad that I'm pregnant."

"You won't start showing for a few months, so there's no rush."

"But if this morning sickness doesn't get better, when I go home for my brother's graduation from high school, they're going to know something is up. I never throw up," Teenie offered.

"I hadn't thought of that. Well, just tell them that you have food poisoning."

Ignoring her husband's suggestion, Teenie continued. "I'm already starting to poof out. Look at my stomach. It's huge!" she groaned. "I've already gained eight pounds. Eight pounds!" she repeated.

"You look great," Brian offered softly.

"I'm going to be in maternity clothes before I'm even out of my first trimester," she sobbed. "I don't want to walk across the stage at graduation with a big swollen belly."

"It's okay, Teenie."

"And when I go to NYU for my law school admission interview, what if they turn me down when they see that I'm pregnant?" she continued.

"They won't do that. Your grades are great, your law school admission test score was great. And that would be pregnancy discrimination, which is illegal. They're going to love you."

"Well, how am I going to be able to go to law school with a baby on my hip?"

"You can just take some time off if you want to. Take a few years off and then go back when the baby is older. I'll finish law school next year, get a job and then you can start."

"But I want to go to school now while I'm still in the school study mode."

"Okay, we'll make it work then. Rashanda and Ian are both in school and they have Christine Marie. They're making it work."

"But their situation is unique. Grace's parents practically live with them and care for Christine Marie, and they have Stella. Between Mrs. Dudley and Stella, Rashanda doesn't have to cook, and they have a live-in housekeeper that does everything. Rashanda's life is totally different! We don't have any of that help!" Teenie barked, the words rolling off her tongue so fast she had to breathe through her mouth to catch her breath.

"We can get help, Teenie," Brian reassured. "My parents will hire someone to help care for the baby while we're in school. Who knows? My mother just may move to Manhattan to help us out herself. It'll be fine, Teenie," Brian replied calmly.

"That's just it. Your parents are always helping us. They're going to get tired of helping us," she sobbed. "I don't know how this happened. I took that pill with military precision." Teenie pressed her index finger and thumb together for emphasis.

"I know you did, doll, but God has a different plan for us, and we're going to go with God's plan."

Still breathing through her mouth, Teenie smiled at her husband.

"Now, are you sure you're pregnant?" he asked.

"Not really, but my cycle is over six weeks late, and I'm never late. My breasts are swollen, I've gained at least eight pounds. I'm falling asleep in class and I'm throwing up every morning. I'm no OB/GYN, but it feels like I'm pregnant."

"Do you want me to go to the pharmacy and buy one of those pregnancy tests so we can be sure?"

"Let's just save the money and go to the student health center."

"Teenie, would you stop worrying about money all the time?" Brian grinned.

"I can't help it. I'm still not accustomed to having access to the kind of money that you're used to having. I'm used to being a poor college student," she smiled.

"Well, you're not any more. You're my wife, and you have access to the same resources that I have at my disposal. I think we can afford to buy a pregnancy test from the pharmacy."

Teenie smiled at her husband.

"There's my girl. I haven't seen you smile all day."

"I'm sorry. I cry at the slightest thing these days," she sniffled. "And my mood swings are almost unbearable. They're even worse when you're not here."

Brian nodded in agreement.

"If I am pregnant, I know everything will work out okay, it's just a curveball in our plan, right?" she sniffled.

"That's right, we'll make it work."

"My dad was just starting to warm up to the idea of us being married. He's going to flip when I tell him that I'm about to be a mother.

ৼৡ

"Excuse me, can you repeat that?" he asked. "I don't think I heard you correctly."

"You're having twins. There are two heartbeats. It's twins. I won't be able to determine if they are fraternal or identical until we do an ultrasound, but you are having twins."

"How can that be?" Brian asked. "Twins don't run in my family."

"Mine either," Teenie offered. "That's impossible!"

"You're almost eight weeks along, and you said that you've already gained almost ten pounds? Didn't you think that was unusual?"

"How would I know? I've never been pregnant!" Teenie barked at the doctor.

Brian squeezed Teenie's hand tightly, fearing she might slap the insolent intern.

"You're an educated young lady. I don't have to tell you how important prenatal care is, especially during the first trimester. Have you been taking prenatal vitamins?"

"No. I didn't know I was pregnant, remember? But I did just start taking a Geritol multi-vitamin every day, and I always eat a bowl of oatmeal for breakfast," she added, her tone softer. "One of my best friends who had a baby a few years ago told me that oatmeal is good for pregnant women to eat. Her husband is in his fourth year of medical school now."

"Well, she's right. The oatmeal has folic acid, so that's good. Geritol is a good vitamin to take, but I'm still going to put you on a pre-natal vitamin," the young doctor scribbled. "Who told you to take Geritol? My younger patients don't normally know to take Geritol," he finished as he scribbled.

"A family friend," Teenie whispered.

"Who was it?" Brian asked.

She found herself inhaling deeply before replying. "Mama Kaye," she mumbled.

"Mama Kaye? Isn't that Maria's pretend grandmother? Why were you talking to Mama Kaye?" Brian asked surprised.

"I wasn't. Maria told me that Mama Kaye told her to take Geritol."

"Why?" Brian asked.

"It's an old wive's tale that if you take Geritol, it will help you conceive," the doctor interrupted. "My grandmother told my mother the same thing."

"Your grandmother is black?" Teenie asked.

"Certainly not," he replied staring at Teenie curiously. "I don't think it's a black or white thing. It's just an old superstition, one of many that my mother follows. She also doesn't believe in putting her purse on the floor because she said that if you put your purse on the floor you won't have any money in it," the doctor chuckled. "Have you heard of that one?"

"Uh, yeah," Teenie stared at the doctor wondering if he were really black and passing for white. "Almost every black woman I know follows that rule."

"Now that you mention the Geritol being a black thing, my mother was raised in Macon, Georgia, and she grew up with a live-in housekeeper who was black," the doctor clarified. "So maybe she learned some of this stuff from Miss Hazel."

"I'll bet she did," Teenie heard herself mumble.

"Is Maria trying to get pregnant?" Brian asked.

"Uh huh. I told you that. They want to start their family now. She wants her children to be close in age to her baby sister, Jeni Kaye, and to Christine Marie."

"That's right. You did mention that, but I forgot. Why were you taking Geritol, Teenie? Were you trying to get pregnant?" Brian asked.

"No. Of course not. Maria said that Mama Kaye said that if you take Geritol it gets your body ready to be pregnant, and the vitamin balances out any negative side effects of the birth control pill," she whispered as though embarrassed to say birth control pill in the presence of a stranger. "I just figured it wouldn't hurt. I was taking the birth control pill every day at the same time. You don't think that the

Geritol counter balanced the effect of the birth control pill do you?" Teenie whispered to her husband.

"You conceived on the pill?" the doctor asked. "I didn't see that noted in your file. The nurse should have made a note of that. It must have been the low dosage mini pill wasn't it?"

"Yes, it was," Teenie sighed wondering how the doctor heard her whispers. "Is there any way that the Geritol could counteract the birth control pill?"

"Certainly not," the doctor said with confidence. "There are no ingredients in one that would interfere with the active ingredients in the other," the doctor explained.

Why does he say certainly not instead of no? That's annoying! Teenie found herself grinding her teeth to stop from screaming this question at the doctor.

"There's only a ninety-six percent effective rate with the mini pill, so four percent of women will conceive even if they take it with military precision at precisely the same time every day. And you're at the peak of your fertility, so you really should have been on the higher dosage birth control pill in my opinion. I reserve the mini pill for young girls who are not sexually active but want to regulate their menstrual cycle or for women who are in their mid to late forties where the odds of conception aren't as high."

"I can't believe I'm having twins. Are you absolutely sure?"

"I'm positive. You heard the heartbeats. Would you like to hear them again?"

"No. I heard them twice the first time."

"Is Maria pregnant?" Brian asked.

"No. At least she wasn't as of yesterday when I talked to her."

"Have you told Maria yet?"

"No. I haven't told anyone yet. I wanted to wait until after the doctor's visit. And I thought we should tell our parents first." Teenie stared at the chipped pink polish on her pinky toes, trying to remember when she had last painted them. The pink polish made her think of Lori. She wished Lori were alive so she could get her opinion. She wondered if Lori would have participated in the elope on April 1st project. She flared her toes like fingers and wished she'd worn socks to the doctor's appointment. Her feet were cold. Shivering beneath the paper hospital gown, she wrapped her arms around her chest and squeezed together her already swollen breasts as Brian chatted with the doctor. I wonder how big my boobs are going to get. Maybe I can get the doctor to measure them now. I'm probably already a C cup. Rashanda's boobs stayed big after Christine Marie was born. I wonder if mine will stay twice as big since I'm having two babies. You are about to have twins! How can you be concerned about your bra cup size?

As was her new custom, the tears flowed uncontrollably. Embarrassed to cry in front of the young doctor, Teenie covered her face with her hands, but Brian noticed the tears.

"It's okay, Teenie. It's going to be fine."

"With twins, her hormone levels are off the charts, and it's only going to get worse so get used to the tears, and the mood swings," the doctor explained to Brian.

"I'm sitting right here, and I can hear you!" Teenie spat. "There's no need to talk around me like I'm a child!"

The doctor continued to write on his chart, but managed to wink at Brian and raise a confirming eyebrow.

"My dad is going to flipping freak out. I can't believe that we are having twins!" She spoke slowly, enunciating each syllable. "I'm supposed to be the first one in my family to get a law degree. How am I going to go to law school next year with a baby on my hip?" she sobbed.

"Hips," the doctor corrected. "You are having twins, so you will have one baby on each hip," he chuckled.

"Shut up!" Teenie screamed.

Three years later...New York City

The knock was firm and decisive. Almost matter-of-fact, not timid like some knocks. It was definitely the knock of a man, that much she knew. Even though the knock lacked the familiar sing song rhythmic pattern to which they'd grown accustomed, she knew it was him. He was a trademark knocker. Everyone else always rang the doorbell. Besides, after their last phone conversation, she expected that he would be on the first flight to New York to see her.

Even though they owned the apartment on Riverside Drive and had their own key, his parents always knocked and waited for them to answer the door. Teenie appreciated the gesture and the independence that it bespoke the young couple, especially now.

"You don't have to knock, Dad," she grinned, reaching out to embrace Mr. Kraft in the doorframe on one of their first visits to see the twins. "It's your apartment."

"No, it's your apartment now, Tanisha. You and Brian need your privacy. You don't need us barging in on you. There's no telling what you two might be doing in here," he continued as she traded hugs with Mrs. Kraft next.

The memory of that visit lingered as Teenie slowly walked to answer the door this time. The doorframe embrace was familiar, but as soon as she laid eyes on him, she burst into tears again. Undaunted, Mr. Kraft cradled Teenie in his arms as he slowly escorted her into the kitchen, waving broadly at the nanny hired to help with the twins. Claudia politely retreated into the living room and began fluffing pillows while the twins napped.

"Teenie, you know why I'm here." Her eyes distant and devoid of even a hint of mascara, she stared at her father-in-law, surprised to hear her nickname roll from his tongue. A stickler for formality, like her parents, Mr. Kraft was one of few people who still called her Tanisha.

"I know that you don't want to deal with any of this right now, but it's necessary," he continued, as he made coffee, reaching for items in the cupboard with the familiarity that comes from owning an in-towner in Manhattan. "Keeping such a large sum of money in your checking account is just fiscally irresponsible. Ninety percent of the funds are not FDIC insured should the banks collapse at this moment. I recognize that's an unlikely occurrence, but no one expected the great depression to happen either. Now, I need you to sign the paper to at least open different accounts so that the money is adequately insured," Brian's father stated firmly, waving a document in her face and placing a pen in her hands. Teenie's hand shook as she signed the document in front of her, the sapphire ring rolling around on her now emaciated finger. She had grown tired of the banker's weekly phone calls to discuss an investment strategy and was glad the check had been automatically deposited into the account opened by his parents when they first wed. The sight of the life insurance check would have caused her to faint or burst into fresh hysterics. "Since my name is also on the account, I will act on your behalf and ensure that the funds are adequately distributed into a household living expense account and the children's trust accounts," Mr. Kraft explained. Teenie nodded her head and pretended to comprehend. "Under the circumstances, Columbia is refunding his law school tuition, and granting him an honorary Juris Doctorate since he was in the final semester of his third year, which I think is very generous and kind of them. And of course, Brian's portion of his trust from our estate will continue to funnel into the account," he continued, pausing as a fresh wave of tears ran down her cheeks.

"I don't mean to be insensitive. But these matters must be handled. You have two children now, Tanisha."

Teenie nodded through the tears.

"I know it seems like you are still living a nightmare, Teenie," he said softly, his hairy hands covering her thin fingers. "This has been rough on all of us. But you must pull yourself together. You have two beautiful daughters who need you. You have to pull it together for them."

She nodded her head up and down again, her hair a tangled mess.

"You are a bag of bones. What did you eat today?" he asked, gripping her thin wrists in his hand.

Teenie stared at him and shrugged. She couldn't remember.

"You haven't eaten anything? It's one o'clock."

"I ate some of Portia's Cream of Wheat," she offered.

"From breakfast? That was over five hours ago," he scowled. "Get dressed, I'm taking you out to lunch. Eleanor Jeniece and Portia Jane will be fine with Claudia. It's their nap time anyway. You need to get some fresh air, and you could probably use a drink. We'll dine at my favorite restaurant in the Helmsley next to the Plaza. They have a good chopped salad and a buttery Chardonnay."

Teenie forced a smile at her father in law, the only one who insisted on using his granddaughters' first and middle names when he referred to them. When the ultrasound confirmed that they were having twin girls, the newlyweds were excited to name the girls, having already agreed to use family names. Both were shocked when they realized that they each had a family member named Eleanor and Jane, so they settled on those names quickly. Brian had an Aunt Portia, and

Tanisha had an Aunt Denise but because they wanted to give the girls the same middle initial, they changed Denise to Jeniece. They wanted to name the baby Jeniece Eleanor but realized that Eleanor Jeniece had a nicer ring to it. They called her Jeniece or Ellie for short. All except Brian's dad, who insisted on calling the girls by their full names.

She smiled as she refused Mr. Kraft's offer for a cup of coffee, never having acquired a taste for Brian's favorite morning beverage. Mr. Kraft placed the steaming mug of black coffee to his nostrils and inhaled loudly as though he were sampling a fine glass of wine. Almost frozen in place, the simple gesture reminded Teenie of her husband who also preferred his coffee black and steaming hot, and also used to inhale deeply before his first sip, savoring the aroma.

"I'd better take a shower," she squeaked, feeling embarrassed that she hadn't showered yet. "It won't take me long." Rising from the table, she swallowed hard determined to fight back the tears as she walked into the bedroom. Smelling under her armpits, she wondered if he knew that she hadn't showered.

The hot water felt good against her skin. She tried to remember if she had showered the day before. She hadn't. She knew that the day before that she had taken a bubble bath with the twins. "People in Europe don't bathe every day," she said aloud. "What should I wear? I'll wear a skirt and blouse," she decided as she smoothed baby oil on to her legs, wondering if she had time to shave. "No time for that. I'll just wear panty hose." She stared at herself in the mirror for the first time in a long time. Her hair was well past her shoulders, longer than it had ever been, and was in desperate need of a shampoo. She brushed it into a pony tail and decided to wear a thick headband. She applied mascara and lipstick before tearing into a fresh packet of pantyhose and getting dressed. The black pencil skirt was now much too large around the waist and hips. She wondered how much weight she'd lost.

The skirt had fit perfectly before the twins were born and then had been snug around her mid section three months after giving birth. But now, the skirt almost slipped off. She tightened a belt around her waist, fastened the belt on the last loop and smoothed out the light blue blouse. She decided that her hands were too shaky to fasten the faux pearls around her neck.

Although she tiptoed down the hallway, the click clack of her heels brought Mr. Kraft to the kitchen door. "Well, aren't you beautiful! You look like a brand new woman, Tanisha!" Mr. Kraft bellowed. "Perfect timing. I just finished my coffee and section one of the New York Times. Mom can get herself ready in under fifteen minutes too. I love that about you Kraft women!"

Tanisha remembered that Brian had made a similar comparison watching Teenie get ready once. "Brian told me that. He said that his mom and I were able to go from zero to ten in under fifteen minutes. And I told him that even in my pajamas and no make-up I was at least a six!" Tanisha laughed.

"That's my girl! Vroom, vroom! Let's eat, I'm starving."

Claudia smiled and waved from the kitchen doorway. "Estas muy bonita, Senora Kraft."

"Gracias, Claudia," Teenie replied, realizing that it had been weeks since Claudia had seen Teenie in anything other than pajamas or sweatpants.

"I love for girls for chew. You no worry nothing. El sol es en el Central Park. We play."

"Esta bien, Claudia."

"That's some spanglish she's got there," Mr. Kraft whispered.

"Her English is actually getting much better, and my Spanish is getting better. I'm actually hungry, Dad," Teenie shared. "I haven't had an appetite in weeks, but I'm hungry."

Once outside, the fresh air raced into her nostrils and filled her lungs quickly, drawn to her like a moth to a fluorescent lightbulb. The familiar New York City street sounds were loud and frightening to her now. She paused on the sidewalk and watched passersby strolling toward Central Park as Mr. Kraft chatted with Clyde, the doorman. She almost lost her nerve when Clyde opened the door to the waiting yellow taxi, his eyes a knowing mixture of warmth and sympathy. She had grown accustomed to that look.

Since the accident, it was the look that she received from everyone who knew what happened. The other residents in the building, all of whom had never spoken to her before the tragedy, now managed to smile and mumble a soft "I'm so sorry," under their breath, their heads shaking from side to side in disbelief. They stopped short of formally introducing themselves to their mocha neighbor, which gave an empty hollowness to their sympathy gesture. Before the tragedy, the other co-op owners almost seemed to gape at her whenever she entered the elevator either alone or hand in hand with her husband. The lined and moneyed faces of the wealthy staring at her as though she were a rare artifact, and they, the curators at the Whitney Museum, studying her intently as though trying to establish an appraised value. Not even the younger looking neighbors bothered to introduce themselves to the only black girl who lived in their exclusive building. Brian didn't seem at all uncomfortable with the glares, but she knew that the disapproving looks, though not embroidered with her name exclusive of his, were reserved exclusively for her. If she managed to make eye contact and smile at a gawker in the elevator or lobby, her smile was met with a blank stare or rolling of the eyes. When, by her pregnancy, it became evident that Brian's experimental dating fling had now been inked with a permanent marker, the expressions turned to sighs of disgust, and tongue clucking. Against her nature, Tanisha learned to avoid eye contact with the neighbors.

Sensing her hesitancy, Mr. Kraft slowly walked to her side and gripped her arm. "Tanisha, you live in New York City. You must get back on the horse," Mr. Kraft said firmly. "Taxis are the central nervous system of Manhattan. He's been gone almost six months, Teenie. We're all grieving, but life must go on."

Her feet frozen to the pavement, she felt like an agoraphobic must feel after finally mustering the courage to leave the comforts of his cozy, eccentric Manhattan apartment, finally tiring of the same take out menu options. She had taken short strolls through Central Park with Claudia and the twins, her tears hidden behind oversized black plastic sunglasses, that were much too large for her thin, oval face. She played with the girls at the playground, pushing them on the swings and playing "Mommy Monster" as she chased them through the playground pretending to be a hungry ogre who must be fed a diet of twins.

"If you're going to live in New York City, you must be able to take a taxi, Tanisha. Either that or you will have to move."

She wondered which logic her father-in-law was using as he decided to intersperse her nickname with her proper name. Staring into her father in law's face, her arm trembling against his hand, she slowly folded her body into the backseat of the taxi.

"You're right. It's time."

One year later...

Almost two years since the incident, the sight of taxis no longer sent Tanisha into a fit of hysterics. Her brow no longer furrowed in anger whenever she saw a yellow taxicab. The grief counselor at church had explained that with time, her anger would eventually dissipate. But Teenie was angry at so many people, she didn't know how to heal. She was still angry at the taxi driver whom she blamed for driving the taxi, and surviving. She was angry at the city of New York for the congestion and traffic that delayed the arrival of emergency personnel to the scene. She was angry with the New York Police Department for their inability to clear a path for the ambulance to get to the emergency room sooner. The emergency room staff at New York General Hospital was on her angry list for not doing enough to save her husband. The police officer who called to tell her that her husband had been in an accident wasn't exempt from the angry list. The New York Department of Transportation was blamed because had the traffic lights been timed differently, the taxi would not have been broadsided. Even though the driver of the other vehicle also died, she was still angry with the driver for speeding up to run a red light. She blamed her husband for sitting in the front seat of the taxi, ignoring her belief that the rear passenger seat behind the driver was the safest seat in a vehicle. He viewed it as one of her odd superstitions like not putting your purse on the floor. Yet whenever they got into a taxi together, he always positioned her behind the driver, claiming that his legs were too long to sit in that seat. He preferred to sit in the front so that he could stretch his legs, yet he never buckled his seatbelt in taxis. Finally, and most importantly, she blamed God for taking her husband and leaving her a widow with two young daughters to raise. It was an accident. Accidents happen all the time. She reminded herself of this whenever she felt the anger rising in her belly like a pot of boiling water. The grief counselor had encouraged her to list her anger in a journal and to review it periodically, crossing off items as she slowly began the healing process. So far, she had only crossed off one item from her list: "I hate the sight of yellow taxis." Moving had helped heal this hurt.

Though one bedroom smaller than the apartment that they had shared on Riverside Drive, and lacking a maid's quarters, her new three bedroom unit was much sunnier than the New York condo and had more expansive views from each of the rooms. She enjoyed awaking to Lake Michigan each morning, and the proximity to Grant Park was good for the girls. She had politely declined an invitation by Brian's parents to spend Thanksgiving in New York, a tradition that the Kraft family had followed for years. Surprisingly, his parents didn't press her on this, but she knew that eventually she would have to return and face the scene of the crime. Thankfully, Brian's mom was having the New York apartment completely remodeled, redoing the kitchen and all of the bathrooms, painting and replacing each piece of furniture. She claimed that she redid all of her homes after twenty years, but Teenie knew that it was just as painful for Mrs. Kraft to return to the place that held a lifetime of memories with her son.

Initially, the sound of the elevated trains had frightened the twins, but now they didn't flinch when the trains rumbled overhead. They enjoyed the occasional ride on the "roller coaster subway," as they called it. Although the condominium that she purchased in Chicago came with a deeded parking spot, Teenie had decided to forego buying a car so that she always had a spot for guests who visited them in the crowded Gold Coast neighborhood. If she limited herself to only one visitor at a time, her parents, Brian's parents or Rashanda and Ian always had a warm, covered parking spot. Justine and AM usually left Ian's car in the hospital parking lot and walked to her place for a visit. Tanisha had grown accustomed to taking taxis around the city, and rented a car for trips to Lake Forest or Wilmette to visit Brian's parents or Rashanda. She hadn't realized how much she missed being near her family, and was glad that she decided to move back to Chicago. It had proved very therapeutic.

The girls had adjusted to the move and enjoyed spending time with both sets of grandparents. Because Chicago was home and had many of the same big city conveniences and nuances: great shopping, theatre, exceptional restaurants, diversity and energy, what Teenie missed most about Manhattan was Claudia. She'd tried desperately to convince Claudia to move with them, but Claudia was a New Yorker and wouldn't budge.

"You find new Claudia, Missus Kraft. I no special. Me love girls and new Claudia love girls too. You see me truth. I be in New York. Cheekago no good place for me. Me family here. Vaya con Dios!"

It had been a teary farewell, but the wise Claudia had proved correct. When Teenie shared that she was moving back to Chicago, Rashanda suggested that she use Stella, her part-time helper, to help with the twins. Now that Christine Marie was in school, Mr. and Mrs. Dudley picked her up and cared for her on days when Rashanda had class and Ian was at the hospital.

Miss Stella won the twins over when she greeted them in Spanish. A stickler for schedules, Teenie tried to maintain the same schedule that the girls had in New York. They had breakfast together, did chores and then school time where Teenie worked with them on phonics and reading. A long walk in the stroller or playtime in the park was usually followed by a quick errand before returning to the apartment at eleven where Stella took over until five o'clock. Teenie used the afternoon to research pre-schools and prepare for the Law School Admissions Test. She had deferred her admission to New York University Law School, and now her LSAT score had expired.

Miss Stella often took the girls on field trips on Friday and visited the Art Institute of Chicago, the Field Museum, the John G. Shedd Aquarium or the Lincoln Park Zoo. She sometimes took them to Northwestern Memorial Hospital to have lunch in the cafeteria with AM.

AM rose from his seat when he saw Stella walking towards him in the cafeteria.

"Hey girls," AM smiled pecking them on the forehead. "Friday is my favorite day of the week, because I get to see two of my favorite nieces in Chicago," he grinned.

"Who are your other favorite nieces in Chicago, Uncle AM?" Portia asked.

"Christine Marie, of course."

"Girls at least say hello," Stella coached.

"Hi, Uncle AM," they both grinned. After several weeks of monthly lunches with AM, and his visits to their place with Justine, the girls had warmed up quickly to AM. "Where's Aunt Justine?"

"She can't join us for lunch today. She had class."

"Is she still in school studying to be a dental hygienist?" Stella asked.

"Yup. I'm so proud of her. She works at Saks at night, and she goes to school during the day. We have to eat fast today because Uncle AM has to observe a surgical procedure in less than thirty minutes. Do you want pizza or chicken fingers for lunch today?" AM asked glancing at his watch.

"Chicken fingers!" the girls screamed simultaneously.

"And I want a chocolate milkshake," Portia added.

"Me too," Jeniece said.

"Can they have a milkshake?" AM asked.

"I guess it's all right. It's field trip Friday, so we'll let them splurge. I'm not hungry, so don't go getting me anything," Stella ordered.

"Not even a small salad?" he asked.

"Nope. I'm fine."

"Can I go with you, Uncle AM?" Portia asked.

"Sure, sweetie. You can be my helper."

"You help Uncle AM, Portia. I'm going to stay here and keep Miss Stella company," Jeniece explained.

"Why thank you, darling," Stella winked.

Busy wiping the table with the napkins from the dispenser and neatly stacking AM's notes and medical book to the side, Stella didn't notice the doctor silently approaching. Jeniece noticed him first.

"Hello," Jeniece smiled. He stood frozen by her table, his head oddly tilted to the side, his tray almost tipping. Startled by Jeniece's voice, Stella looked up.

"Hello. Is there something we can help you with?" Stella smiled, noticing his dark gray coat, the color worn by the attending physicians.

"I, um. I'm not sure," the doctor stammered staring intently at Jeniece.

"Did you lose something, doctor?" Stella suggested, tilting her head and placing a protective arm around Jeniece's shoulder, slightly uncomfortable by the intensity of his gaze toward her young charge. A sparkle in his hazel eyes made him appear more youthful than the salt and pepper flecks of gray that were haphazardly sprinkled through his thick black mane and mustache.

As though waking from a trance, the doctor shook his head and smiled. "I'm so sorry to bother you. I noticed her as I was leaving, and she just looks familiar to me," he paused.

Stella furrowed her brows tightly and slanted her eyes at the handsome doctor. "Oh, are you a pediatrician? Does she remind you of one of your patients?"

"Yes. That's it. She looks like one of my patients," he replied quickly snapping out of his trance. "But no, I'm not a pediatrician, I'm an anesthesiologist with a pediatric specialty."

Comforted by his reply, Stella smiled. "She hasn't been here very long, and I don't believe that she's had surgery, so she couldn't be one of your patients unless you worked in New York. Did you ever have surgery, Jeniece?"

"What's surgery?" Jeniece asked Stella.

"It's an operation to make you feel better," the doctor explained.

"No. I never had an operation. I already feel better," she replied to Stella, politely ignoring the doctor hovering at the table.

"Well, I'm glad to hear that. You are a very pretty little girl," he added.

Jeniece smiled without making eye contact and continued to count the sugar packets in front of her.

"The nice doctor just told you that you're pretty, Jeniece. What do you say?" Stella asked.

"I smiled thank you to him Miss Stella. Mom says that we can't talk to strangers, but we can smile at them," she whispered.

The doctor and Stella chuckled quickly.

"But if someone pays you a compliment, it's okay to smile and say thank you."

"Thank you," Jeniece replied, smiling widely at the doctor.

"What did you say her name was?" the doctor asked.

An out of breath Portia raced to the table before Stella could respond.

"Miss Stella, we have coffee for you because Uncle AM said that you can't just watch us eat," Portia bursted.

"That was supposed to be a surprise, Portia-Smortia. Uncle AM asked you to keep that a secret," AM added walking up behind her carrying a tray of food.

"Thanks, Uncle AM," Jeniece squealed reaching for her chocolate milkshake as AM placed the tray of food on the table.

"Oh, hello, sir. Were you looking for me? Am I late? Do you need me to scrub in to view your next case now? My pager didn't go off or anything, and I know it has fresh batteries," he explained, checking the pager clipped to his waistband.

"Hello. Calm down. Is this your family?"

"Yes, well, no. I mean sort of," he stammered.

"That was a yes or no question, intern. Either it is your family or it isn't. Which one is it?" the doctor asked firmly.

"Stella is a family friend, and the girls are my friend's daughters. They're twins."

"I can see that," the doctor said firmly. "She called you uncle, but they're not related to you?"

"They're not, sir. But their mother is one of my girlfriend's best friends, so they call me Uncle AM."

"Uncle AM? What does AM stand for intern?"

"It's a nickname that my roommate gave me a long time ago, sir. Because I'm a morning person."

"Thank you, intern." The doctor's tone was firm and dismissive, his gaze intense and disinterested. His serious tone and gaze softened when he stared from Portia to Jeniece. "What's your mother's name?" he asked.

"My mother's name is Beryl, sir," AM answered robotically. "And they can finish lunch without me if you need me now. I had a big breakfast, so I'm really not that hungry."

"Not **your** mother's name, intern. What's **their** mother's name?"

"Teenie Kraft," AM responded quickly as though accustomed to rapid fire questioning at the hands of the doctor. "Actually, her real name is...."

Like watching a waterfall in slow motion, the tray tipped forward, cascading remnants of salad and silverware to the floor, his empty soda can bounced on the now upside down salad bowl. "Tanisha," the doctor whispered almost to himself as his chin tilted into his chest following the gravitational pull of the tray slipping from his grasp.

"That was funny," Jeniece laughed. "Do that again!"

Like a lithe acrobat, the tall doctor quickly bent at the waist and scooped the bowl and can back on his tray. "I lost my grip. I'll send someone over to clean this up. I will see you in surgery, intern," he finished as he walked away without offering a formal goodbye.

"Yes, sir, doctor," AM replied to the back of his head.

Stella stared at AM curiously. "That was odd. Was that your boss?"

"Not exactly, but sort of. I'm an intern, so any doctor here is my boss."

"What's his name?"

"That's the problem, I don't remember. There are so many doctors at this hospital, that I can't keep their names straight. I'm on my anesthesiology rotation now, so I'll meet him this afternoon."

Chapter 13

Forever

"We's gone have us some trouble up in here. Mark my word. I knews it when da phone went a ringing. 'Cause ain't nuthin' but bad news and troubles bold enough to come a calling during the bewitching hour. Dems dere the hours betwixt eleven at night and eight in the morning," he muttered, rubbing his new goatee. "Yes siree, only troubles comes a knocking whilst the birds is still hunting for their morning meal. And don't let it be no full moon out yonder. That's double trouble right dere, that's fo' sure," he laughed playing with mock suspenders and teetering on his heels.

"He's so melodramatic," Rashanda dismissed, waving her wet nails in the air, her trademark bubblegum pink nail polish resting on a paper towel on the large stainless steel island that now seemed crowded with a parade of decadent desserts: caramel cake, coconut cake, german chocolate cake, sweet potato pie, pound cake, peach cobbler, banana pudding and a two tiered tray of red velvet cupcakes with cream cheese frosting.

The girls laughed at Ian's antics. Rashanda, Maria and Justine sat in the metal stools tucked beneath the island, a glistening new pot rack suspended high atop the center. Refusing an offer to join the girls in the island huddle, Grace claimed that she had almost bumped her head on one of the lower hanging pots, so she had voluntarily repositioned herself at the kitchen table, and offered the vacant island stool to Tomoko. But her yoga partner and volleyball coach chose to stand, as though afraid to take her place at the table.

"Can't I just have one cupcake, Shanda?" Ian begged. "No one is going to eat all of these desserts. Or at least let me have a scoop of peach cobbler. She made two platters. We're going to have leftover sweets for days."

"You can have one small cup of peach cobbler, but no ice cream, Ian," said Rashanda. "And then you need to go outside and keep an eye on things."

"It's all under control," Ian acknowledged as he scooped from the tray cooling on the stove.

"I like the beard, Dr. Hall," Grace smiled. "It makes you look older and erudite," she emphasized. "I'm trying to expand my vocabulary and this week my word is erudite," she explained without prompting.

"Thanks, Grace. Before I grew the beard, my patients sometimes mistook me for an intern, but with the beard, I feel like I look more mature and scholarly," he paused to chew. " I look more erudite, to borrow your new word," Ian smiled.

"So you think we're walking into a snake pit and trouble is a brewing, huh Dr. Hall?" Grace asked.

"I'm just saying that my spider senses are telling me that trouble is a foot. When the phone rings before eight o'clock in the morning, or after eleven o'clock at night, there's nothing good on the other end. It's generally bad news or something that could lead to trouble. Trust me," he chomped.

"Ian, why don't you go in the backyard and help them set up the volleyball net," she suggested.

"Am I being dismissed?" asked Ian. "In my own house? I

think I'm being dismissed in my own house. So much for a man being the king of his castle."

"Well, if you want to get technical it's Grace's house, and yes, you are being dismissed, sweetheart. Leave so we can talk about you behind your back like we always do."

"You are still the king of the castle, Ian," Grace smiled. "You guys don't move out for another month."

"I'm so excited for you," Maria gushed. "You're going to love Oak Park. It's diverse, and near Oak Brook Shopping Center, so you'll be near excellent shopping," she rattled. "And it's near the city, but far enough away that you won't hear bang bang shootem ups when Pookie and Ray-Ray have been over served at the local tavern. My mom and Richard love living in Oak Park, and Jeni Kaye is in a great Montessori pre-school."

"We just found out that Christine Marie got a spot in that school. One of the doctors at the hospital suggested that we put her on the waiting list a few months ago, and a spot just opened up."

"That's so cool," Maria gushed. "You're going to love it. Will you miss living on the north shore a little?"

"I will. I will miss having Lake Michigan as my backyard," Rashanda sighed, staring through the French doors leading from the kitchen to the backyard.. "It's so beautiful in the summer when people have their boats out on the water. It looks like a postcard."

"It's peaceful and pretty in the winter too," Ian added. "I'm going to miss having Lake Michigan at our backdoor, but you know what I'm going to miss most of all? I am going to miss Auntie Grace paying that Roycemore private school tuition," Ian chuckled.

Rashanda scowled at her husband and shook her head. "You

can dress them up, but you can't take them out. Even as a doctor, he's still uncouth. Ian, I can't believe that you just said that," scolded Rashanda. "And in front of company, no less."

"They're not company. They're family. You didn't even let me finish my speech, Rashanda," Ian explained, swallowing his last bite of peach cobbler, he placed his right hand over his heart. "Grace, allowing us to live in your house rent free for these last few years has been such a blessing. It's how we were able to save for the down payment on our Oak Park house so quickly when I was making peanuts at the hospital. Thank you. As the king of this castle for thirty more days, I knight you," he waved his empty fork towards her head and bowed.

"You are so silly," Grace blushed. "I'm glad that I could help you. Just remember that I always get free medical advice and procedures from you, Ian and free legal advice from you, Rashanda, and we'll call it even."

"That's a deal!" Ian grinned. "Now, I will leave you ladies to your gossip, but if your little scheme doesn't go off exactly as you imagined, just remember that I warned you." Ian scooted out the kitchen door as Rashanda motioned towards him.

In the backyard, the caterers scurried beneath the white canopy tent, draping tables with lavender tablecloths and carefully placing eight gold cane backed chairs around each square table. The powder blue sky was spotted with thin cloud cover that provided a sheer veil for the sun. Grace had arranged for a tent with sides and heaters in case the meteorologist's forecast for clear skies and temperatures in the mid seventies proved inaccurate. The heaters were on standby in the garage, just in case the weather took a sudden turn for the worst. The tent flaps had not been fastened down, providing an unobstructed view of Lake Michigan.

"I'm glad that we were all able to be here on your mother's actual birthday, and that it fell on a Sunday over spring break."

"I know, right? I can't believe that it's this warm in April in Chicago. My mother likes to celebrate her birthday on her actual birthday, so I'm glad it all worked out because everyone that we invited was able to come. A seventieth birthday celebration is significant."

"What's the deal with the volleyball nets? Did your mom really say that she wanted to play volleyball at her birthday party?" Maria asked.

"That's what she said," Grace shrugged. "Obviously, at her age, she doesn't plan to play, but she wanted a volleyball net set up for us to play. She knows that I'm into volleyball now, so she wanted us to have a good time. I can't wait to show you guys how good I am. I'm quite the spiker now thanks to Tomoko's coaching."

"This is going to be fun. But help me understand something," Tomoko said. "I know that I'm the new girl in the group, but do any of you think that Ian might be on to something? I've only met Teenie a few times, but from what Grace has told me about her, she might not be too happy with this little scheme," Tomoko considered. "What if she gets pissed and storms out?"

Rashanda, Grace and Justine stared at Maria. "Tomoko does have a point, you guys," Grace admitted. "You know how Teenie is. She does not like surprises."

"Most control freaks don't," Maria sighed. "But Teenie has softened up. She agreed to elope remember? When I suggested that to her, I never thought in a million years that she'd go for it. Honestly, I was shocked when she agreed to it. I really was. I thought she would laugh in my face and try to talk me out of doing it," Maria paused. "So that's a sign that Teenie has mellowed out.

Remember, she also didn't freak out when she learned that she was pregnant, and not just with one unexpected baby, but two," she demonstrated, holding two fingers in the air.

"Not quite true, Maria. Teenie did freak out," Rashanda corrected. "But she pulled herself together. She really had no choice. It wasn't something that she could control."

"Maybe we didn't fully consider that she may have just closed that chapter in her life. After David and Rachel got married, she stopped returning his phone calls and pretty much just let the friendship lapse like a magazine subscription," Rashanda remembered.

"Okay, that was a little melodramatic don't you think?" Maria asked.

"It's true," Rashanda defended.

"It's true, but their lives had changed so much. It's hard to be friends with someone who is now married and has a child," Justine added.

"Justine makes a good point," Maria nodded, stirring a large glass pitcher filled with lemonade.

"You guys still managed to be friends with me when I got married freshman year and had a baby in college," Rashanda offered.

"But that's different," defended Maria.

"How's it different? I was the only married mother in the group, but you guys are still my friends."

"Are you sure we don't need to help do anything else, Grace?" Maria asked, hoping to change the subject.

"Nope. We're all set. I can't believe that my mother insisted on doing all the baking herself. She actually wanted to cook everything, but I put my foot down and had a caterer prepare trays. It's her seventieth birthday, she shouldn't have to sweat in the kitchen. I know how much she likes fresh squeezed lemonade, so thank you guys for juicing all of those lemons!"

"Your mother made all of these desserts?" Tomoko asked.

"Every single one," Grace replied.

"From scratch," Rashanda and Justine added simultaneously.

"Jinx, you owe me a Coke," Rashanda smiled.

"Who's all coming to the party?" Maria asked.

"All of our parents will be here," Rashanda said. "Maria, your mom called to see if she could bring Mama Kaye, so I said of course," she paused. "Last night, Teenie called to see if Brian's parents could come so they could spend some time with the twins and with her parents."

"Are you serious? Teenie's in-laws are going to be here, and you've invited David Barton? What if she starts going off?" Justine asked.

"That's what Ian was talking about. He thinks it's one giant bad idea, sparked by that phone call from Justine that came after eleven o'clock at night, proving his theory that when your phone rings that late, it's usually drama brewing," she sighed. "We shall see, 'cause it's too late now."

"Can we just drop it?" Maria groaned. "The ship has sailed out of the harbor now."

"I'm kind of confused. Can we start at the beginning?" asked Tomoko. "How did you connect the dots, Justine?"

"Yeah, tell us that story," added Grace. "You told me a little about AM being involved, but you didn't finish explaining exactly what happened."

"That's because you cut me off to go to a yoga class," Justine reminded.

"You know we take our yoga very seriously at the God's Grace Yoga Studio," Grace smiled. "Namaste."

"Teenie and her girls do a yoga class together. It's so cute to watch them practicing their little downward facing dog when we go to their house," Justine chimed in.

"If you're going to tell the story, start talking. Teenie will be here any minute. You know how prompt that chick is," Rashanda reminded.

"The twins slow her down now. I've seen it. Teenie will be all set to walk out the door, and one of them will spill something or need to be changed, or their hair will need to be re-brushed. It's amazing to watch how children naturally mellow out even the most neurotic people."

"Anyway, almost three weeks after Stella took Portia and Jeniece to the hospital to have lunch with AM, he told me about the doctor that came over to their table asking all of these questions, and how he was staring at the twins like he knew them," explained Justine.

"Why did he tell you that weeks later?" Grace asked.

"He was complaining about this particular doctor always being in a bad mood, and how the other interns were afraid of him and how he heard that the doctor was going through a nasty divorce and in a custody battle with his ex-wife so he was always biting interns' heads off and eating them for lunch. The interns had nicknamed this doctor, "DC" which stood for Dark Cloud. AM shared that Dark Cloud seemed like such a nice guy when he was talking to the twins at the hospital. That's when I said, 'when did Dark Cloud see the twins?' and that's when he told me that Dark Cloud came over to the table in the cafeteria when Stella brought the twins to have lunch with him."

"Did you know it was him then?"

"I had no idea because he always uses the doctors' nicknames. For instance, there's a really pretty Haitian doctor named Dr. Lisa, but they nicknamed her "CQ" for Caribbean Queen. There's a chubby doctor that they call "HD" as in Humpty Dumpty. There's a doctor who has really bad corns on her toes, yet she always wears open toe sandals so her nickname is Iowa. Get it?"

"Because corn is grown in Iowa?" Grace replied.

"Bingo! They nicknamed Dr. Barton 'Dark Cloud' because he was always in a bad mood like he had a dark cloud over his head, so that's what AM always called him. AM never used his real name."

"Why do they give nicknames to the doctors?" Tomoko asked.

"So they can talk about the doctors and not worry about getting caught. It's a hierarchical thing with the interns too. They don't share the nicknames with the nurses, because some of the nurses will tell the doctors. If a doctor gets wind of the nickname, the interns change the name. Ian's intern class did the same thing," shared Rashanda. "The attending physicians and residents usually know about the nicknames, they just ignore it because they did the same thing when they were interns."

"That's when AM remembered that Dark Cloud had known Teenie's real name was Tanisha," added Justine. "Just like that. He said it really casually. And I said, 'what are you talking about?' and he said, 'he asked me what the twins' mother's name was, and I said Teenie and then I was about to tell him her real name was Tanisha Kraft, and he dropped his tray, but before he dropped his tray I heard him say Tanisha really softly. I wondered how he knew her real name was Tanisha, but then I forgot about it.'"

"Men!" Rashanda groaned.

"John is the same way. They are so not gatherers. That was a material fact. John will spend hours talking with someone in the law library, and then I'll ask him where the person is from or where the person went to undergrad, and he won't know. How do you not learn where someone is from after studying with them for three hours? Basic," Maria finished.

"Ian, AM, John, they're all cut from the same one cell cloth. Teenie said Brian was the same way. They can't multi-task either, but don't get me started on that," Rashanda said. "So that's how Ian got involved. When AM described Dark Cloud, Justine got suspicious and called Ian to ask him what Dr. Barton's first name was."

"Exactly. And as soon as he said David, I got suspicious," Justine said.

"You did not! You didn't remember that Teenie's David's last name was Barton right away," Rashanda clarified. "As soon as I heard Ian say, 'his name is David Barton' I knew that it was Teenie's David Barton."

"True. It didn't click for me right away because it's been a minute," Justine confessed. "I hadn't heard his full name in a long time. I think AM may have called him Dr. Barton, but that didn't click for me. Besides, I thought David was still living in Washington D.C."

"Exactly. We all did. Teenie hasn't mentioned David in years, and once she married Brian, I never brought David up anymore. I tried once and she just said they didn't keep in touch. So Rashanda and Justine three-way called me so we could figure out what to do," Maria explained. "We would have called you too, Grace, but we couldn't do a four way call," Maria explained quickly.

"What's he doing back in Chicago?" Tomoko asked.

"Practicing medicine, obviously," Maria replied sarcastically, her eyes rolling into her head in an exaggerated fashion. Grace sighed softly and exchanged a knowing glance with Justine and Rashanda.

"Be nice," Rashanda whispered to Maria, smiling softly at Tomoko as Tomoko joined Grace and sat at the kitchen table.

"I am being nice. He's practicing medicine in Chicago. That's what he's doing," Maria shrugged, swiveling on her chair to ensure that her back was to Tomoko.

"Tomoko meant why is he back in Chicago. You know what she meant, Maria," Rashanda scolded.

"Then she should have worded her question differently. 'Why is he practicing medicine in Chicago?' would have been a better question," she said flippantly.

"Are you still planning to go to law school, Maria," Grace asked softly. "Did you take the LSAT?"

"I did, but I didn't do that great, so I'm going to take it again," she sighed. "We decided to cash in that Dante diamond to help pay for John's law school so we wouldn't have any student loan debt. Our plan is to start our family now and then I'll go to law school when he finishes. I want my baby to be close in age to my sister, so Jeni Kaye has someone close to her age," she paused. "When you think about it, that sounds so bizarre. My child will have an aunt just a few years older than she is. But I really want to have a baby before going to law school. My mother went to school after she had her children. Law school will be there when I'm ready for it."

"How's that going?" Rashanda asked.

"The LSAT studies are tough. The analytical reasoning section is kicking my butt. I cannot seem to figure out how to diagram the logic problems quick enough. If the design is obvious,

I do okay, but if I have to set up the diagram, it takes me forever. John is helping me, but his brain thinks differently than mine. I do great on the reading comprehension and logical reasoning sections, but the analytical reasoning trips me up."

"I had a hard time with that section too," Rashanda offered. "I think everybody does. I'll share the tips that I learned in my LSAT review course. I didn't do great on that section, but I did well enough. I meant how's Project Stork coming along?" she whispered.

"Oh, still no stork sightings," Maria sighed. "But we're practicing," she smiled. Maria waved her hand across her face, the universal gesture for 'I don't want to talk about this now' while simultaneously tilting her head towards Tomoko. "I'm working at a law firm as a recruiter to pay the bills while John is in school," she tossed in quickly.

Maria was the only girl in the group who hadn't received Tomoko warmly. The girls couldn't decide if Maria was made uncomfortable because Tomoko was a lesbian or if Maria just didn't like Tomoko. Maria had never really been especially close to Grace, so their relationship was not altered materially when Grace came out of the closet.

"Anyway, where was I?" Rashanda asked, nodding understandingly toward Maria. "Oh, I remember. We were talking about David Barton. I didn't know how to go about getting in touch with David at the hospital, so I had Ian take us to his office one day. As soon as I saw him, I recognized him," Rashanda admitted. "Even though I hadn't seen him in over ten years. He's gained some weight, and his hairline has receded a little, and he has gray at the temples," she described. "But other than that, he looks the same. He didn't remember me until I told him that I'd met him at the skating rink with Maria and Todd when we were in high school. He stared at me at first, and then it clicked for him and he remembered exactly who I was. He seemed to get really nervous."

"Why did he get nervous?" Tomoko asked, obviously intrigued by the story unfolding before her.

"Maybe nervous isn't the right word. He became uncomfortable. I think he thought he was just meeting Ian's wife and her friend, and when I told him that I'd met him before, and he realized my link to Teenie, he just looked uncomfortable."

"He did," Justine added. "When Rashanda told him that we all went to middle school and high school with Teenie, he smiled, but it was almost as though he was embarrassed. I think he realized that we probably knew every detail about their relationship."

"Friendship," Rashanda corrected. "If Teenie were here she would correct you and say 'friendship' because they never had a relationship," Rashanda emphasized, her fingers making mock quotation marks in the air.

"Whatever, Dude," Justine laughed. "All I know is that his entire demeanor changed when he realized that we were Teenie's friends. He stood up and started pacing like a lion in a cage."

"Did he really start pacing?" Grace asked.

"He sure did. I forgot about that. He came from behind his desk and started pacing," confirmed Rashanda.

"Did he ask about Teenie right away?"

"Yup. I told him that Teenie had moved back to Chicago to be closer to her family."

"He stopped pacing and shared that he'd moved back to Chicago because his father had a stroke, so he was preparing to take over his dad's medical practice. He didn't say anything about the divorce though so I didn't ask. I didn't want him to know that his business was on the hospital gossip mill."

"Did you say anything, Justine?" Grace asked.

"Not really. I had heard all the stories about him, but I'd never met him, so he didn't know me from a can of paint. I just went with Rashanda for moral support, and I wanted to finally see what this David Barton character looked like."

"You'd never seen David?" Maria and Tomoko asked simultaneously.

Maria glanced over her shoulder and smiled at Tomoko, her lips parting slightly as though she considered playing the jinx game with the newest member of their circle. But just as quickly, her lips came together tightly and her jaw moved as though chewing on the words waiting to escape from her mouth.

"Nope. I never met him. I was never around when she hung out with him," Justine shrugged. "I think sometimes I was at my dad's for the weekend, and then when we moved to Rogers Park I was so geographically undesirable that you guys forgot about me," she fake sniffled.

"And the Oscar goes to Justine. Actually, I think Ian outperformed you with his little slave routine earlier. Everyone is being overly dramatic today. Maybe it's these warm April temperatures," Rashanda noticed. "Did you ever meet him, Grace?"

"Nope," Grace added. "Justine and I never met him."

"Did he explain why he hadn't been in touch with Teenie in all those years?" Tomoko asked.

"Why would he feel the need to do that?" Maria spat coarsely. "If you've been listening, Tomoko, we told you that Teenie was the one who cut off all communication with him when he got married and had a baby. She stopped returning his phone calls, and then she got married and had twins so she didn't have time for him anyway. Take it from me, if someone stops returning your phone calls, that's a clue that they are not trying to maintain a friendship. There was no reason for him to keep calling her after that," she finished, her voice just a tad softer and slightly less abrasive.

"Did you tell him that Teenie was a widow?" Tomoko asked Rashanda, seeming oblivious to Maria's caustic tone.

"I wanted to, but I didn't know if it was appropriate for me to tell all of her business like that. I couldn't remember if he even knew that she had gotten married. While I was trying to decide what to say next, he started checking his watch real obviously, which Ian noticed, so he gave me the high sign that it was time to go. He thanked Dr. Barton and we left," paused Rashanda. "Teenie has been friends with him for so long that it was odd for me to watch Ian suck up to the same guy that I roller skated with well over ten years ago," Rashanda nodded.

"You guys should have rehearsed what you were going to say," Maria added.

"Teenie is usually the one who scripts us in situations like this. We tried to call you, Maria, but you didn't call us back in time," Rashanda explained.

"I couldn't believe that we were leaving so abruptly. It just felt like something else should be said, so as we were leaving I told him that if he called her, Teenie would probably be glad to hear from him," added Justine.

"Teenie would be glad to hear from whom?" Teenie asked standing in the kitchen doorway holding the small hand of a twin in each of hers.

Chapter 14

The Light

Cradling warm breath in his cupped hand, he hoped that the absence of a pram confirmed his hunch. For that's all it really was. A hunch. A hunch or a hope. For him, it was both a hunch and a hope. He rhythmically massaged his fingers with more warm breath, feeling slightly foolish, and wondering if he should abort. It had been a whimsical decision made in haste.

When the charge nurse informed him that the operating room would not be available as originally scheduled, delaying his procedure by at least one hour, he viewed it as a sign. Without hesitation, mumbling over his shoulder for her to share this delay with the interns and other physicians involved, he grabbed his jacket and walked briskly to the cafeteria. He watched as she hustled the girls into the restroom. In that instant, he realized that had he paused (or dilly dallied as his mother often said) he would have been too late. He would have missed his moment. This was his second sign. Content with his swift decision making, he walked down the escalator, wearing a mischievous grin for a mask. Once outside, he stood in front of a large pane window that afforded him a view of the escalator. His adrenaline rushing, the chill was unmistakable. He stuffed his hands into his pockets before instinctively reaching back to hold the door for a woman pushing a pram.

As he smiled at the young mother, he marveled at how the word pram, a word that he'd once described as a snooty substitute for stroller, had managed to creep its way into his vocabulary. In the hospitals surrounding the nation's capitol, he'd heard the word used with a greater frequency than he did in the Midwest. The international patients as well as those from Asian and African nations all used the word pram along with some of the more affluent white patients, mostly those bred along the eastern seaboard, he learned when he researched the trend. The less affluent white patients and even the affluent African American patients who found themselves strolling through the hospital on their way to the pediatric clinic still referred to a baby carriage as a stroller. Her use of the word pram should have confirmed his suspicion that she was a member of the ultra privileged class, her mall job not withstanding. He spit the bitter thought of her from his lips, remembering that a prior youthful display of quick decision making had earned him the nickname Dark Cloud.

His frigid fingers found their way back to his mouth and formed a funnel for more warm air. He trembled as the hawk whipped around the building and bullied its way into his jacket. Defenseless, David wondered if Chicago was the only city that nicknamed its wind "the hawk" or if it was a universal term for frigid winds. He tried to remember if he'd heard anyone in Washington D.C. refer to the wind as the hawk. He couldn't remember. He tapped his feet to create body heat as the hawk reentered the ring for round two, causing him to shiver and wish that he had paused long enough to wear a sweater on top of his cotton shirt. David seldom wore a sweater to the hospital, even though he knew that wearing a thin leather jacket against the hawk was like an amateur entering the ring to box with Muhammad Ali better known as "the Champ" in his prime, neither would prove a fair match against the more experienced prize fighters, both strong and ferocious enough to earn their own nicknames. His time spent dealing with the lake effect elements was limited as his commute consisted of a brief drive from his building's heated parking garage to the heated doctor's parking garage at Northwestern Memorial Hospital with seldom a stop in between. If he did stop unexpectedly, he knew that he had a leather jacket riding shotgun in the passenger seat. He deemed it fate that he had at least worn his jacket into the hospital that morning instead of leaving it in the car as was his custom. He told himself that was yet another sign that his mission was meant to be. In actuality, it was a coincidence that he'd worn the jacket, placing it around his shoulders to run inside the drugstore to buy a birthday card for his administrative assistant. The sun hadn't made a cameo appearance in several days, so the sunglasses were not necessary, but he donned them nonetheless, glad that he had found them tucked inside an interior jacket pocket. He checked his outer pockets hoping to locate an abandoned pair of gloves, but knew that effort was futile.

Even the inflections in her voice sounded like a ghost from his past. He closed his eyes and listened.

"I want to walk, Miss Stella," the soft voice pleaded. "I don't want to take a taxi. Mom doesn't like us riding in taxis unless it's really far, remember? It's not that far. We walked here. Let's walk back," she pleaded. "Mom likes for us to get exercise after we eat."

David smiled as the child confirmed his hunch that they didn't live very far from the hospital.

"It's just so chilly now. I guess if we walk quickly, we'll warm up. It just feels like the temperature dropped since we had lunch," Stella said, gripping one girl by each hand. "I should have brought the pram," she nodded.

"We're too big for the pram," the twin protested. "Mom says that we are big girls now, and we should walk."

"I miss the pram," the other twin sighed and yawned.

David raised one eyebrow hearing the word pram peel from the lips of the portly African American caregiver and her two young biracial charges. His thoughts raced. Your hunch is preposterous, David. It's a hunch and a hope. If you quiz that little intern, and you're wrong, he will think you're a stalker. Don't give those interns any reason to come up with another nickname for you. Dark Cloud suits you. Like Darth Vader, the sniffling interns tremble when you enter the room. Keep it that way. Follow the hunch. If you're wrong, no one is the wiser.

The trio crossed the street at Huron and headed south on Columbus Drive. Their pace slow and carefree, Stella and the girls were bundled in winter coats, boots, hats, scarves, mittens and gloves, unthreatened by the wind whipping wrappers and litter from the overflowing trash can at the corner of Grand Avenue and Columbus Drive. He was careful to keep at least a street block of distance behind the trio. At the Chicago River, David watched as Stella gripped their hands tighter to walk across the bridge, the wind swirling bolder in the openness that was the river. He slowed his pace when he noticed that the pedestrian traffic had thinned and watched as the group slowly ascended a metal stairwell from lower Wacker Drive and vanished out of sight. He remembered that the stairwell was located just a few blocks from Grant Park. He counted to ten and then quickly ascended the same stairs two at a time, hoping that the climb had winded the elderly caregiver and slowed her pace. It had. Her gait now visibly slower, she headed south and crossed at the corner, bending to whisper something to the twin who lagged behind and had wished for the pram. He found himself facing the Fairmont Hotel and watched as an elderly black doorman greeted Stella and ushered the girls into a tall building on the corner overlooking Grant Park and directly across the street from the Fairmont Hotel.

୨୦୯

"Hey Teenie," Rashanda squealed. "You made it!"

"Look at how big my little pookies have gotten," Maria cooed rising from her stool. "You two are looking more and more like your Auntie Maria every day. You are little red foxes just like me. Come give your mom's prettiest friend a hug," she said as the girls ran into her arms.

"Auntie Maria," the twins sang as they ran into her outstretched arms.

"What about me? Am I just chopped liver now?" Teenie teased. "I haven't seen you in a few months, and I don't even get a hug?"

Maria released her bear hug on the twins and gave Teenie a squeeze. "You need to gain some more weight, Tanisha Denise Carlson-Kraft," Maria observed. "You are a bag of bones."

"I'm working on it," replied Teenie. "Between the running and the yoga, I'm back down to my purse snatching weight, so I've been trying to eat more bad stuff. In fact, I've been eating crunchy Cheetos again," she added. "You know I swore off the Cheetos and junk food when I gained that freshman fifteen at Yale, but looking at the desserts on the counter, I will be gaining some of that weight back today, that's for sure. Holy moly!" she squealed. "Look at all of this food. This is great."

"It's a bit out of control, if you ask me," Maria offered.

"No one asked you," Justine replied.

"Most of us can't eat sweets and not gain weight anymore," she acknowledged, patting her mid section. "So I will be watching you guys eat. Teenie, I think you're skinnier than you were in high school," observed Maria. "I hope I get my figure back after having a baby," she sighed. "And you had twins!"

"You will," Teenie reassured. "Your mother got her figure back, so you'll be fine. I also lost quite a bit of weight when Brian died. Some people overeat when they are stressed, and some forget to eat," she shrugged. "I had to be reminded to eat."

At the mention of Brian's death, Maria's face suddenly turned sad, and her head tilted to the side warmly. Teenie smiled and winked at her friend before turning to greet the other girls. "Tomoko! Grace! Justine! Rashanda!" she sang loudly. "Hail, hail, the gang's all here! It's so good to see all of you," she beamed brightly. "I've been looking forward to this all week. You have no idea! Rashanda, the house looks beautiful! Where's Christine Marie? The twins have been worrying me silly about when they would see Christine Marie," Teenie stated, working the room and embracing each of her friends as Portia and Jeniece made the rounds like their mother and hugged each woman warmly.

"Christine Marie is in the backyard with Ian helping get set up for the party," Rashanda shared eyeing Teenie curiously. "Portia & Jeniece, go on out back. You can help Uncle Ian put up the volleyball net," suggested Rashanda as she opened the French doors and pointed. "Or you can play on the new swing set that Auntie Grace bought for Christine's last birthday, even though she knows we're moving and don't need a play set."

"What?" Grace shrugged. "That backyard is huge, and it was just screaming for a play set. Besides, I like to swing, so I can play on it when I come to Chicago."

"Have you decided what you're going to do with the house when Ian and Rashanda move out?" Teenie asked.

"My parents will still be in the guest house, so they can keep an eye on it. I may allow charities to hold functions here. Justine's friend Kendal is going to be having a chapter member party here this summer," she added.

"That's right, I forgot Kendal talked to you about that. It's the tenth anniversary of his coming out, so he's going to throw a grand party. He always does some wild theme for his parties, so it should be a lot of fun," Justine smiled. "Kendal will be here this afternoon. Grace told me to invite him to her mom's birthday party."

"Oh great! I've wanted to meet the infamous Kendal that I've heard so much about," Teenie gushed.

"He's been looking forward to meeting you too. I'm warning you, he will probably give you a nickname and invite you to his summer bash himself," paused Justine. "If he likes you, he'll give you a nickname," she corrected, her eyes slanting toward Maria.

"You can count me out," Maria said loudly. "A lawn full of gays and lesbians parading around is not my idea of a good time. I'll be in Philly anyway, so I'll miss that freak show."

"That's enough, Maria. You're being rude," Rashanda scolded.

"I am a grown woman. I can say whatever I want, and I'm entitled to my opinion. In my opinion, I don't think it's natural for women to be with women, and men to be with men. There I said it. Nothing personal Grace and Tomoko, but I think it's gross," she shared, staring directly at Tomoko.

Grace tilted her head and stared at her fingers, her head shaking from side to side. It was Tomoko who spoke.

"It's okay. We are accustomed to this type of behavior, many people do not understand. My own parents do not understand. I just hope that we can be friends, Maria."

In typical Maria dramatic fashion, she rolled her eyes at Tomoko and spun around on her stool, her back facing Tomoko and Grace.

"It's getting way too heavy in here. Let's all go back to our happy place everyone. Today is a day of celebration," Teenie encouraged.

Rashanda watched as Teenie pranced around the counter,

inhaling the desserts on the island, and grinning from ear to ear.

"Aren't you in a good mood, missy," Rashanda noticed suspiciously.

"I try to stay in a good mood. Happy people have more fun."

"Something seems different about you, Teenie."

"I'm the same old me," she smiled. "You're just so accustomed to seeing me moping and grieving. I feel like a storm cloud has been following me around for the past two years, and now it's finally sunny again. It's literally sunny in my life and a brilliant light has filled my heart," she smiled, gripping her hands to her heart. "Look outside! It's the first week in April, and it's sunny and in the seventies. How can you not be in a good mood on such a beautiful day? My best friends are here, and I am just happy. I feel like Mary Tyler Moore twirling at the end of her show. I wish I had a hat to toss into the air," she bursted.

"Nobody watches that old show," Maria groaned.

"I love that show you little sourpuss. Besides, it's been too long since we were all together for a happy occasion, and I've really missed you guys."

"Today is the day that Rev. Dr. Martin Luther King, Jr. was assassinated," Justine shared.

"Well, thanks for that random downer," Maria scowled. "We could have done without knowing that."

"April 4th is the day that he died. Operation Push hosted a prayer breakfast in honor of him today. I saw it in the paper this morning."

"It is, isn't it? How ironic. I didn't realize that," she paused. "Well, it's a day of celebration today. We'll make sure that we give a toast for Dr. King at today's festivities," she smiled. "It's your mom's seventieth birthday, and the temperatures are in the seventies, and it's a beautiful day!" gushed Teenie. "The girls and I are late because church was late dismissing. It was a powerful message though, so I'm glad we went."

"My mother always says that taking time to enjoy God's Sabbath day of rest and going to church adds sunshine to your Sunday even when it's cloudy. She made that up so that Neal and I would willingly go to church," Maria added brightly. "At least she's in a good mood," she mumbled under her breath to the back of Rashanda's head, staring at Teenie curiously. "Rashanda is right, Teenie. You just seem a little different. Maybe it's your hair. That's what it is. Your hair is much longer. I love your hair long, by the way. I don't think I've ever seen your hair past your shoulders."

Her fingers instinctively raked through her longer tresses. "It was the twins. My hair grew like crazy when I was pregnant with them. It was the added estrogen in my system and the prenatal vitamins, so I decided to keep it long. Brian liked it longer," she smiled. "I can say his name now. It took me many hours of therapy to even say his name without crying. It's okay if you guys say his name too," she added. "Don't swallow it or apologize if you bring him up. The therapist told me that was part of the grief process."

"Are you still in therapy?" Tomoko asked boldly.

Maria stared at Tomoko and rolled her eyes in an exaggerated manner. "What kind of question is that to ask someone? That's personal!" Maria screamed. Rashanda covered Maria's mouth with her hand before she could finish her rant.

"It's okay, I don't mind answering that. Not anymore, Tomoko. I still participate in the grief counseling group at church, but I'm not seeing the psychiatrist any more," she explained while exhaling slowly through her nose. "It's time to get ourselves in party mode, ladies! Is everyone coming that you invited, Grace? Who all did you invite again?" Teenie asked.

"Well, all of our parents will be here. Except Justine's father, of course," corrected Rashanda.

"That would be a mess since my mother is bringing Bob," Justine added.

"I can't believe that Andrea is still dating that realtor guy. Apple-tree. You're dating a white guy, and so is your mother. I guess the apple doesn't fall far from the tree," Maria giggled to herself. The group ignored her.

"Yup, they're still going strong. He wants to get married, but she doesn't. I think she'll marry him eventually, but she's waiting until my youngest brother is eighteen and moves out."

"That's what my mother did," Maria added. "She waited until Neal went away to college, and then she lived on her own for two years before marrying Richard. My mother had never lived on her own since she married my dad when she was nineteen. Thank goodness I lived in a dorm for a couple of years, so I lived alone a little bit, but then I had that roommate, so maybe that doesn't count."

"Apple-tree," Tomoko said. "Your mother married young and so did you."

Maria stared at the newest member to the girl circle, unsure how to respond. Grace grinned at Tomoko's bravado.

"Of course, Maria's dad isn't coming either since Liz is bringing Richard," added Rashanda.

"Your mom is definitely bringing Jeni Kaye, right?" asked Teenie. "I want Portia and Jeniece to get to know her."

"Yup, they're bringing Jeni Kaye since the invitation said that it was a family party. Mama Kaye is also coming because I haven't seen her in a while," Maria added. "My parents are scooping John from the airport. They should be here in about an hour."

"That's perfect," Teenie grinned. "I haven't seen John since Brian's funeral."

Again, there was a slight awkward silence when Teenie mentioned the funeral.

"Speaking of Brian," Maria paused. "Rashanda just told us that Brian's parents are coming to the party."

"Uh, huh. They are," Teenie nodded. "Since we're so close to Lake Forest, I thought I should invite them so that they can spend time with the twins. They're going to take the girls home with them for a sleepover tonight. I want you guys to get to know them better since you will be seeing more of them whenever I entertain. Even though Brian is gone, his parents are my girls' grandparents, so they're family. Plus, they're cool, so they'll fit right in. In fact, they're bringing a few more people with them. Their friends wanted to meet the twins," she stammered somewhat nervously. "The more the merrier, right? Caterers always prepare more than enough food," she smiled.

"Maybe we should just tell her so she can get mentally prepared," Rashanda blurted.

"Get mentally prepared for what?" Teenie asked, straddling the bar stool and joining the girls at the island.

"You're right," Maria nodded. "I'll handle this. Teenie, before we tell you what's going on, just know that I take full responsibility for this idea. I know you don't like surprises, but since you're in such a good mood, I don't want you to go off and ruin the party vibe up in here," giggled Maria nervously. "It's Grace's mother's seventieth birthday, and we haven't been together in a long time," she cleared her throat before continuing. "At the time, we thought that it sounded like a good idea. Sometimes things seem like a good idea in your head, and in theory, but in reality or practice, the same idea turns out not to be such a good idea. It might still be a good idea. We really won't know until we know. You know what I mean?" she continued without waiting for a reply. "Now keep in mind that when we conceived this idea, we didn't have all the facts. For instance, we had no way of knowing that you were going to invite Brian's parents to the party. With that added piece of information, we would have made a different decision. Just keep that in mind as you consider the options before you."

"Maria, this is not an opening statement in court," Rashanda groaned. "Teenie, what she's trying to say is that we invited one of your, uh old friends to the party. I don't know if we have time to go into it now, but almost a year ago Justine and I ran into an old friend of yours," stammered Rashanda, her eyes squinting as Teenie's grin grew wider and wider.

"A very old friend," Maria echoed. "A friend that you haven't mentioned in a while, but someone that we thought that you might be happy to see again. But even if you're not happy to see this person, please promise us that you are not going to erupt like a volcano."

"We thought it would be safe to invite the friend to the party since there will be so many other people here," Justine added as Rashanda and Maria nodded in agreement. Tomoko and Grace watched from the kitchen table. "That way, if you're not happy to see this friend, you can ignore this person and go on about your business."

"Exactly," Maria agreed. "We thought it would be fun to surprise you."

"You guys know I hate surprises."

"We know, we know. But just this one time, we need you to go along and play along."

"Well, if it's supposed to be a surprise," paused Teenie, her face serious and stern. "Why are you telling me?"

"Because you're in such a good mood, and it's Mrs. Dudley's birthday party, and it's a festive occasion," Maria rattled nervously.

"They don't want you to ruin the mood by going off when you see their surprise," Tomoko added.

Maria glared at Tomoko and swallowed her words as Grace whispered something to her yoga partner.

The other girls stared at Teenie for a reaction, but looked away as the French door leading to the patio creaked open and Portia and

Jeniece ran inside with Christine Marie on their heels. "Mom! They're here! Deebo and Lydia are here!"

"Are you serious? They're at least an hour early. Where are they?" Teenie asked quickly, jumping to her feet.

"They call their grandparents by their first name? What kind of name is Deebo? Or did she say Dumbo?" Rashanda asked.

"I think she said Deebo," Maria shrugged. "Is that a nickname, Teenie? I've never heard you call Brian's parents by their first names. You just call them Mr. and Mrs. Kraft."

"I call Brian's parents Mom and Dad," corrected Teenie gently. "Deebo and Lydia aren't Brian's parents."

"I saw the car pull up. They're here! Deebo and Lydia are here!" Jeniece squealed again jumping up and down. "They pulled up to that little house in front of this house. Should we go get them?"

"That's a good idea, sweetie. Why don't you do that," Teenie grinned mischievously, covering her nose and mouth with her hand.

Rashanda and Maria stared at each other and shrugged. "They must have parked in the driveway at the guest house. Everybody does that when they first visit this big house," Rashanda deduced, standing to her feet. "I'll get the caterer to station one of the workers outside near the guesthouse so they can wave the cars back to the main driveway so people don't park way up there and have to hoof it way back here. Are these the Kraft's friends that you were talking about? I hope they're not old and infirm. That's at least a quarter mile walk from the guest house."

"No..." Teenie started before being interrupted.

"Wait a minute. I thought you said that his parents' friends were coming to meet the twins," Maria noted. "How do the twins already know what kind of car they drive and know their names?"

"I have something to tell you guys."

"What's going on Teenie?" asked Rashanda.

Teenie stared at her friends and took several deep cleansing breaths like she'd perfected in yoga class. She breathed the air in through her nostrils and exhaled through her nostrils in a measured rhythmic pattern, stalling for time as she chose her words carefully.

Grace and Tomoko walked over to the island and leaned against the sink. Maria folded her arms across her chest and tilted her head to the side. Justine helped herself to a glass, filled it with ice and turned on the faucet.

"Pour me a glass of water too," Teenie requested, her eyes shifting from friend to friend as she bit her lip. She chugged her water and waved her glass at Justine for more. "Well, one of the reasons that I'm in such a good mood is that I can finally tell you guys what's been going on with me," she paused without sipping from the fresh glass of water that Justine placed in her hand. The only noise that she heard was the sound of her own measured breath. "David Barton is here."

"How'd you know that we invited David Barton?" Maria exhaled. "We were so worried that you might flip out and act a fool, and you knew the whole time. You let us give that little speech and everything," she exhaled with a giggle. "I'm so relieved. Wait a minute? Who told you? Rashanda told you didn't she? Rashanda, you still cannot keep a secret. I knew you would tell her," Maria ranted.

Rashanda waved her hand in Maria's face to silence her and stared at Teenie suspiciously.

"How do you know that David Barton is here?" Justine asked.

"I've been waiting for the right moment to tell you guys, but I wanted to tell everybody when we were all together, but we're never all together at the same time, so when Grace said that she wanted to throw a seventieth birthday party for her mother, it made sense."

"What made sense?" Maria asked. "I'm confused."

"I knew this would be the best way to tell everyone. It couldn't have worked out more perfectly, if I'd penned it in a novel. When Maria said that she was flying in for Mrs. Dudley's party and everyone would finally be at the same place at the same time, I knew it could work."

"What could work?" interrupted Maria.

"If you would stop interrupting me for a second, I'll tell you," she breathed. "David and I have been dating for over a year," she paused.

Without exception, every jaw in the kitchen fell ajar, and each girl found herself speechless. "When Grace told me that she was planning this birthday party for her mom, I called Mrs. Dudley and asked her if it would be okay for us to share in her seventieth birthday celebration, and announce that we are dating. She loved the idea. She really loved the idea of keeping it a secret from everybody."

"Oh my God, Teenie. You and David Barton have been dating for over a year? And you didn't tell any of us? Why?" Maria asked.

"There's more to the story, so I may as well let the cat all the way out of the bag," she giggled. "David and I are getting married!"

A hushed silence washed over the room.

"Are you serious? You're kidding right?" Rashanda asked.

"Nope," Teenie giggled.

"You guys are getting married?"

"Yup."

"When?"

"Here. This afternoon. It's a birthday party and wedding combo platter," she grinned. "Surprise!"

"Seriously, Teenie? You're kidding aren't you? You hate surprises."

"I know, that's what makes it so much fun. You guys were trying to sneak and surprise me, but instead I surprised you. David talked to my parents last week. My dad was excited because my parents know that we've been dating. They're the only people that know that we've been seeing each other. Well, that's not true. David's parents and his sister Claire knew, and Laura and Monica knew too," she listed.

"Laura and Monica? Your white friends from Yale? Those girls you met at camp?" Maria's face furrowed into a deep frown, a look of perplexity racing from one raised eyebrow to the next. "You told them before you told us? Why would you tell them first?" demanded Maria.

"I needed to tell someone, and I'm really close to them. What's the big deal? Plus, I knew that if I told one of you guys, it would be on the grapevine lickity split since none of you heifers can keep a secret. The only person who could keep a secret was Lori, may she rest in peace."

"What's a heifer?" Tomoko asked.

"Is she really this clueless? A heifer is a female cow. Duh. It's slang in the black community. Grace, if you're going to have her around, you need to teach your friend some black slang," Maria dismissed rolling her eyes at Tomoko. "Teenie, I can't believe that you told some random white girls that you were dating David Barton before you told us."

"You know what, Maria? You need to grow up," she spat. "Laura and Monica are not some random white girls. They are my friends," Teenie scowled at Maria, her tone stern and loud. Raising her palm as though signaling a yield, she placed her index finger to her lips and took a sip of water followed by a long cleansing breath and painted on a slight smile before continuing. This time her tone was firm yet softer, almost mom like. "Laura and Monica are as important to me as each of you." Teenie fanned her hands wide. "I've practically known them almost as long as I've known you guys. They will be here this afternoon, and I expect you to be kind to them, Maria. A little tolerance goes a long way, my friend. People are people. Life's too short for all of your silly hang-ups and what not. Learn to enjoy the world through a nonjudgmental lens," she grinned patting Maria's shoulder.

"Teenie's right," the voice stammered slowly. "You need to be nicer, Maria, and stop being so mean to Tomoko," Grace said firmer, borrowing the wind from Teenie's correction of Maria. "Tomoko hasn't done anything to you, and I'm sick of you yelling at her like she's a dog. If you can't treat my friend with respect, you can get out of my house, Maria!" Grace barked, her voice rising with each word.

Checkmate. The girls stared from Grace to Maria, unaccustomed to docile Grace demonstrating anger. Justine covered her mouth with her hand to suppress a giggle that wanted to escape like air from a deflated balloon.

"What's all that about? Did I miss something?" Teenie whispered to Rashanda.

"Just Maria being Maria before you got here."

"Okay, everybody, let's calm down. Today is my wedding day. I've had a rough couple of years, and I'm finally smiling again. See?" she grinned in a grimacing smile so wide that her back molars were displayed which made all the girls smile and laugh. "There will be no fighting or kicking people out of houses. I am declaring today an argument free zone. Today is a double celebration," she clapped. "As such, it's time for a group hug. Everybody come on into the circle of love. The bride needs a hug. Give me some love. Rapido! Vamos!" she ordered in Spanish. The girls encircled each other and giggled, Maria found her arm around Tomoko's shoulder.

"Do they know that you're getting married?" Maria asked softly as they huddled around the dessert island.

"Laura and Monica? Nope. I kept it a secret from them too. They just think they're coming to spend time with the twins and get to know you guys better."

"Well, at least they don't know all your little secrets," sighed Maria. "You are like a stealth secret keeper. I talk to you almost every day, and

I had no idea you were spending time with David Barton," she pouted, her lower lip poked out as far as she could extend it.

Teenie embraced her childhood friend, softly stroking her back. "It's been killing me too. I really wanted to tell you guys, but I wanted to wait and make sure that it was real. That it wasn't some weird rebound thing. David and I have so much history together," she sighed. "And with him being divorced and me being widowed I just wanted to experience getting to know him one on one without any well meaning distractions."

"I totally get that," Justine agreed. "That's why I didn't tell you guys that AM and I were dating again right away."

Her lower lip now in its proper place, Maria replied. "Chick, you didn't tell us that you and AM were an item until AM had transferred to Northwestern Medical School and moved back to Chicago."

"Wow!" exclaimed Rashanda. "Teenie is getting married! Today! And here we were worried that you'd be mad at us for inviting David Barton to surprise you! This is surreal!"

"I'm so happy for you, Teenie."

"Thanks, Grace," she sighed. "This is going to be the best day ever. My Grandma Bootsy and my aunts, uncles and cousins that live in Chicago are coming up, but they just think they're coming up to meet the twins' grandparents for the first time. They met them briefly at Brian's funeral, but there were so many people there that they didn't get to spend any time getting to know them. I told them that it was a bar-b-cue, so no one will be dressed up for a seventieth birthday party. My uncles will probably come in with a case of beer, because they do not roll empty handed so have a cooler ready. I'm warning you now, they will flirt with each of you, whether your man is with you or not," Teenie smiled. "My brothers are bringing their girlfriends so you'll get to meet their chicken heads."

"Why do you call them chicken heads?" Maria laughed.

"They're not chicken heads. They're all pretty, and two of them are smart, but one of them is as simple as a penny. I will let you guys determine for yourselves who Simple Simon is," Teenie paused.

"Is your brother still dating that Keri Peck white girl from high school? Tell me he's not, and please tell me that Byron and Allen are dating black girls."

"No, Jack, Jr. and Keri broke up in college. And yes, they're all dating black girls, not that it matters," Teenie swatted Maria's shoulder. "My brothers don't know that we're getting married, and neither does David's sister and brother. His brother isn't coming, but Claire is bringing her family. Her son Barton is going to be the ring bearer."

The look on her face was animated and almost exaggerated. "Ooooh, oooh, oooh," she crooned like a chimpanzee. "There's one more thing that I forgot to tell you. When we told David's parents that we were getting married, his mom pulled me into their study and told me that she was glad that I was marrying her son," Teenie fanned. "She pulled me into this big bear hug and said how happy she was that I would be a part of their family. But then, her face got serious and she told me that she already knew a member of my family," Teenie paused.

"Who?" Maria asked. "One of your aunts? From the sorority, right?"

"Nope. My mother. David's mother already knew my mother."

"Billie? How does she know Billie?"

"David's mother was my mother's psychiatrist!" Teenie shared. "Can you believe that?"

"His mother is a shrink, I mean a psychiatrist?" Maria corrected.

"Yup. She's a psychiatrist. All these years I never knew what type of doctor his mother was. I was really just getting to know them when David got Rachel pregnant and got married, so I stopped coming around the family, and she practices under her maiden name as Dr. Elliott (Elle) Ernestine Dudley, so even if I had known the name of my mother's psychiatrist, it wouldn't have registered. Is that tripped out or what?"

"How did she know that Billie was your mother?"

"Well, even though my mother doesn't see her professionally any more, they still keep in touch. She came to my mother's graduation open house when she got her degree, and Mrs. Barton saw my high school graduation picture in the living room. She didn't say anything to my mother because by then David was married to Rachel, and she wasn't sure if my parents had even met David."

"Does your mother know that her psychiatrist is David's mother?"

"She does now. I told her as soon as I left David's house. David wanted his parents to meet mine after he asked my dad for permission to marry me, so his parents invited my parents to join them for dinner at their country club. Portia wasn't feeling well, so I didn't go."

"He asked your dad for permission to marry you?" Grace asked.

"Yup," Teenie smiled.

The group awed in unison. "That is so incredibly sweet," Maria added. "My dad was pissed with John for not doing that. John wanted to do it, but I told him that it was old fashioned, and that you don't do that when you're eloping or it defeats the elopement element of surprise."

"Brian wanted to call my dad too, but I told him the same thing. Remember when you called and told your dad that you and John eloped on April 1st? He thought it was an April Fool's Day prank? I still have our double wedding photo in a frame on a shelf in the bedroom that I use as an office," Teenie shared, staring at the Tiffany sapphire ring that adorned her right ring finger and twirling the ring from side to side with her thumb.

"Were you embarrassed to find out that your new mother-in-law is your mother's psychiatrist?" Maria asked.

"I wouldn't say that I was embarrassed," she paused. "I was definitely surprised. I probably would have been embarrassed had I known this in high school," Teenie corrected. "I used to be ashamed of my mother's mental illness, but I'm not anymore. She takes her medication, and my dad helps her manage it. My mother wasn't embarrassed when she found out either. She likes David's mother and they still keep in touch. I think it's sad how we place a stigma on people who have mental health issues. People aren't ashamed when they have cancer or other illnesses," she paused. "Laura and Monica's mother have mental health issues too. Did I tell you that? Laura's mother is bipolar like Billie, and Monica's mother suffers from severe depression," she shrugged.

"Do you think it's hereditary?" Grace asked.

"I've researched that a little, and the data is inconclusive. While I was managing my grief, there were days that I didn't want to get out of the bed, so the doctor put me on an anti-depressant. I was worried that I was developing a mental illness," she confessed. "But the doctor told me that was normal during a grieving process. I plan to watch the twins closely and get them whatever help they need just in case. And it will help that their grandmother is a board certified psychiatrist, so she can help diagnose any symptoms," she grinned. "The twins will have three sets of grandparents. How about that? Before I forget. Claire is pregnant again. Did I tell you guys that already? She's still in her first trimester. It's been so hard keeping all of these secrets. There's so much that I've wanted to tell you guys, but I couldn't," rattled Teenie. "I'm so glad that this day has finally come. Grace, before I forget, since I've invited like thirty extra people, David and I insist on splitting the party costs with you fifty-fifty," added Teenie. "My dad said he would pay for the reception, but David said he would do it. They were arguing over who would pay. Can you believe that? My cheap father was insisting that he would take care of it."

"It's a daddy-daughter pride thing. You're still his little girl," Rashanda reminded.

"I won't accept money from any of you. Don't be silly," Grace dismissed, waving her hand across her face. "We were doing all of this for my mom's birthday celebration anyway. Now we have two reasons to celebrate. Consider it my wedding present."

"Grace has more money than she knows what to do with, Teenie. Let her pay the bill," Maria offered. "Tomoko, are you and Grace still planning to start that foundation?" she asked sheepishly.

"It's Grace's foundation actually," Tomoko replied startled. "Her attorneys are drafting the papers."

"This is the charitable foundation that you talked about, right?" Teenie asked.

"Yup. I thought that it was time that I started contributing to charitable causes that are important to me too. I'm not going to alter any of the ones that my grandparents started, but I wanted to start a foundation of my own."

"Are you going to call it the Grace Dudley Moore foundation? You legally added Moore to your name didn't you?"

"I did, but I don't want to use my legal name. I'd rather not let people know that I'm linked to the Moore wealth. I want to protect my privacy for a little while longer. Tomoko and I have been trying to think of foundation names. We thought about naming it the Lydia Moore foundation after my biological mother. Do you guys have any suggestions?"

The girls stared at Teenie.

"Why is everyone looking at me?"

"Because you always have cute naming ideas. Remember, Project Strong?" Rashanda asked.

"Lori's Angels?" Justine added.

She brushed the top of her shoulder with her fingertips. "I guess I am ever the clever one aren't I?" she bemused in a bad British brogue. "What is the philanthropic thrust of the foundation? I can't just come up with a name without knowing some background information. What are your key objectives?"

"We want the foundation to promote harmony and understanding," Tomoko said proudly, and with finality, nodding her head for emphasis, like a declarative punctuation mark at the end of a sentence.

"Harmony and understanding?" Teenie repeated. "That's too broad. I need you to be more specific. What type of harmony and understanding?"

"Racial harmony, respect for diversity, tolerance for gays and lesbians," she listed boldly.

"And even acceptance for people with mental health issues," Grace suggested. "We want to use the foundation funds to help people get along and understand each other better. To help eradicate stereotypes and prejudices through education and communication."

"What about calling it the Lydia Moore and Charles Lovett Foundation. It would be a way to link your parents even though they were forbidden to be linked because of the social stigmas of the times?"

"I had the same idea, Teenie," Grace beamed. "But Chip thinks it would dishonor his late wife to do that since he and my mother had an affair. But you get the idea. I want the foundation funds to be used to educate and inform in a hands on real way where people spend time with different types of people, and after the experience their attitudes are transformed. Their eyes are opened and they realize that people are people."

"I get it. Like what happens at summer camp," Teenie offered.

Grace and Tomoko's eyes lit up excitedly as Tomoko applauded and raised both thumbs in the air. "Exactly! One of our ideas is to offer a summer camp experience. It's like you're in our heads, Teenie."

"A camp for kids, right?"

"Yes, and no. We were thinking we would sponsor a summer camp for kids and a separate camp for adults. We'll work with school guidance counselors and invite students from different backgrounds and neighborhoods so they have a chance to mix and mingle with kids from different races and different socioeconomic backgrounds."

"That's a good idea, but how will this be different from the camps offered through the YMCA? Those camps are usually filled with kids from different backgrounds," Maria challenged.

"Yes, but the YMCA camp offers a traditional camp experience, and they don't usually address issues of tolerance. Our camp would target leaders at various schools and would allow them to talk freely about their hangups, stereotypes, fears and prejudices, and then we would work with the campers to plant seeds of tolerance to help change those attitudes, and give them the tools to take what they've learned back to their schools and neighborhoods and plant more seeds of tolerance. We're finding that some of the poorest kids in Champaign are white and there are many affluent African American kids whose parents are on staff at the University of Illinois and those kids attend private school. But when most of the white college students see the black kids, they assume the black kids are the poor kids. So we want to mix it up and help break up some of the obvious stereotypes that exist. The black kids aren't always the poor kids, the Asian kids aren't always the smart kids. We want to have a camp where all kids feel welcome and they can learn about other groups in a safe, non threatening environment."

"During the school year, we'll allow companies to have diversity training sessions at the camp, and the participants would sleep in cabins and be taught to embrace that time in their youth before the world's prejudices filled their brains," added Tomoko. "Encouraging them to embrace their inner child, that magical time when kids just played with other kids at school or on the playground regardless of the person's race, socioeconomic status or sexual preference."

"I get it," Teenie chewed on her bottom lip. "I really like the idea. Let me think about it for a while and I'll see if I can come up with something cute and catchy."

"This is all well and good, and I'm glad that you guys are planning to be all altruistic and save the world, but I'm starving. Do you have anything to snack on, Rashanda?" Maria shared.

"Camp Colorblind!" Teenie blurted. "You should call it 'The Camp Colorblind Foundation.' People who are colorblind only see shades of gray. They don't see color or differences. Just images. Get it? It works on several levels," she said definitively.

Grace and Tomoko stared at each other. "The Camp Colorblind Foundation," Grace repeated. "I like it. It's really cute."

"That's really cute," Tomoko smiled.

"What do you guys think?"

"I love it."

"Me too. It's perfect."

"I'll have my attorneys run that title through the licensing department and see if it's available. I knew you would come up with something clever and cute, Teenie. Before I forget, my mom knew about the wedding secret the whole time?" asked Grace.

"She did, but she assured me that she would keep it a secret."

"That's my mom. Ethel and Greg Dudley are great secret keepers.

I remember my mother telling me that when they worked for my grandparents, they learned that it was best to keep silent about the affairs of the rich and privileged," Grace said. "Now it makes sense why my mom didn't make a fuss when I told her that I wanted to have her party catered and have a tent setup in the backyard with a Dee jay and balloons. And when she told me that she wanted to invite the parents of Christine Marie's classmates at school, and the Roycemore teachers, I thought that was odd," Grace laughed. "She was upping the catering count to cover for your extra people wasn't she, Teenie?"

"She was. I think your mother was more excited than I was when I told her our idea to just surprise all the guests and get married at her birthday party. She was tickled pink," Teenie grinned. "I love your mom."

"Teenie, we are not dressed for a wedding," Maria observed, her eyes wandering the kitchen and staring at the display of casual spring attire.

"Yes, you are," Teenie smiled. "We wanted everyone to be casual. I'm so glad that your mom agreed to the backyard bar-b-cue theme, so everyone could come dressed casual. By the way, you guys are all my bridesmaids and you're going to be standing at the altar with me. Laura and Monica will be bridesmaids too. I figured that you would all have your hair and nails done for the birthday party anyway," Teenie acknowledged knowingly. "Portia, Jeniece, Christine Marie and Jeni Kaye are my flower girls. Tomoko, I want you to read a poem that we've selected."

"Are you wearing that?" Maria asked eyeing Teenie's khakis suspiciously. "Please tell me that you're not getting married in that," she groaned.

"Shut up, Maria! I have a simple white sundress with a white cardigan that I'm going to wear, but I probably don't need the cardigan now because it's so warm today. David is just wearing tan slacks and a white shirt. We're wearing matching flip flops. It's a no fuss affair," she smiled. "I plan to change back into my khakis or jeans after the photos so we can play volleyball. I'm also wearing the pearls that Brian gave me for our first wedding anniversary," she smiled, softly fingering the string of pearls encircling her neck.

"Do the girls know?" Rashanda asked.

"No. The twins cannot keep a secret. Brian's parents know," she paused.

"Are they okay with it?" Maria asked.

"They are. They met David a few weeks ago. I wanted them to meet him, so he came with us when we drove the girls to visit them in Lake Forest. They really like him. I called and told them that we were getting married after we told our parents. They're happy for us." Teenie nodded her head affirmatively. "They said that they are glad that I've met a kind man who loves me and the twins."

"Now I understand why my mom wanted to meet with the florist herself, she was working with you to get the flowers right. It's all coming together now," Grace added.

"Speaking of the florist, they're setting up the bouquets at your parents' house as we speak. We'll all have matching bouquets of tulips. I need to get over there and check on things. I told Deboe to park at the guest house until I told you guys what was going on," she paused. "Now that you guys know, you can come with me and say hi to Deboe."

"Why do you call him, Deboe? Is that his nickname?"

"Not really. Once he met the girls, I didn't want them to slip and use his real name, so we came up with a nickname for them to use in case they slipped and said his name around any of you. We didn't want to arouse any suspicion. I still call him David."

"You are so sneaky," Maria said, swatting Teenie's shoulder. "How long did it take you to get serious again? I want to hear that story," Maria insisted.

"There's no time now," Teenie explained. "I wanna go and peek at the flowers, and let David and Lydia know that you guys are now in on our little secret. But mums the word to the other guests!"

"Who's Lydia?" asked Rashanda.

"Oh, that's right. I forgot that I haven't explained everything. I've kept so many secrets that I can't remember what you guys know and don't know. David and Rachel finally worked out the custody battle and visitation schedule. Lydia is David's daughter with Rachel. She flies to Chicago as a UAM every other weekend to see him. She's a great girl. She'll be spending six weeks with us during the summer. The twins love her already."

"What's a UAM?" Tomoko asked.

"It's an unaccompanied minor. It's how the airlines classify and code minor children who are flying without an adult," Maria explained gently, smiling softly at Tomoko. Justine and Rashanda exchanged shocked glances, shifting their eyes and shrugging at Maria's uncharacteristic display of tenderness. "How does Rachel feel about David marrying you?" Maria continued.

"She's happy for us. She knows that I didn't break up their marriage. She broke up their marriage, so she has no beef with me. She's remarried now too."

"Chick! I hope you are not planning to slip away with Mr. Barton tonight for a honeymoon extravaganza, because if you are, we are going to kidnap you so you can bring us up to speed on all of your little secrets!" Maria announced. "Like, have you already had a honeymoon extravaganza with Dr. David Barton?" she giggled.

ৡৡ

Teenie stroked Portia's hair softly. "We're going to shampoo your hair in the morning, Portia-Smortia. I think there are cobwebs nesting in your mane."

"Mom! Don't talk about spiders! You know I don't like spiders. They give me the creepy crawlies."

"Hush, Portia," Eleanor Jeniece instructed. "Let mom finish her story."

"You're not the boss of me, just because you're eight minutes older. That doesn't make you the boss of me, does it Mom?"

"No, it doesn't, shadow," Teenie smiled, using the nickname that David had given Portia shortly after they got married when he watched how Portia trailed Tanisha from room to room in the old house. "I'm the only boss."

"What about Dad? Dad's the boss too."

"That's right. Dad's the boss at work, and he's the boss of you guys too, but not of me. Dad and I are partners," Teenie explained rubbing her swollen baby.

"So that's how you met our second Dad? He sent flowers to our downtown apartment and that's how you met him?"

"Well, I knew him before he sent the flowers. He sent the flowers to say hello to me because he and I hadn't talked in such a long time."

"What kind of flowers did he send again?"

"What's mom's favorite flower?" Teenie tested.

"Tulips!" the girls squealed simultaneously.

"That's right. He sent me tulips."

"How did he know where we lived?"

"Remember I told you that he saw you in the cafeteria having lunch with Uncle AM and Miss Stella and he decided to go for a walk to get some fresh air, and he just happened to see Miss Stella walk into our building. He asked Fred, the door man if we lived in the building."

"I miss Fred and our Chicago apartment," Jeniece whined. "Can we stay there this weekend, Mom?"

"That's a good idea, sweetie. Let's have a tourist weekend. We'll go to the Shedd Aquarium and the Art Institute."

"Let's go to the dinosaur museum too, Mom," Portia added. "I want to see the dinosaurs again. Maybe we can have lunch with Uncle AM and Dad at the hospital."

"That sounds good, but I don't know if we can go to all three museums, since the baby is due in two weeks. It's hard for me to walk around for a long time. Look how swollen my toes are," she pointed, wiggling her feet. "My fingers are so swollen that I can barely get my rings off. I have a Constitutional law exam on Tuesday, so I will have to study this weekend, but I will have Miss Stella come to the apartment and spend some time with you guys while I go to the Loyola law library."

"Is Miss Stella going to still help you when the baby comes and when you become a lawyer, Mom?"

"That's our plan, sweetie. She likes taking the train to Oak Park every day, so she said that she'll come and help with the baby for as long as we need her. I still have seven more classes to take before I graduate from law school and I need to study so it's time for bed girls."

"Say the wedding vows that you and Dad said again, Mom. I want to hear the vows again, please!" Portia pleaded, rubbing Tanisha's round belly and bouncing on the bed.

"I thought you had them memorized," Teenie teased. "Let me hear you say them."

"I want you to say them, Mom. Portia always forgets some parts."

"Okay. After I say the vows you two are going to bed. Close your eyes and let's hold hands," Teenie suggested as she closed her eyes and remembered back to that warm April day on the lake. "I'll say my vows first, and then I'll say your dad's vows," she explained with her eyes closed. "David, you are my best friend. I am elated that God has brought us together, and I know that our journey will be filled with love and grace. I am excited to walk this path with you holding my hand. I love you and am honored to be your wife."

"Now do the deep voice imitation and do Dad's part," Portia giggled.

Teenie coughed to clear her throat and lowered her voice. "Tanisha, I knew that...."

The girls giggled at her falsetto baritone and felt a firm warm hand grip theirs joined by a deep voice.

"Dad! You're home," Jeniece squealed rising to her feet and embracing David in a bear hug as Portia tumbled out of the bed and encircled David's other leg.

"I'm home a little early, but you two are up past your bedtime," he smiled. "But I'm glad because I missed you, and now I get live hugs and kisses from all my girls."

"Mom was telling us the wedding story again," Portia explained as Teenie slowly swung her swollen legs over the side of the bed and stood up.

"I can see that," David smiled. "I've been watching you guys in the doorway," he confessed. "Don't get up, Teenie. I'll put the girls to bed, I know you need to study."

"That works for me, but I have to pee," Teenie confessed.

"You and that bladder," David smiled.

"Your big head son uses my bladder as a pillow."

"Do we know it's a boy, Mom? Did you find out?"

"No, I didn't find out. Your dad knows, but I told him that I didn't want to know. I like being surprised."

"Say your vows, Dad," Portia ordered.

"I'll say them after your mom uses the bathroom."

"I can hold it. It's only fifty words," Teenie smiled.

"How do you know exactly how many words it is?"

"Because your mom said our vows had to be no more than fifty words," David explained. "You know how your mom is about rules," he winked.

"You agreed to that too," she grinned. "We wanted our wedding ceremony to be short and sweet and not go on and on. It made the vows easier to memorize that way," she smiled her arms around her husband's waist.

David removed her hands and kissed the back of each one, his eyes boring into hers as the twins looked up into his face.

"Tanisha, I knew that you were special when we met. Although I didn't understand the rules that you placed on our friendship, I wouldn't change a thing now. I thank God that our paths led us here. I will honor, cherish and protect you for the rest of my life."

David embraced his wife and kissed her passionately on the lips, her arms instinctively encircled his neck.

"What's a honeymoon baby, Mom? Miss Stella said that you are having a honeymoon baby."

"I am having a honeymoon baby," Teenie admitted, her eyes suddenly wide as saucers. "I think we're having a honeymoon baby today. Either I just peed my pants or my water just broke."

The End

ABOUT THE AUTHOR

A native Chicagoan, JC lives in the Memphis, Tennessee area with her husband and their three children.

Other books by JC Ellis:
Boys, Beauty & Betrayal
Camp Colorblind
Chemistry & Chaos
Dancing with God's Grace
Sunshine on Sunday

Visit JC Conrad-Ellis' website for interactive blogs:
www.blackdiamondseries.com

Follow JC on Twitter
@dearjcellis

LOVE, SECRETS & PEARLS

Like a cherished piece of jewelry or beloved family heirloom passed down through generations, the bond shared between Tanisha Carlson, Maria Wesley, Justine Wellington, Grace Dudley, Rashanda Jordan and Lori Perkins has become more precious with time.

In Love, Secrets & Pearls, the sequel to Sunshine on Sunday and the final book in the Black Diamond Series, the girls have blossomed into young women and continue their journey linked arm in arm. While adding more souls to their circle, the ladies embrace the reality that love is uniquely defined, secrets have healing qualities and healthy friendships should be treasured like a sentimental string of pearls.

Through it all, forever friendship clues are revealed that readers will want to replicate in their own lives as the girls affirm that a strong friendship circle of support is as important as a good bra and as comforting as a warm quilt.